Open Ticket

REBECCA CLEMENTS

Copyright © 2014 Rebecca Clements

All rights reserved.

ISBN-10: 1500722235
ISBN-13: 978-1500722234

First published by Christine M. Baker in the UK, 2014

Book cover design by Gulab Chaggar, 2014

The right of Rebecca Clements to be identified as the author of this work has been asserted by her in accordance with Copyright, Designs and Patents Act 1988.

All characters and events in this publication, other than those clearly in the public domain, are fictitious and any resemblance to real persons, living or dead, is purely coincidental.

All rights reserved. No copies of this publication may be reproduced, stored in or introduced into a retrieval system or transmitted, in any form, or by any means (electronic, photocopying, recording, or otherwise) without the prior written permission of the publisher. Any person who does any unauthorized act in relation to this publication may be liable to criminal prosecution and civil claims for damages.

This book is sold subject to the condition that it shall not, by way of trade or otherwise, be lent, re-sold, hired out or otherwise, without the publisher's prior consent in any form of binding or cover other than that in which it is published and without a similar condition including this condition being imposed on the subsequent purchaser.

1

Thursday 25 November 2004

Douglas rasps, 'got your passport?'

The slow oozing of the morphine drip continues. Eva nods and blinks fast.

He drifts in and out of consciousness. Sometimes he smiles, eyes closed, as if at a private joke she can no longer share. Eva grips herself around her middle, listening and watching for every little sign of his passing. Douglas' eyes open, search her face, squinting and bleary. 'It's good, lassie. Like a good malt. I won't hold you up long.'

The heating is turned up high for the late November morning, but still she cannot help but shiver. She will perform the final act of love, the washing and laying out of his body. Alex will not be able to complain she had left his father in a mess for him to clear up. *I do this for you, Douglas, so you know that the hands which touched your body for the last time belonged to someone you loved and who loved you.*

The beep of a text intrudes. 'Can you pick up my dry cleaning before 6?' Alex.

Her Eurostar train will have arrived in Paris by then. She and Roz will have melted into the crowds, ready for the next link to Prague.

Douglas raises a hand and his dry lips are forming some word.

'It's OK. Just rest,' she whispers, smoothing his hair.

His fingers that used to be steady enough to wield a scalpel now tremble as they descend slowly to the blanket.

Douglas' note had been written a few days earlier when his hand was still strong enough to hold the pen steadily. Brief. Direct. He wanted to protect her from blame and repercussions. She had wanted to leave a note of her own as well but Douglas had said, 'what's the point? The more you say, the worse it could be for you. Let Alex think what he wants to think. Let me absolve you. The rest doesn't matter.'

This morning, when Douglas had had more strength left in him, he and Eva had talked properly for the last time.

'I wish I could come back to visit your grave.'

'Sure, lassie, but I won't be there anyway. You must be where you need to be. I just hope that what you find will bring you what you want.'

No time or energy for continuing that conversation now. His breath is leaving him slowly and her body and mind are drained. Whatever might still be left unsaid would have to be conveyed by a squeeze of the hand. *Can he even see me properly now through this morphine fog? Have I given him enough of a dose to ease his exit?* And then other thoughts crowd into her mind uninvited - *has Roz packed? Has she left a note of her own?*

She knows she should be thinking only of Douglas and how she has just shattered her professional oath to protect life, and not about what is to come for her and Roz. She should be thinking of what she is going to do when her own time comes soon, when the doctors will purse their lips and admit that it's time to put her own affairs into order. *Who will be there at my own end? Will I have to beg Roz to do what I am now doing for Douglas?*

Just how far off that day might be, no one can tell her. In that lies both a blessing and a curse. If she is going to leave Alex and set off on this particular journey, she cannot afford to procrastinate.

Eva wakes with a jerk. The suffocating heat of Douglas' bedroom had induced drowsiness for a few moments and she leans forward urgently seeking proof of his continuing life. Breath that is barely there, but still present.

She glances at her watch, anxiety mixed with guilt at the slow pace of Douglas' passing and the nagging deadline of her departure for the train. She recalls how some of the other nurses in her team used to fret about the bed-blocking by patients hanging on to their last shreds of life, their needs competing with the urgency of new hospital admissions. Death had become just a part of the medical production line for some of the nurses and doctors, disconnected from the feelings they had about the patients as human beings deserving of dignity.

She almost misses Douglas' last seconds in her distracted musings but turns her head to him just in time to hear his last major intake of breath. A final kiss of goodbye, stroke of the cloud of white hair and she sets herself to work washing his body, wishing she did not have to rush these last moments with him.

In her haste she kicks aside her handbag and her passport falls out. As she performs her tasks a tide of anguish threatens to choke her at the injustice of the situation. She will miss Douglas' funeral, memorial service and all the rituals that would have brought some comfort and closure. She loathes Alex for the pain his affair had brought to his father as well as to herself. And she resents the illness that is slowly obliterating her own flame and is forcing her to make choices no one should have to make.

The process is finished. Douglas looks handsome again now that the absence of pain has relaxed his features. Her fingers trace his prominent cheekbones and the heavily-veined hands whose grip used to reassure his own patients, once upon a time. Reluctantly, she draws the white bed-sheet over his head. His note is propped up against the night-lamp.

She doesn't want to leave him. She sinks to her knees and offers a silent rebuke to the God who has allowed such needless suffering.

A muffled beep from her handbag. Roz's text tells her she has left home for Waterloo station and urges her to hurry too. She remains on her knees, reluctant to leave but now under pressure to make her planned move. She had wondered last night what this moment would feel like when it came. Everything and nothing. Just an aching void.

She knows she should go now. But her body disobeys, keeping her rooted to the spot, paralyzed with fear of the journey ahead.

A key rattles in the front door.

2

Nine days earlier: Tuesday 16 November 2004

As Alex McKinley manoeuvred his Ford Focus into one of the consultants' reserved spaces in the hospital car park at seven-thirty in the morning, he glimpsed Camille hurrying through the main entrance and for a moment he stopped breathing. They had already agreed never to be spotted entering or leaving the building together. Even large city hospitals like this were close enough communities to make any kind of personal relationship nearly impossible to hide. There was no margin for error. For now, this brief sighting would have to satisfy his longing for her, a thirst that could be assuaged later in her flat nearby after they had both completed their dayshifts. In the meantime, there would probably be plenty of patient-centred dramas to focus their respective minds.

As he got out of his car Alex brushed off a small cobweb from the wing mirror absent-mindedly. Whilst his taste in cars was considerably plainer than that of his more flamboyant colleagues, his exacting attention to the Focus' cleanliness was second only to that of his personal grooming. The dark blond hair was trimmed regularly and had just the right dusting of early grey strands to convey the impression of wisdom and gravitas to his child patients and their anxious parents. Today would bring one of the twice-weekly outpatients' clinics, with an overstuffed waiting area spilling out on to the corridor and threatening to block the scurrying nurses, physiotherapists and administrators. The doctors themselves would stroll at a more leisurely pace, having learned the ability to read files and papers whilst negotiating deftly around groups of people without making eye contact.

Alex dedicated his life to saving children he didn't want to have himself. He enjoyed solving their health problems when he could, but chose not to experience the messiness and angst of parenthood. He spent his days observing the fear and occasional grief of mothers and fathers bewildered by what even modern medicine sometimes could not cure. His little patients' faces were those he saw in his mind's eye on waking and often in his dreams. For every nine he saved in the operating theatre it was the unsuccessful tenth he remembered only, and measured his success and self-worth by.

His first appointment of the day was with a new referral. The nine-year-old boy had been suffering from blackouts in school PE classes. Scans had revealed an unusual heart problem. More monitoring would be agreed and review dates arranged. There was some comfort to be drawn from this familiar approach which helped to deaden any feelings of worry on his part about his patient's prognosis. Alex's calm and measured tones reassured little Callum's mother that her trust in Alex and the medical system would be well-placed. It wasn't for Alex to prick this bubble of hope too soon. Every case was a personal challenge to him, every success an affirmation of his capabilities. But the end of each day brought a sense of relief to him that he was not in the parents' shoes of having to cope with the uncertainties of 24/7 parenting.

Had Alex's colleagues been aware of his affair with Camille Mauriac, the registrar seconded from Lyon to progress her experience in pediatric surgery under his supervision, they would have been astounded. This image of a dedicated but seemingly-dull surgeon suited his circumstances well. Camille was clever enough to maintain an ice-cool veneer of polite professionalism with him as with the rest of the pediatrics department. In such ways they suited each other perfectly. Neither was willing to risk their reputation, to endure the sideways looks and sniggers that would have been inevitable. Each of them had seen colleagues suffer from those effects before. Their deal was simple: they kept their private passion and their professional life compartmentalized. Neither of them had asked for or made any promises about a joint future. Alex did not attempt to justify to himself his adultery, his betrayal of Eva's trust in him. It was what it was, and didn't need further scrutiny. Eva would never need to know. At some stage Camille would have to return to

Lyon and he would accept that when the time came.

The day progressed much as any other day. Every minute of Alex's time was accounted for, scarcely room to draw breath. He saw Camille only in the morning as she formed part of his ward round team and sat in on the debriefing session later, busy with her notes. They took care for their eyes never to meet for longer than was absolutely necessary. There was a brief distraction during the meeting when his eyes thought they glimpsed a slight tremor in her hand as she wrote but his attention was called away in a different direction almost immediately.

For people in their positions the concept of a lunch-break didn't exist – a sandwich sent for and consumed whilst writing up notes or researching a case at the desk. The outpatients' clinic in the afternoon overran as usual. By the end, even Alex's normally even temper was starting to shift to a more abrupt manner, as his inner needs to be with Camille started to rise. It wasn't about having enough time with her before he had to return to his own home – Eva understood that long hours were part of the landscape of the job. But the wrestling match between the Alex that everyone thought they knew and the new element emerging within him was getting tougher to control every day.

Six-thirty-five. The last case file was closed with relief. Alex emerged from his consulting room and stretched his aching back. The nurses and administrators had already gone. A quick chat, then, with some of his colleagues. Camille's door was still closed and he resisted the temptation to enter. Instead, he reverted to the system they had created for their situation. He called out his standard cheery good-night to his colleagues, and exited into the damp darkness of the car park.

He waited until he saw Camille leave the building, get into her car and finally drive out. He waited another two minutes before driving out himself, nothing that could draw attention to his actions. He ensured that in following her car to her flat he took a slightly different route. As in his operating theatre, details were important.

Camille seemed to be fumbling with her keys as she negotiated the lock of the apartment building's main entrance. Alex frowned. Every minute counted for him as his desire increased. Once she was finally inside and he allowed another couple of minutes to elapse, he left his car. Ever-watchful for passers-by or the twitching of curtains he moved swiftly and inserted the copy key she had given him in the lock. The lift ascent was smooth and quiet. The flats seemed to be well-insulated enough for no sounds to escape from the doors he passed before he reached number sixteen.

Closing the door behind him he breathed a small sound of relief, as he always did each time he completed this ritual of deception successfully. Camille's bag was lying carelessly on the hall floor. This clutter irritated his current tense mood and he snatched it up. In his haste some of the contents of the half-zipped bag spilled out, and as he bent down to scoop them up one of the objects caught his eye. A white plastic pen with a rectangular clear window. With two blue vertical lines showing. He stayed crouched down, numb, and his gaze slowly rose to Camille's face as she stood in the living room doorway, her face frozen in misery.

'I don't understand,' Camille kept repeating between her sobs, 'I have always been so careful. Now this....'

Alex sat on the edge of the sofa, continually rubbing his long bony hands together as if trying to shift a particularly stubborn stain.

'What are we going to do?' she whispered.

'You have to deal with it. But I can't be part of anything you do. If you need some money - .'

'I don't want your bloody money!'

He looked up at her at last. 'That's as much as I can do. Just be discreet about it. You could find an excuse to return to Lyon.'

'So, that's it? You just get rid of me now?'

'Camille – we always said – look, I'm sorry, there's nothing else I can do.'

'And what would your precious wife say about this?'

'Leave her out of this.'

Camille sank to the floor, her arms hugging her knees. 'Jesus! What kind of man are you?'

Alex rose and strode to the door. Turning, he said, 'I'm not blaming you. But I can't give you what you want. If you keep the child, I will help you financially on the understanding that my identity is protected. That's as far as I can go. Think about it.'

He hurried down the back stairs and, once back in his car, slumped in his seat and gripped the steering wheel hard. He thought of Eva, of the childless marriage they had both agreed to thirteen years ago, of her illness that would soon rob him of her solid unquestioning companionship. He thought of his father's own imminent demise and had a sudden vision of life alone and a void that not even his career could perhaps fill. But not even that prospect could sway him towards a future with an unwanted new partner and child. What had she been playing at? Camille was a mature educated woman, not some teenager ignorant about contraception. Unless she had planned it, of course. Why on earth did some women still consider that an acceptable bribe to a stable relationship? He had seen others before him fall into similar traps. But their subsequent love of the child had given them compensation which could never fit with his own needs and wants.

He needed a plan. He could concoct a professional reason to engineer her return to Lyon. He could draw up a legal agreement with her for financial support in return for anonymity and a promise that Camille would not divulge anything to Eva. But all options that occurred to him contained the same flaw – Alex McKinley knew he was no longer in control of his personal life.

3

Wednesday 17 November 2004

Douglas winced as Eva manoeuvred his pillows into the right position for him to sit up straight in bed.

'Sorry.'

'Ach no, lassie. What more can I expect now, eh?'

'Do you want me to read the papers to you or have a go yourself?'

'Just pass me my glasses, there, let's see what the world's been up to whilst I was asleep.'

'Or I could put the TV on?'

'No! I canna stand those blathering idiots on breakfast TV. I'll take my news straight, like my malt.' His eyes twinkled. 'I don't suppose - ?'

'At this hour? Certainly not! You're incorrigible, Douglas!'

'And you're a bossy boots, nursey, but a fine one.'

She patted his hand and he placed his other hand over hers. The warmth of his touch lifted the greyness of the autumnal morning.

'And how are you feeling today yourself, my dear?'

'Fine,' she lied.

The headache had come again upon awakening. One day it would be the big one. One day Alex might wake to find her lifeless beside him. It occurred to her that he might find that easier to cope with than his father would. Their fates were intertwined – when Eva was gone Alex would have to decide whether Douglas should go into a hospice or have a live-in nurse. Douglas had refused to discuss the matter. 'Don't listen to the naysayers, Eva, you just keep on living your life and I'll not be in your way for too long.'

But so far Douglas' stubborn spirit had allowed him to live

long beyond the oncologist's expectations. Eva knew from her own nursing background that predictions in terminal illnesses could never be certain about duration, only the eventual outcome. No miracles were prayed for. Her ranting at the unfairness of why her own life should be cut short before she had even reached forty had been intense but contained. There were no children's futures to fret about. Alex had reacted – like Alex. Eva had felt like one of his patients: she received what felt like a well-rehearsed speech about living life every day and making sure she was comfortable. She could have made a scene, could have screamed, 'why aren't you crying, like me? Don't you feel anything anymore?' But where would that have got her? A silent accommodation over thirteen years of marriage, her acceptance that however deep his feelings might run on any subject there was an impenetrable veil he had chosen to cast over them. *This is what they do*, she had said to herself on many occasions, *this is how guys like that cope with the strain of their work. So much is expected of their ability to cope with others' pain.* Some of that had rubbed off on her too, over the years, as she had worked in different hospitals and hospices whilst she tagged along behind him in his transatlantic career path. But when had Alex stopped being human?

'We're the same, you and me,' said Douglas, 'we're hard to kill off.'

He made her laugh and he didn't mind when she cried. There were a lot of relationships you couldn't say that about and Eva had often envied the quiet contentment of Douglas' marriage to Catherine. Douglas would tell Eva sometimes that she reminded him of his late wife. Eva remembered Catherine's bubbling optimism and the depth of Douglas' grief when he lost her to breast cancer ten years earlier. Like his son, Douglas had buried himself in his surgical career. Unlike his son, his humanity was never far from the surface.

Had she lived long enough, Baba would have met and liked Douglas too. Alex? Maybe not so much. Eva had only been eighteen when her grandmother Baba had passed away. Suddenly alone in the world, Eva had clung to her closest school-friend Roz. Roz the wacky. Roz the devourer of men and red wine. Lacking the anchor of Baba's strict but loving steer in her life Eva threw herself into Roz's whirling path and their college years – Eva at nursing in

University College Hospital in London and Roz in art at Central St Martins School nearby - passed in a drunken blur which made their respective successful graduations even more remarkable than their lack of class attendance. Only the daily reality of nursing and meeting Alex sobered Eva up. By that time too, Roz had been swept off her feet by Howard Berrington and the mesmerizing prospect of his generous family inheritance and burgeoning career in politics. Looking back, Eva could recognize that Roz's sudden abandonment of her in favour of Howard had probably thrown Eva in Alex's path in her desperation to find a new life partner. Eva could not now undo the subsequent thirteen years of tedium, each of them quietly dedicated to their professional duties, life lived on the flat surface rather than the undulations. Whilst self-pity had never been a fault of Eva's, since the day of her own diagnosis two months ago the recurring thought of what-if was her constant companion. She could start again, somewhere, and make the most of what life-span was left to her. But there was Douglas to consider as well. *And where could I go anyway? What would be the point? What would change?*

'Yeah, Douglas,' she smiled, 'we'll go on forever.'

'Sure, now, so what about that wee dram, then?'

What will I do when you're gone? That question made itself comfortable in the deep recesses of her brain.

Same day

Camille washed her face after emerging from the toilet. The puffy and blotched face that greeted her in the mirror was a stranger. Her normally glossy chestnut hair was an untamed frizz this morning. Was this what pregnancy did to you or was it only the crying fit she had just had? Alex had barely acknowledged her presence that morning. The word 'unprofessional' hung in the air between them, a word that she admitted to herself could now be applied to both of them. *The man has ice in his veins*, she thought, and then wondered why she was so surprised at how he had reacted to her news. Alex's cool exterior had been part of his attraction for her, a pleasant contrast to her previous experiences of possessive lovers in Lyon. He had been brutally honest in his terms: no disruption to the normal flow of his life, no question of leaving his wife (at least she had glimpsed some clue of inner pain when he told her about Eva's terminal illness), no scandalmongering at work. That was what she had signed up for.

But this, now. This changed everything. Camille Mauriac's own carefully-managed life up to that point was about to unravel because of a cluster of cells growing in her belly and the heartbeat which would soon be revealed on a scan. And since last night's broken sleep and the emptiness of yesterday spent staring out of the window of her apartment at the cheery bustle of others' lives, new thoughts were beginning to creep into her mind about how life could be different now.

'We have to talk about this,' she whispered to him as they walked some distance behind a group of noisy Foundation Year 1 doctors. He threw her a look which would have silenced her even a few days ago. But not now.

'Alex, there is a way we could do this together. Your wife, in her condition, she'll understand and - .'

His face loomed over her. 'Not a word. We're done here.' His pace quickened so that he forged ahead of her. Another colleague joined him en route and her chance to continue the conversation disappeared. Camille's face burned and she came to an abrupt stop, causing a nurse to bump into her.

'You all right, love?' enquired the nurse.

'Of course!'

The nurse raised her eyebrows but continued on her way. Camille leant against the wall and closed her eyes briefly. *We're not done yet.*

Douglas wheezed as he tried to chuckle. 'I think you'll find you're buggered now, Alex.'

Alex frowned, his hand hovering over his chess-pieces, but the old sod was right. Checkmate.

'You're slipping, boy, being beaten so quick by a dying old man. Hope your mind's sharper when you have a scalpel in your hand.'

Alex attempted a smile. 'Well played, Dad.'

'Bad day?'

'A few challenges.'

'Wouldna be fun without a few of those now, would it? Any case you want to pick over?'

'No. It's fine. Honest. Nothing that can't be sorted out.'

'Dinner's ready,' came Eva's voice from the kitchen.

'Ah well, you can give me a return match later.'

Eva entered with a tray. 'Douglas, you need to rest after this.'

Douglas sighed. 'You're no fun, the pair of you.'

Eva then brought in trays for Alex and herself. Six months earlier when Douglas moved in with them after his chemotherapy programme had gone as far as it could, all of them had agreed that Douglas' final weeks (months now, and still counting) should be spent with the ones he loved. She had observed that Alex and Douglas had a complex relationship of mutual respect and gruff affection, with the dynamics constantly shifting between them and the old man still able to demonstrate that his mind, if not his body, was still in top shape. Eva had given up her nursing job at a nearby hospice without demur. Douglas was the father she had never had. Nursing him was no chore of duty but an act of love. The house had been modified so that Douglas' life was fully integrated with theirs. Alex's long days at the hospital and unsocial hours had given Eva and Douglas time and space to talk and share. She now knew all about his humble origins on the biggest and roughest social housing estate in Glasgow. He, in turn, had probed her about her Czech origins and how she and Baba had come to England, fleeing from the turmoil of the Prague Uprising of 1968. And he was one of the few people in her life to whom she had shown the contents of Baba's oak box.

Watching Alex and Douglas now, conferring on the chess game just played whilst they ate, Eva had a rare glimpse of a warmth within Alex and was grateful that Douglas' personal tragedy had united them rather than torn them apart. She didn't want to think about the empty space in the house, both physical and emotional, that Douglas' eventual passing would create. And one day, one day, Alex would have two empty spaces to contend with. Was it better to be the first one to leave? No, Alex would struggle to provide the right care for Douglas if she went first. She caught herself marvelling at how she could be so dispassionate about her own fate, and at this unexpected sense of contentment tonight, the three of them a protective and loving unit.

Clearing the trays in the kitchen, Eva continued to muse at the sink when the shrill doorbell broke her train of thought.

'I'll get it,' called Alex.

She continued to clean the kitchen, humming to herself and planning in her mind the next day's schedule. Miriam, the relief nurse who would take care of Douglas whenever Eva needed to go out, had been booked from ten till two. That would give Eva time to have her monthly lunch with Roz, the font of gossip and self-appointed expert in putting the world to rights.

Behind her, in the hall, a muffle of angry voices. Frowning, Eva dried her hands and walked through.

'Just go home!' she heard Alex say.

'No! You have to listen, now!' The words were spat out by a blonde woman whose pretty face was blotchy and distorted by anger and tears.

'What's going on? Who's this, Alex?' Even as she spoke the words a feeling of nausea was rising inside Eva.

Alex looked away, silent. The blonde woman turned to Eva. 'I'm sorry, but you need to know this.'

Her heart was racing and with the taste of vomit creeping up her throat, Eva leant back against the wall and stared at Alex. He looked towards her, his face taut, a blood vessel at his temple visibly throbbing.

'Tell her, Alex!' Camille begged. Then she turned to Eva. 'I am sorry for you. I did not mean this to happen.'

Eva's face flushed and anger replaced the nausea inside her. 'Get out of my house! Whatever there is to say, I'll hear it from *him*.'

Alex looked aghast, opened his mouth to protest but nothing came out.

The women's gaze met. 'Please leave now,' said Eva, keeping her voice as steady as she could. Camille was the first to look away. She turned, cast one last look at a sullen hunched Alex and hesitated at the door. Eva sprang forward to wrench it open and stood silently as Camille bowed her head and slipped out.

Her energy boost dissipated, Eva slumped against the door. 'You bastard!' she exhaled.

'Eva - .'

'You complete and utter fucking bastard!'

'It doesn't mean anything - .'

'Mean anything? So, why do it anyway? Don't want to fuck a dying wife anymore, do you? Jesus Christ!'

'It's not about you - .'

'Oh really? Midlife crisis, then, is it? You poor bugger! Didn't think you were that stupid!' Eva sank down on to the floor, her fingers kneading the carpet. 'Are you still seeing her?'

'No.'

'So, why - ?'

'She's – she's pregnant.'

The nausea returned and threatened to erupt from her mouth. A moan came, but no words. She shook her head in disbelief and was suddenly seized with a bout of uncontrollable laughter. Alex's eyes narrowed as he stared at her.

'Oh! Oh, that's rich, isn't it, the man who never wanted the complications of children. Oh, that's sweet justice!' Her laughter ebbed away and she choked on her words. 'You bloody hypocrite! That's what you are! Playing the bloody hero at work, but oh, if they only knew - .'

Alex's expression turned to alarm. 'Look, I'll sort it out. It won't affect us - .'

'Oh really? You think I want to stay under the same roof with a scumbag like you?'

'Keep your voice down!' he hissed and they both looked towards the dining room. Eva closed her eyes and winced. Alex ran his fingers through his hair repeatedly. 'I'll sort things out, I promise.'

'How? You know what? I don't care!' Even as the words came out she knew she was lying. 'I don't care because, because…..' She looked towards the dining room entrance and thought, *there's a dying man in there whose arse you are not fit to wipe, Alex McKinley.*

Alex cleared his throat. 'I have to go in tonight. Might be better if I go early – I'm on-call tonight anyway and - .'

'Do what the fuck you like, just get out of my sight!' Eva staggered to the dining room door and leant against it for a moment, eyes closed, her back turned away from him, and she heard Alex's slow shuffle up the stairs. She edged into the dining room and looked across to where Douglas was still at the dining table in his wheelchair, saw the controlled fury and grief in his eyes. 'I'm sorry you had to hear all that,' and then she dissolved into tears.

Douglas shook his head in silence. She approached him and lay her hand on his shoulder where he immediately grasped it. She then sank down beside him and placed her head in his lap, sobbing into the tartan blanket which covered him.

The front door closed quietly behind Alex as he stepped out into the driving rain. For the first time since his mother died, he felt tears running down his face.

4

Thursday 18 November 2004

Eva woke to an empty space beside her and the nausea returned as she recalled the previous night's events. She had remained huddled up to Douglas for an hour after Alex had left the house. Douglas had remained silent for a long while, his eyes so fixed on a spot on the wall she feared that maybe he had had some kind of mini-stroke. But eventually, he spoke and his voice was mostly steady.

'I canna tell you what to do, Eva. But only this – if you still feel you can bear to spend the rest of your days with this man, you must think about what you will lose, and how that will feel one day when there is no more time to put things right.'

A chill had run through her at that point, and a truth she had been hiding now clamoured to be heard. Since the day of her diagnosis nearly two months ago she had been waiting to die. Every morning she had woken and wondered *will it be today?* Alex had carried on his life as if she had nothing more than a cold. The tightening of his face when she had told him her news – too busy with his own surgical patients to accompany her to the oncologist appointment - had been replaced by empty gestures of sympathy, the hand on her shoulder whenever he left the house. She had been living on autopilot, absorbed by Douglas' daily needs, obliterating herself.

'You need to live,' said Douglas, 'for yourself now.'

The words cut through her like a laser. 'Douglas, I can't leave you alone, with him, I couldn't do that.'

'Then I should leave you.' His hand grasped hers suddenly.

'No, Douglas!'

'Please, Eva…'

'You can't ask me to do that.'

'It's what I want, lassie. Please let me go like a man.'

She gazed at him, as always in awe of his insight born of having had to make life or death decisions for his patients for decades. Never sentimental, just mature compassion. *Alex is half the man of his father.*

'It would be a mercy, a great gift, Eva. Try to see it that way, if it helps.'

'No! I don't want to talk about it, do you hear? Now, we need to get you into bed, no arguments.'

And the old Eva, the nurse of fifteen years of chivvying her recalcitrant patients, re-asserted herself and steered him to his bed in a resentful silence. As she made him comfortable, his voice was silent but she felt his eyes on her back as she left his room. She leant back against the closed door and ran her hand over her face, trembling, wanting to banish the thought which had now taken root.

In the privacy of her bedroom Eva searched in the back of her wardrobe for the box. Baba's box. The intricately-carved clusters of oak leaves and acorns on its lid, the musk of old memories when she raised it and the sadness of the sparse contents. Three cracked black and white photos taken in the 1960s, the edges curled with age. A handsome couple in their twenties, hugging for the camera – here was her father, killed during the 1968 Prague uprising one month before she was born, her mother who had died soon after Eva's birth on the flight across Europe accompanied by Baba. It had always been hard for Eva to conjure up any feelings for people she had not touched or smelled, with no voice tone or familiar phrases to recall. Baba had had to fulfil multiple family roles and had risen to that challenge. The school bullies who had teased Eva and misnamed her a bastard through their ignorance had nevertheless feared Baba's tall and hefty presence at the school-gates, and Eva had been proud to be her granddaughter. Her triumphs at school had been met with a mere nod of approval, – *'of course, you have this from me, yes?'* – and any failings had earned her 'the look' that said, *do better next time.*

Baba had given her the box when Eva turned fifteen and it had become her talisman. Apart from her parents' photo there were two others. One, a tall woman, maybe late thirties, with striking good looks, blonde hair and a sculpted face, gazing imperiously at the camera. Baba would dismiss her as *'someone we knew, not important.'* The other photo was of a group of people amongst whom she could make out a younger version of Baba, and next to her a huddle of men and women whom Baba had described as friends and co-fighters in the Czech struggle of that time. Baba's first-hand account of the Russian tanks rolling down Wenceslas Square and the sacrifices these persons had made for their fellow countrymen had created more depth and colour than any history book could achieve and Eva had always regretted that she had never recorded those stories. There was always something else going on in her teenage life and, besides, there would be time later. But 'later' had never come. Baba should have lived beyond her fifty-eight years. Just the photos to look at now, to look beyond the faces and try to guess at their lives.

But Baba's box could not comfort her tonight and she stayed awake throughout the dark hours, heard the rain pebbling the conservatory glass roof, and tried to think what Baba would do. It was clear to her what Baba would do. She would have left Alex without a backward glance and sued him for everything she could get. But what would she have done about Douglas? Could she take another's life, even at their begging? But the alternative for Douglas was a living death. Alex would surely bundle his father off into the care of others, unwilling or incapable of taking on the responsibility himself. One visit a month with a book and a box of treats until the end-day came, to a nursing home that reeked of pee and guilt? What else was possible? A live-in carer to keep Douglas at least in a comfortable and familiar environment, at the expense of fees and the awkwardness of sharing his house with a stranger who was paid to give physical care but no more? Either way, Eva's own absence would probably lead to Douglas' early demise, so why hasten that day? Why blacken her soul?

He said it would be a great mercy, a great gift. When the dawn came eventually Eva was no closer to resolution.

As she entered Douglas' room with his breakfast tray she had a sense of a void, that he was gone, and for a fraction of a second she was relieved to have her burden released. But a sudden wheeze from within his nebulizer confirmed his obstinate clinging to life and she felt a flush of shame rise through her. Once she had removed the nebulizer she saw a slow smile spreading.

'I dreamt I was with Catherine again. It was grand.' His eyes were filled with that pleading look from the night before.

Eva covered her eyes with her hand. 'Douglas, please…..'

Anger now replaced the pleading. 'I never took you for a sentimental fool, Eva! Do you not think people already do this? Are you just too scared you'll get found out?'

'For God's sake, Douglas, do you think I can just flip a switch without thinking?'

'Woman, we let people die horrible slow deaths every day in hospital. Don't you think that, just once or twice, a doctor or nurse hasn't given the morphine drip a quick nudge to end someone's misery? We let our pets die with more dignity than our parents!'

'Don't start that argument now, you know there's no end to it.'

'No. You have to make the ending that makes most sense to you, eh?'

'We wouldn't be having this conversation if Alex - .'

'I'm not talking about him! He can dig his own grave. Listen. Your day, every day, is precious now. And he has done you a favour, woman, he is waking you up to the fact that your life with him is worthless.'

'Stop it! You'll wear yourself out now, Douglas. Eat. We'll get you bathed and then Miriam will be here to take over by ten.'

Douglas lay back on his pillows, eyes closed, his breathing rapid. 'I canna stand that woman. She smells of bleach and good intentions.'

'Sorry, but I'm seeing Roz today.'

'Oh, that crazy redhead.'

Eva managed a smile and felt the tension between them dissolve. 'Shut up, you know you fancy her rotten.'

'Ah, she's no time anymore for an old man like me.'

'Well, she moves in grander circles these days. Howard's just been promoted to the Shadow cabinet.'

'Nasty piece of work,' snorted Douglas. 'All that crap about restoring the country's moral balance. I wouldn't be surprised if he bats for both sides himself.'

Eva looked at him sharply. Roz had kept the secret of Howard's rentboys as an insurance policy to protect her own status. Rumours had floated for years in the press but nothing had stuck.

'And what will your Roz have to say about what happened last night, then?'

Eva helped him ease into his wheelchair. 'I'm sure she'll have plenty to say about it.'

'And what do you think she would tell you to do about this whole situation?'

'Listen, whatever she or anybody else says, my answer will be the same, Douglas.'

His eyes glazed over. 'Then we'll all be the sadder for it.'

Alex groaned as his bleeper woke him. Every time he had managed to fall asleep the damn thing had shattered his slumber and now he felt like hurling it through the window. He dreaded seeing Camille even more than the prospect of returning home in the evening. Even as he was rudely awakened he had a fleeting vision that it had all been a bad dream and that life was continuing in its predictable rut. He didn't deserve his life to be so shit. Camille had been a single aberration to his good judgment. And now he was going to pay big time.

One day, however soon, he knew he was going to be facing life alone and he didn't necessarily want Camille to be filling that void. The trouble was, he wasn't sure how he would fill it. Exhausted and drained from the compassion he had to show at work, there was nothing left to give to anyone else. Eva had understood, all these years, that it was part of the deal when you had relationships in their professional field. She had always allowed him mental and physical space and sometimes, in rare moments of self-reflection, he wondered why she had never asked for more than the basic marital companionship he could offer her. She could have taken a lover, anytime, someone to spark off. But maybe her intense commitment to her own work had been enough for her too. It had never occurred to him to ask.

His guilt this morning was about hurting her as a good friend and wondered how he would face the shame of his father's opinion when he returned home. Douglas must have heard it all. He couldn't avoid them forever.

There was a knock on the door. 'Mr. McKinley?' came a

female voice. 'You're wanted in theatre. There's a problem.'

'Yeah, yeah, I'm on my way.'

His face in the mirror was droopy and exhausted and new lines had appeared overnight. That had to be fixed. The world out there had to trust that he was in total control.

When he came out, with his cloak of confidence restored, he almost immediately saw Camille at the end of the corridor. She stopped in her tracks and then quickened her pace towards him. There was no way he could avoid her now.

'Alex, last night, I didn't mean to - .'

'Not now! I'm due in theatre. Later.'

As he hurried past, his head down, she yelled after him. 'You can't run away from this!'

Two porters passing by exchanged glances and Alex broke into a fast run, reaching the lift as the doors were closing.

5

Same day, late morning

For the last couple of years, after agreeing that their respective lives had kept them apart too much, Eva and Roz had started a ritual of meeting for lunch on the third Thursday of every month at Gianni's Trattoria in Bloomsbury. It was around the corner from where they came to live during their college years, with University College Hospital for Eva nearby and Central St Martins College of Arts and Design a little further away for Roz, but still close enough for a fifteen-minute stagger in the morning fog of a hangover.

The location of this lunch ritual was important. It reminded them of carefree times, forecasting each other's brilliant future in a haze of cigarette smoke and cheap Chianti. When they were broke they ate plain pasta in olive oil with a bit of salad thrown in and a glass of tap water on the side. On solvent days they could add meat or fish. They never starved, either way. Sometimes they would offer to do the washing-up or wait on tables in return for free food. Not that often, though. Gianni may have had a big heart but he was a shrewd businessman behind the gap-toothed smile and bear hug. But he didn't know that his wife Maria would sometimes slip the girls small shots of grappa at the end of their meal.

As Eva walked through the quiet back streets, scattering fallen autumn leaves as she strode, it was the beauty of the architecture around her that drew her down this route. The mixture of Georgian and Victorian London had always held her in thrall, the timeless elegance of portals, the curve of a portico, the symmetry of sash windows that generations before her had stood at to view their world. But since her diagnosis with a brain aneurysm two months earlier, connecting with people from her early life had taken on a new urgency. She followed the same route as ever, passing the British Museum by just after eleven-thirty and reaching Little Russell Street, looking up at the flat on the first floor which she and Roz had shared for nearly five years, all through college and then the first years of their working lives. Life was then mostly about having fun whilst doing the bare minimum of study and work upon which to create a professional future. They had still thought and behaved much as they had done through their school years in Finchley. Roz and her mother had moved down from Manchester's Moss Side after Roz's alcoholic father had died from liver failure. There had been an aunt in Finchley, a reason for her mother to make the long move south so that someone trustworthy could care for Roz whilst her mother worked all hours to make ends meet. Roz and Eva had clashed at first but discord had soon transformed into an invisible bond between them, two girls both far away from their roots.

The house in Little Russell Street looked much the same as ever, still needing a lick of paint but not quite as scruffy as it used to be when they had lived there. They wouldn't be able to afford to rent that flat these days. Well, Roz could, with Howard's money. The flat overlooked the back of St. George's church, an eighteenth century Hawksmoor jewel. The vestry at the back was still being refurbished, Eva noticed. An out-of-date poster fixed to the wall listed Russian theatre and dance classes, a red arrow pointing towards a chipped door down a short flight of stone steps.

Eva had often wondered whether she and Roz would still be living in that flat, if Roz hadn't broken the spell and fallen in love with Howard's money. Eva had felt abandoned after that, and hooking her wagon on to Alex's soaring medical career trajectory had seemed the only way to go on. Alex and Howard, rising stars in their respective spheres. Looking back, it seemed that they were both looking for bright personable women to enhance their status. It was painful now to recall that she and Roz had actually congratulated each other on their excellent choice of life partners. Gianni and Maria had wished them all much joy and many babies. Well, there had been no babies and only short-lived joy. Roz had discovered the duplicities and hollowness of Howard's life and had turned for comfort to Scotch and cocaine. As for Eva, she had searched in vain for the depth behind Alex's charming exterior and had come to accept that the only way for comfortable co-existence was to pursue her nursing work with the same vigour and high level of commitment that he gave to pediatric surgery. Living with a hero whose patients thought he walked on water had been the substitute for a family of their own.

However many times Eva had walked this route to Gianni's, she never failed to pause to gaze up at the house. The window on the left had been Roz's bedroom. Eva's room had overlooked a small courtyard at the back. The walls between the two bedrooms had been very thin – a cheap, botched conversion – allowing little privacy when they had brought home a man. Not that that had bothered them unduly. They had shared most things. Sometimes they had shared the men too.

Gianni's Trattoria was in Museum Street, an oasis of calm between the blaring thoroughfares of New Oxford Street and Great Russell Street. The restaurant had made no concessions to passing trends over the previous twenty years. These days it sat nestled between a sushi bar and an interior design shop. Much had changed around here, but not Gianni's or the surrounding bookshops with their teetering piles of obscure titles, in defiance of the competing brands of major book chains. In the adjacent streets you could now eat Indian, Korean, Thai and burgers the price of steaks. But Gianni's food range had not altered since the late-1980s when Eva and Roz had moved here and even then the menu was out of step with the times by at least ten years. The décor also reflected Gianni's resistance to the attempted influence of the interior designer next door. Perhaps that's why they loved it. Gianni and his food had always represented an anchor in their lives.

Gianni spread his arms wide as he greeted Eva at the door. 'Eva! *Cara!*' The hairy muscled arms nearly crushed her in their enveloping embrace. Maria waved from the small bar at the back.

'Roz, she is not here yet – you have a drink, yes? Maria!' he gestured, 'something to warm her up – look, she is blue from cold!'

Maria came with a shot glass of grappa which Eva sipped dutifully, even though its fierce heat made her cough. Maria laughed and kissed her on both cheeks, smoothing her windswept hair.

'Eva! How are you? You look tired, *cara,* and too thin. You should rest more.' She ruffled Eva's wiry chestnut-brown hair. 'Come, Paola is here. She has brought the baby. Come see.'

Eva felt she had to say yes. They were all so proud. This was their fifth grandson now, Paola and her brother Guido having obediently started their respective family production lines nearly ten years before. More family to carry on the business, Gianni had said, it was best to breed your own workers. The baby boy looked pretty much like all others Eva had ever seen, but they all cooed over it, pointing out possible family resemblances that escaped her. She watched their obvious love for each other, and remembered their tight embraces when she had told them her own news eight weeks earlier, their deep concern a welcome antidote to Alex's bewildered emotional distance.

'I'm sorry, Paola, I should have brought a present.'

'Eva, you do not need to, you know that,' she replied, dimples forming in her cheeks as she smiled. 'Next time, if you like.' Then she hugged Eva too. Eva screwed her eyes shut, luxuriating in the boundless affection from someone she regarded as almost a sister. 'Eva! You are so skinny – look at me! Look at what this baby has done to me!'

But Paola was laughing all the same as she slapped her rounded belly and hips. She encouraged Eva to pick up her baby son but as Eva's hands reached out tentatively towards the pram the door behind them crashed open.

'For fuck's sake!' Roz stumbled through the front entrance, hitting the doorjamb with her golf umbrella, her wild red hair tumbling over her face. She brushed it aside with a rough gesture. 'Bloody rain! Look at the state of these boots!'

Eva saw the smile on Paola's face tighten. Gianni strode towards Roz. *Bellisima!* he exclaimed. 'How is Madame today?'

'Yeah, yeah, Gianni, love you too,' Roz returned his kiss. 'Hi Eva. Sorry I'm late. Fucking awful traffic on the A40.'

There was a shuffling noise behind them. Eva turned around and saw Paola wheeling the baby's pram through the kitchen door, followed closely by Maria.

Roz strode up to their usual table and scraped back a chair. Gianni had already placed an open bottle of his best red wine on the white tablecloth. Roz Berrington would be paying as usual, with Howard's credit card, no need to ask and no expense to spare. Eva copied Roz's order of antipasti, veal and salad, noticing how Roz's hand was shaking as she raised the wineglass to her mouth.

'How's tricks?' she asked Eva, her eyes not on her but roving over the street scene through the plate glass windows. 'You look like shit, by the way. Don't you think you should get some more help to look after Douglas? He's wearing you out. Must be like having a baby around.'

Eva glared at her, jerking her head towards Gianni who was still at the bar.

'Whoops! Sorry,' Roz said, lowering her voice. 'So, go on then, what's new?'

Eva had thought of sending Roz a text in advance, something like: *my life, or what's left of it, is now totally fucked up by the one person I should be able to rely on.* But some things had to be said out loud.

Roz drained her glass and immediately started to refill it. 'I know you – something's happened. Come on, woman, cough it up.'

Eva fiddled with her wineglass for a moment, silent, then raised her eyes to meet Roz's. Roz' own eyes widened. 'Oh Christ, they haven't given you a date, have they? Oh shit, Eva!'

Eva burst out laughing, then stopped abruptly. 'No, not that.'

'Thank Christ for that,' Roz mumbled as she lit a cigarette, one hand over the other. 'Nothing could be as bad as - .'

'Alex has been having an affair with someone at work and now she's pregnant.'

Roz coughed over her cigarette, speechless for once, and then started to laugh.

'Jesus Christ, Roz!'

'Sorry, sorry,' Roz stifled her mirth and a shadow suddenly crossed her face. 'Oh my God, and I thought it was…. I can't believe that! Alex? *Alex?* What a dark horse! Christ, what a shit! What a hypocrite! How could - ?'

'There's nothing you can say that I haven't said or thought already,' said Eva curtly. 'Oh, and I think Douglas could match you for language on this one.'

Roz closed her eyes and shook her head. 'Bastard.' Then her eyes flew open. 'I take it you've thrown him out? Eva? Please don't tell me you're going to forgive and forget or something dumb like that?'

'You think I could?'

'I think you're too tolerant, that's always been your problem. Bloody hell, Eva, he doesn't deserve any better!' She drew heavily on her cigarette. 'Hard to believe though, him. Come on, tell me everything.' Roz's green eyes blazed when Eva's recounted Camille's visit to the house but she allowed Eva to finish the story. And then Eva told her about Douglas' request.

'Shit,' was Roz's sole reply. They sat in silence, Roz's gaze fixed on the window, their starter dishes untouched in front of them whilst Eva found herself emptying her own wineglass faster than she intended.

Eva broke the silence at last. 'I suppose you're going to tell me Douglas is right?'

'Do you think he is?' asked Roz after a moment, lighting another cigarette slowly.

'To tell you the truth – I really don't know. Does he have the right to ask? I probably would, in his place. But how could I do that to him, to anyone, just to make my life easier?'

'He wants it for himself as well as for you. He wouldn't last long if you left. You both know that.'

'I couldn't enjoy the rest of my life knowing I'd done that.'

'Christ, Eva, you're hardly enjoying your life as it is now, are you?' They glared at each other. Gianni approached the table slowly, but paused and turned away.

'Easy for you to say that!' Eva snapped. 'What the hell do you know about life, swanning around like - .'

And then she watched as Roz slowly pulled up the left sleeve of her cashmere sweater. The bruises were vivid, great purple blotches with yellowing edges, running up the inside of her forearm. Roz held Eva's horrified gaze and raised her eyebrows.

'Oh my God, Roz! When did this happen? Why the hell - ?'

'Last Saturday. I teased him in front of his grand friends at a dinner party and this was my reward later.'

'Has he done this before?'

'No. Threatened, yes. But not actually done anything before now. So, what the hell do I know about enjoying life, right?'

'Why didn't you ring me? You should have gone to the police.'

Roz blew a smoke ring high above Eva's head, pausing to stare up at her creation admiringly. When she looked at Eva again there was an emptiness in her eyes.

'Biding my time.'

'You'll leave?'

'Have to figure out a plan first. Leave him – let's say – something to remember me by.' She stubbed out her second cigarette, grinding it into the ashtray slowly.

'Where would you go?'

Roz laughed, just a little too loudly. 'Wherever his money will take me!'

'It'll be messy. He won't let you get away with much.'

'He may not have much say in it.' A smile flickered across Roz's face, quickly replaced by a frown. 'Seriously, Eva. You can't stay with Alex when you don't know when…..' Roz's voice trailed off and her hand reached out to the red wine bottle whose contents were now significantly depleted.

'I don't much care about what Alex gets up to now, to be honest. But I can't leave Douglas like this.'

'So, you've answered your own question, then.'

When Eva had told Roz about her illness and the uncertainty of the timescale Roz had immediately started nagging her about creating a bucket list. But Eva had never had any overwhelming desire to scale Mount Everest, take a trip in a hot-air balloon or any of the standard must-do-before-I-die things. But learning more about Baba - finding Baba's homeland and the family that were hers too – that would feel like the right thing to do. Where to start and when?

'We both have a reason to leave now,' said Roz softly.

'What if - ,' started Eva. 'What if I go away just for a short while, get some nurse in to help?'

'And one of you dies during that time?'

'How can you be so cold about it? Don't you think I've already looked at all the options? Whatever decision I make, someone has to pay.'

'For once, why don't you make sure it's not you?'

'Because I'm not you, Roz.'

Same day, late evening

Alex paused with his key in the front-door lock. His workday had been as long as he could make it, but he couldn't stay away from home forever. Besides, the workplace contained Camille's brooding presence and threats to expose him to his colleagues. Whichever way he turned he was surrounded by the evidence and consequences of his temporary lapse in judgment.

The night had been a maelstrom of broken sleep, nightmares and the comparatively welcome interruptions from his work environment. Functioning on autopilot, he had mused about how easy his life had been up to this point. A career path that had evolved almost of its own will, the easy undemanding relationship with Eva, the thrills of making decisions on the knife-edge in the operating theatre. His mind had always been as steady as his hand when it held the scalpel. He had transformed the lives of many children and their families and those problems he could not help he was able to justify in the names of medical science and bad luck. The backdrop of his personal life had been a smooth screen against which to project his professional persona.

In the early hours of the morning, greeting another rainy dawn, he tried to think if there had been a time when things had started to change without him realising. He couldn't picture any gradual shifts, any pattern changes. Just suddenly, a few weeks after she had arrived from Lyon, he had found himself looking at Camille in a different light and it was as if some long-buried yearning within him had erupted and demanded instant satisfaction. The Alex McKinley who would weigh up the risks and benefits of each medical intervention with great care had vanished in an instant.

His first and only aberration. No feelings of love to justify himself. He had rolled the dice and lost. The ground was opening up beneath his feet now and he was facing what he had always dreaded in life: the lack of an easy option. Abandoning either his wife or his lover would come with a heavy price. And then it came to him, whilst he was scrubbing up in theatre, rhythmically and methodically soaping his hands, forearms and elbows. Eva was upset. He could understand that. But like him, she was stoical and pragmatic. She understood the value of stability and continuity. She would hurt for a while but would surely weather the storm. And it wouldn't cost him that much in effort to redeem himself in her eyes. His father – well, there was little of his lifespan left and Alex could stay away from him to avoid the recriminations. Douglas would bark and bite, lecture him on the sanctity of marriage but there was less and less strength in him now.

Surely Camille would not wish to harm her own career and reputation by exposing their difficulties? He could talk her round too. There could be ways he could engineer her next career move to their mutual advantage, preferably back in her own country. Some financial settlement to smooth the way, perhaps. It was not the child's fault. If she chose to keep it and interrupt her own career, of course.

So, time to take a deep breath, rehearse his speeches and move on with calming things down. But his hand still shook as he turned that front-door key.

The house was in darkness. He paused briefly outside Douglas' room, listening to the hum of the medical equipment keeping him alive. He could see a light on in the bedroom he shared with Eva. For a moment he wondered about making up the bed in the spare room. It could still come to that if she refused to share their bed with him. But this scene would have to be played out at some time anyway. Putting it off wouldn't make it any easier.

Slowly, he pushed open the door. Eva appeared to be asleep, a book fallen from her hand. For a moment, he watched her carefully, noting the gentle deep rise and fall of her chest, suddenly fearful of the moment that would come one day when it would be still forever. He hesitated and felt a creeping doubt, a sudden desire to turn and leave, but then her eyes fluttered open and she focused on him.

'Can I come in?' he asked.

She screwed up her eyes, and he wondered whether she had taken something to help her sleep. Then she blinked several times and nodded briefly. Alex edged forward and sat on the bed. He tried to remember the opening lines he had rehearsed.

'Eva. I'm so sorry for what I've put you through. I've been an idiot, I know. But I want to put things right between us, if you'll let me try.' *Word perfect*, he congratulated himself.

Eva seemed confused, tilting her head to one side. He

frowned. 'Eva, listen, I said - .'

'Heard you the first time.'

'But - .'

'Made up the bed for you in the other room.'

Shit. 'Of course. I understand. Look, tomorrow I can stay home in the morning and we can talk.'

'About what?'

'Us. Everything. How we can put things right.'

'We? I've done nothing wrong.'

'Eva - .'

'I want to sleep now.' She rolled on to her side away from him and switched off the bedside light.

Alex took a deep breath. *OK. It can keep till the morning.* As he settled down in the spare room, he thought, *don't lose it, keep calm, just follow the plan, she'll come round.*

6

Friday 19 November 2004

In her dream, Eva was walking through a cemetery with Baba. Not the Baba she had known. Her grandmother was of her own age, no lines of care yet on her peachy skin, her hair the same shade of chestnut brown as Eva's. It was warm and sunny. Baba laughed and invited Eva to dance with her. As she looked into Baba's eyes she saw a change - not the deep brown eyes that Eva remembered but instead the same quirky feature as she had herself, one green eye and the other brown, the legacy from her father as Baba had told her. Then Baba became more serious. As they walked slowly amongst fallen gravestones, the lettering faded and in a language consisting of symbols rather than words, she pointed out several of them and told Eva about who they had been. But Eva couldn't hear her words. The air seemed distorted, the light grainy and all sounds were muffled as if the world had been wrapped in cellophane. She kept asking Baba to repeat herself but her grandmother became increasingly irritated and accused her of not being interested in what she had to say. Eva strained her ears, making out the odd name here and there, feeling heavy and stupid. And there was a sense of urgency, as if she were revising for an exam and if she didn't absorb this information today a door would shut, opportunities would fall away and she would be stuck in a kind of limbo forever. 'Can we hurry up please, Baba, because I've got to get back to give Douglas his morphine dose.' Baba had laughed. 'He's here, can't you see him, look, behind that tree.' And Baba had waved at a man who looked like an older version of Alex but not Alex, or Douglas, for that matter. Eva felt her heart thumping, crushing her ribs. 'Baba, you've got this all wrong. I've got to get back.' But Baba was walking towards the man, waving at him, ignoring Eva. Eva looked around her wildly. Where was the gate they had come through? A mist was descending, and from somewhere there was a clamouring, like an alarm to tell them that the cemetery would be closing in five minutes and….

The clock alarm was insistent. Eva's eyes flew open and for a second she couldn't think where she was. Her head felt like concrete, her tongue dry and there was a metallic taste in her mouth that she recognized as fear. Douglas' morphine dose. She had to get downstairs and fix him up for the morning or his pain would quickly become unbearable. She usually woke before the alarm. The small dose of diazepam she had taken last night to help her sleep had furred up her brain. She wanted to turn over, sleep more, but that would have to wait. The dream had already receded into a blur but she kept trying to grasp at the images.

Another thought broke through: *was Alex still home?*

As she passed the spare room Eva could see a chink of daylight through the slightly-ajar door. The curtains must be open. Which would mean he had already left for work. But hadn't he said last night he would be home this morning? Eva's heart sank at the thought of facing him. What could they possibly have to say to each other now?

As she descended the stairs she could hear murmurings. Pushing open the door of Douglas' room the sight that greeted her was Douglas propped up in bed, with what looked like a fresh morphine drip doing its work and Alex sitting opposite in an armchair, shoulders hunched, and hands together. Both men looked up as she entered.

'It's all right, I've done the necessaries. You can go and get some more rest,' said Alex.

She looked at Douglas, who nodded silently. For a fraction of a second, she heard 'done the necessaries' as 'I've done what he wanted you to do' and she felt sick. She stood, waiting for something to happen, for Douglas to fall asleep forever.

'Eva, are you all right, lassie?' rasped Douglas. 'You look awfully pale today.'

'I'll get you some tea.' Alex was past her on his way to the kitchen before she roused herself from her stupor.

'And can I guess what might be going through your mind, then, my girl?' whispered Douglas.

She approached his bed and examined the morphine drip.

'No,' said Douglas quietly. 'No change yet.' He shifted slightly. 'We were just – talking. Maybe you two should go and do some talking too.'

'I've nothing to say to him.'

'Yes you do. It's just a question of which way you jump on this matter.'

'I'm not going to argue with you anymore. I'm too tired.'

There had been enough arguing the day before to last her the rest of her life. Roz had needled her, pressed her to take action, and Eva had ended up walking out with tears streaming down her face and a thumping in her head that she feared. Then, returning home, Douglas had been unusually crotchety and had nagged her with equal vigour.

'Shut up or I'll put us both out of our misery right now!' she had screamed at him.

He would have known she didn't mean it. But at bedtime, when a restless first hour had driven her to the medicine cabinet and the diazepam, she wondered whether it could have been a close-run thing. Isn't that what sometimes happened to people, she thought? Some unexpected trigger that leads to an irreversible action?

Alex returned with a mug of tea for her. He touched her elbow, searching her face, and gently steered her out of the room and into the sitting room next door. He sat opposite her in an armchair. 'You must hate me right now.' The words were slow, careful, his gaze just a fraction above her head.

'You have no idea what I'm feeling.'

'I don't blame you - .'

'Well, that's big of you!'

He swallowed hard, the colour in his face rising. *Yeah*, she thought, *this must be really fun for you*. And suddenly she felt sorry for him. Because she knew, ultimately, he was going to be alone in the world. And maybe sooner than he thought. She relaxed. Something was releasing inside her and she felt strangely calm.

'Eva, I want to put things right. I know I've not been around much – not that I didn't want to be, you must believe that – but I will make changes, whatever it takes. I won't insult you by trying to explain why some things have happened.….'

She let him ramble on. *It must have taken a lot for him to do this. Well-rehearsed. Not bad, actually. Pity it's a waste of his breath.*

Once he had finished, he looked at her, desperation clear in his face. 'S- o-o, what do you think? How can we make this work, Eva?'

You poor bugger. And then she smiled. 'Let's take this one day at a time.'

Alex exhaled loudly. 'Thank you.'

See you in hell.

7

Saturday 20 November 2004

The second slap splits my bottom lip and flecks of blood spray on to my white silk shirt.

'Now Roz,' *says Howard, his face just a couple of inches from my face so that I can smell the whiskey on his breath mingling with his overpowering aftershave. 'We're not going to say another word about this. Is that understood?'*

I nod, wiping the blood off my chin with a trembling hand.

'Good girl.' He straightens his bowtie and smooths his black hair as he peers into the mirror over my dressing-table. He stares past his reflection and into my eyes.

'Go and get yourself cleaned up. I don't want the Leader's wife asking me awkward questions. If she says anything, tell her you tripped or something. I'll expect to see you downstairs in ten minutes. The car's waiting.'

He slams the door behind him and I hear him on his mobile as he runs down the stairs.

At least he didn't leave me with any more bruises this time. Very clever. No. No, he's not. He's very stupid, actually. The Leader of the Opposition's wife is no fool. This latest injury will be hard to hide. The murmurings will start. Actually, I wish he had left bruises on my face too. That would really fuck up his chances and then everything would start to leak out....I'd love to tell them. Everything. Screw up his career good and proper, and what would his dear mamma have to say about that? Would his 'little boys' stay with him then? Well, maybe, unless the money starts to run out too.

But I should have been more careful. I shouldn't have made idle threats. The bastard knows I can't afford to leave. Shit, this bloodstain will never come out properly. The shirt's had it. What the fuck? I can afford to buy a hundred more. Nice thought, that. Money may not make you happy, but it bloody well helps when....

There's a knock on the door. I freeze — what will he do now? Then Wanda appears, her eyes taking in the state of my face.

'Mrs. Berrington, what has happened?'

'I'm fine, Wanda. Just find me another shirt whilst I fix myself up.'

'Oh!'

Her blue eyes are wide as saucers. She must have heard our rows before, surely, guessed at what's been going on? There are few secrets we can keep from the staff. Howard doesn't care, doesn't even seem to notice that these other people exist in our house. The bastard cheapskate won't even pay the going rate for English staff, but gets them flown in from Eastern Europe instead.

'I help you, Mrs. Berrington.'

'S'alright, I can manage. Thanks anyway.' *I wince as I dab my mouth. It's going to be a tricky camouflage job.*

I slide into the backseat of the car next to Howard. He's busy on his mobile, as usual, barking orders. I huddle down into my silver fox fur coat and watch the car lights on the A40 slide past, blurring in the soft rain. They're talking on the car radio about a hard winter starting next month. I wish it would snow properly. It used to, I'm sure it did, when I was a kid in Moss Side, scrabbling for handfuls of the stuff in our backyard, never enough for a real snowman. Pathetic country, this. Enough snow to make the transport system grind to a halt but not enough for a half-decent snowman. When Mum and I moved to London and I met Eva and her granny, the old woman used to tell me stories about knee-high snowdrifts in Czechoslovakia and how they had made cheap wooden skis out of crates. Howard took me skiing once, in Val d'Isere, when we were first married and still making a pretence out of doing things together. He had been embarrassed when I couldn't stand up straight on my skis. Me, I thought it was a great hoot. It had been fun, back then. Howard was good-looking, funny and a great screw. Still is, for all I know. But it's not my bed he shares anymore and the wit he now reserves for his Very Special Friends.

I know too much about him now, stuff I wish I didn't. But this life has had its compensations, still has in some ways. Eva thinks I exaggerate, that I've got too much time on my hands. Maybe. No kids, no ailing parents to nurse. Now it's just me and the bottom of the whiskey glass and the line of white powder on silver foil to tell my secrets to. The car pulls up outside the

Connaught at last. 'Good evening, Mr. Berrington,' says the doorman, nodding. 'Mrs. Berrington.'

I spot the doorman looking at my mouth. I lift my turquoise silk scarf quickly to cover it. Once we enter the hotel, the addictive smell of power and money fills my nostrils. I drain the proffered glasses of champagne too quickly. Howard shoots me a warning look but I move away and circulate with my painted-on smile and the well-rehearsed phrases. It's like a choreographed dance, with me and the other Shadow Cabinet wives playing out our roles. We all loathe each other really but we - or rather, they - are too well-brought up to let it show. But what if one evening I were to let something slip? Howard is keeping a watchful eye on me as we each work the room in our own individual styles. You could say that this is my very-well paid job.

But by the fifth glass of champagne I'm starting to think that it's payback time. With every throb of my bottom lip and every time I have to offer up the same rehearsed excuse of a clumsy fall off my horse (I don't even ride, for fuck's sake), it's another nail in the coffin.

On the way home in the car at two a.m. I slump sideways in the backseat and I can feel Howard's bottled-up fury beside me. He has no real cause tonight. After all, I said nothing untoward, but maybe he could tell from the quiet smiles and looks of sympathy they throw him that everyone's expecting Something to Happen. But how will he do it? He has to maintain the illusion. Still, he must know some good doctors, they'll be thinking, somewhere where she can disappear quietly from the scene, spread the word about a mental breakdown and then a discreet divorce in the fullness of time, perhaps?

Well, I'll not be going quietly.

Passing through Notting Hill, Howard suddenly raps on the driver's screen. 'Take me to the flat and then take Mrs. Berrington home.'

Oh, I get it. Need one of your boys now, do you? Well, at least I'll have peace and quiet tomorrow. Take the dogs out. Bit of fresh air. Put my feet up.

Check the contents of his safe.

8

Sunday 21 November 2004

The text alert woke Eva from a deep sleep. Grunting, she groped for her phone and squinted at the screen. *For God's sake, Roz, it's five in the morning and…..*

She read the text a few times to make sure she'd understood it correctly. 'Come today, Woodberrow. Watch naughty videos with me. Bring passport.'

Eva rubbed her eyes. Roz had obviously been on a bender. She probably wouldn't remember sending this text by tomorrow. Eva snuggled down and tried to get back to sleep without success. Her mind started to tick over – *naughty videos? What's that all about? And why bring my passport?*

She would ring Roz later, just to make sure she was OK. Roz had always seemed to know her limits with booze and coke, enough sense left in her not to risk an overdose. But a creeping sense of dread wrapped itself around Eva's heart. Accidents were always possible. And what had Howard maybe done now?

She sat up. The clock said five-twenty-two. The house was quiet, save for the reassuring gentle hum of Douglas' breathing apparatus she could hear remotely through the baby alarm on her bedside table. She would need to be downstairs by six anyway to check on him. Now would be a good time to phone, maybe, although as she hit the speed-dial button she figured Roz would probably have passed out by now and might not appreciate being woken.

Roz answered on the second ring. Alert, calm even.

'Roz, are you all right?'

'Never better, chick. Come up to Woodberrow as soon as you can. I've got something to show you.'

'What the hell's going on? And what's this about a passport?'

Roz's laugh was strange, controlled, and empty of emotion. Eva shivered and drew her duvet around her.

'OK, maybe not right now. But come anyway. We need to talk.'

'What has Howard done now?'

The phone went dead.

Roz didn't sound drunk. She didn't sound high or hysterical. And yet Eva felt a dull ache in her stomach, that tug that she knew meant something terrible was about to happen and she had no way of stopping it. It was the feeling that she recognized from her nursing experience when she knew that something had gone dreadfully wrong with a patient's treatment and that the situation had reached the point of no return. But at this moment, she couldn't guess whether it was about Roz or herself. She only knew she had to go and go now.

She roused Alex from his slumbers in the spare room. She wasn't sure whether she was making sense, as he screwed up his eyes but he eventually nodded. To be on the safe side, she scribbled down Douglas' care instructions for Alex to follow and left the note pinned on the kitchen cork noticeboard.

Half an hour later, Eva reversed her Peugeot 206 out of the drive and drove through the empty West London suburbs lashed by relentless rain which made it hard to see the road. But this was a route she knew well enough. Howard's manor house in Woodberrow had been the scene of several Tory party fund-raising events to which Roz had sent Eva begging invitations to help her get through the awful artificiality of playing the gracious hostess. But wouldn't Howard be there today, playing his weekend country squire role?

The rain had stopped by the time Eva reached Woodberrow forty-five minutes later. Her car's headlights illuminated oaks and chestnuts still burdened with the last remnants of dripping foliage, and large pools of water forming along the edges of the narrow lanes. The lanes became rougher for a while, until she turned left at a sign for the church and then soon after on her right the familiar stone pillars loomed into vision, topped with lion statues and with tall iron gates already open as if expecting her arrival. The road surface transformed into the smoothness that announced wealth and status.

Throughout the journey Eva had talked herself back into a state of calmness and practicality. Roz had not sounded as if she were in danger. She had a track record of melodramatic gestures. This would probably be some overstated event. But as Eva parked outside the Jacobean manor house and saw the front door already open an icy grip returned to her heart.

As she climbed out of her car she saw a light come on in the open hallway and a figure appeared. Roz was standing there, swaying slightly, clad only in skimpy black lace underwear. As Eva approached her, Roz's puffy face and split lip came into focus.

'Bloody hell, Roz – is he still here?'

Roz threw back her head and screamed with laughter. 'Oh, you're going to love this, chick! Come and watch the show!'

Eva's heart was pounding against her ribs as Roz ushered her into a small oak-panelled room she had not seen before. An armchair stood with its back to them and for a fleeting moment Eva expected to see Howard's dead body slumped in it and was relieved to find it empty. Roz saw the expression on Eva's face and subsided into giggles.

'You didn't think that, did you? Oh my God, what is going on in your head, woman?'

'I might ask you the same thing! Jesus Christ, Roz, you've scared me shitless! What are you up to?'

'Not me, chick, Him. Come on, get yourself comfortable.' She picked up the remote control for the DVD and settled on the floor, pulling Eva down beside her.

The image on the screen was grainy and it took Eva a few seconds to work out what was going on. And to recognize the face of one of the naked men lying in the middle of the group of young boys as Howard. After a minute she turned her head away.

Roz looked at her. The beam of smug satisfaction slipped from her face and she switched off the TV screen. 'Sick bastard, isn't he?'

Eva closed her eyes. 'How the hell did you get this stuff?'

'Let's just say, I have my own connections.'

Eva wanted to blot out the images of terrified-looking

prepubescent boys. She took a deep breath and shook herself. Roz passed her a glass of Scotch and Eva drank it down without tasting it. 'What are you going to do?' she asked Roz eventually.

'Well what do you think, chick? You surely don't think he should get away with this?'

Eva shook her head and then took in her friend's damaged face. 'Can you cope with the backlash too?'

A smile spread slowly across Roz's face. 'Well, I won't be here, will I? And you're coming with me.'

Weak sunshine filtered through the trees as Eva drove back into Whittington Avenue and parked outside her house in the early afternoon. Looking up at the windows she felt sick as she realized that this could be the last week of her life here.

One day she might have to account for what would happen this week. She looked at her hands, those which had held the dying fingers of others in her nursing career, and wondered whether she really had it within her to use them to precipitate the death of the person she most loved.

She wished her choices were as clear as Roz's. Roz had plenty of reasons to leave now, and the satisfaction that the DVD she would post to the police with a covering note just before her departure would be her sweet revenge on the man who had used her for thirteen years. Roz had the rest of her life to carve out a new existence somewhere else. The only crime she would be committing would be about the money she was about to steal from Howard's safe to kick-start her new life.

Eva's hands shook as she texted Roz. 'Can't do this. You go. We'll catch up one day.' But even as she hit the 'send' button Eva knew there would be no catch-up. She would be counting the days until her disease took her, hoping it would be sudden enough not to have time to look back and think, *could have, should have.*

Unless Douglas went first.

She and Roz had drunk too much, dreamed too grandly, laughed too loudly. It had seemed so obvious in the comfort of a Scotch-fuelled haze. Eva had protested, 'I'm not supposed to drink too much, the doctors said,' and had then burst into waves of giggling with the next glass she emptied. 'But you're a long time dead,' Roz had retorted and they had clung to each other, laughing and crying at the same time. 'Prague it is then,' Roz had held up her glass in a toast, 'here's to cheap booze and fags, and no questions asked.' After all, if Eva was going to finish her life anywhere, why not back in her homeland, maybe amongst long-lost relatives? Who knows what else might be found there? Eva had smiled at her friend's childlike exuberance and the idea started to grow in her mind. A lifetime dream fulfilled, perhaps? 'You'll hate the cold winters, Roz. Fuck that, fur coats will be cheap there, won't they?'

It had all sounded so easy.

Now, sitting in her car outside her house, the illusions shattering with each cup of espresso she had drunk to ensure a safe drive, Eva's mind was exhausted and empty. She had been a fool. Roz could follow her own dreams, but Eva wanted to be able to live with herself each morning she woke.

When she turned the key in the front door she had a sense of returning reluctantly to prison.

Alex was hurrying down the stairs. 'Eva, where the hell have you been? You know I've got a work shift starting - .'

She bristled, startled out of her stupor. 'No one's going to die, Alex, just because you're a bit late!'

'What's happened to you? Are you drunk?'

She brushed past him. 'Go on. Off you go.' She hurried upstairs and shot into the bathroom, holding back the vomit just in time.

A soft knock. 'Are you OK?'

'Yes. Go on. I'll be fine.'

'Look, why don't we go out tomorrow for dinner? I'll get Miriam in to look after Dad.'

'Sure.'

Why not? What else can Alex do? He's trying to re-build bridges, looking to restore the ease of his previous life. Isn't everyone looking for that easy life, the one with no hard choices to make? Once she was sure he was gone, Eva crept out and went down to see Douglas. She stood in the doorway, watching him doze as his chest rose and fell slowly, deeply. His mouth was slightly open and there was a faint wheeze-cum-snore, like the softness of a puppy content in its slumber. Suddenly, his eyes jerked open and he focused on her face.

'You're back.'

She smiled, eyes brimming with unshed tears.

'I want to do this, Eva. I want to be with Catherine again. Soon.' His voice was strong and clear today.

She thought of all the times a pair of pleading eyes at the hospice had silently begged her for a quick and painless acceleration of their final journey. Relatives who had railed against the senseless prolonging of suffering of their beloveds. The lectures of her superiors who said that they had no right to play God. Behind her in the hall, Eva could hear the shrill ringtone of an incoming text on her mobile. She looked around and then back at Douglas.

Slowly, as the tears trickled down her face, she nodded.

9

Later that same day

'When will you go?'

Douglas' tone was as casual as if he had been asking Eva when she planned to take a holiday. But her leaving date would have to be the same as his own final day of life. The two events were inevitably intertwined. Staying even a day longer would mean discovery by Alex. And neither of them could predict how Alex would react. Over the years she had been with Alex and during the inevitable discussions of their work that conversation had never taken place: 'would you, ever? Been tempted?' Even in the years preceding his specialization in pediatric surgery, where the lust for life overcame for many the agonies of treatment, there must have been times when compassion overruled duty? But then, it was only one of many possible conversations that had never arisen. Everything superficial – what had happened that day, who was moving jobs where – and Eva saw the patterns, the avoidance of anything that required an opening-up of one soul to another. Always in a hurry, often overlapping shifts with each other, exhaustion at the end of a shift leading to one or both of them falling asleep in front of the TV.

Since Douglas had come to live with them Eva felt they knew each other better than she and Alex. Douglas was never afraid to raise contentious issues, thrived on debating them. In the hours he and Eva had spent together she had learned so much, acquired new perspectives on life and faced up to assumptions she had made. It was through Douglas that she had reluctantly come to the painful realization that she and Alex had an empty life together and her bitterness at her own medical diagnosis had been the more acute for it. A wasted life. She should have left him straightaway to enjoy the rest of what was left to her. Now, the thought of silencing Douglas' powerhouse of a brain forever at her own hands was more than she could bear.

In answer to his question: it had to be soon, before she found even more reasons to stay and fester. She had told him about Roz and he had grunted in sympathetic understanding.

'Now, tell me about your plans. I want to know that you will be enjoying yourself somewhere faraway.'

But she had no plans. In their drunken ravings the day before, Eva had enthused about Prague and how she would finally track down the missing parts of her family's jigsaw puzzle. Roz had wanted to know about the nightlife and what kind of swanky place they could find to live in. But neither of them had a clue where to start. In the cold light of day, someone would have to make some plans.

A text came from Roz, checking that she was still going ahead, asking about next steps.

'You do it. Got enough on my mind.' E.

'Plane or train?' R.

'How the hell do I know???' E. *Can't the bitch see? How does she think I'm feeling?*

It was Douglas who turned out to be the clear-headed one. 'Leave no trace. Not the plane. Think about a circuitous route. Make it hard for people to find you.'

He was right, she knew, she had to get a grip and look beyond the next few days. That evening he made various suggestions, enlivened by the prospect of her journey and destination.

'Make sure you take enough cash. No credit cards. Don't use an ATM abroad – too easy a mistake to make. Do you have enough money?'

'Some small savings. A joint account with Alex.'

'Empty it. He'll earn it back quickly enough.'

So clinical, so decisive.

'Now, when shall we do it, Eva?'

She didn't want to name the day, the time.

'Don't be foolish, woman! This has to be done right. Whilst Alex is out of the house. Enough time for you to get away before anyone tries to follow you.'

She checked the calendar for Alex's work schedule. Home every evening until Thursday when he would be working during the day and then straight into on-call for the evening and night.

'Thursday it is, then,' said Douglas firmly and they locked eyes. She drew on his strength and found calm and reassurance through it. Suddenly it all seemed so simple and right.

They ate dinner together as always, leaving a portion for Alex when he would return around midnight. Douglas quizzed her all evening – about Baba, the stories she recalled from her childhood, and they looked through the old photos again in Baba's box. 'All these years, not knowing. How could you stand it, my dear? Did you never think of visiting before?'

Baba's going to live forever, Eva had thought, *and one day we'll go back together.* But they didn't. Life events swept them along until, one day, Baba wasn't there to be asked and there was no one else to help. She had tried looking online at family history sites. Nothing. As if the family had never existed. And records might not even be in Prague – their origins were in the hinterland, not the city.

'Ach, you'll find something if you keep asking. You just have to be there, that's all. It's not as if you don't know the language, lassie.'

Eva laughed at that. She hadn't spoken Czech in eighteen years. Her language level, even before that, had been limited to basic domestic topics. She didn't even feel Czech.

Douglas was on good form that evening, cheerful, ebullient even. Eva reflected that she had seen this before in terminally-ill patients. Once they knew it was likely to be down to a matter of days, a new spirit would often arise, relief that came from the certainty that pain would soon be gone, and an eagerness to enjoy the last few days with their loved ones. Not all cases, for sure. But more than she would have reckoned.

Once dinner was finished he asked for a single malt. A large one. *What the hell, what difference would it make now?*

'Bring me paper and pen,' he said, 'I want to write the letter now.'

She swallowed hard. This would make it feel real. 'Maybe I should do one too?'

'No! You must leave this to me. My life. My decision.' The final absolution. Sound of mind, if not of body. Brief, business-like in tone. Hard for his fingers to manage the pen. She offered to type it. *No, it must be handwritten*, he insisted, *would look better that he could write it independently and unaided.* Afterwards, he lay back exhausted by the effort and with the effects of the malt whisky kicking in.

'I should leave a note for Alex. Maybe tomorrow, when I'm a little stronger. Oh, I shall sleep well, tonight, lassie. Thank you, for everything.'

And then her tears came again, and he shushed her with comforting words. 'Live, Eva, live. Cherish every little drop of life. Your Baba would surely have wanted you to do that.'

10

Sunday to Tuesday

The reality of what was to happen started to sink in. When Alex returned late, drained and uncommunicative, Eva saw him in a different light, someone to be pitied for the chaos which was about to break around him and over which he would have no control. Father dead. Wife gone. Lover? Would Camille try to help him build a new life? Would the baby be a fresh start for him? Alex was used to being in control, the architect of his own destiny. But destiny was about to deal him an unexpected hand.

In a dreamlike state, Eva went through the motions of Douglas' routine care. They did not speak much, a quiet companiable state existing between them. The persistent soft rain outside provided a gentle background hum. Alex apologized to Eva for his short temper earlier, an act almost unheard of in their relationship. Eva chose to treat this as a sign of his desire to re-connect and when he suggested, tentatively, that he return to their bed she did not demur. What was the point in arguing any longer? *Let our last days together be free of angry moments*, she reasoned and peace drove out hate from her heart from that moment. Because these would be their last days together. How could she return, having done what she intended to do? And who knew how many more days of her own she had left, anyway? Spending them in prison was not part of her plan.

But, strictly speaking, she had no plan. The next morning when Alex had gone to work there was another flurry of texts exchanged with Roz.

'Try the train. Paris first, and then? Do we need to book?' E.

'No clue. Will find out.' R.

'Are tickets named?' E.
'What?' R.
'How no trace us on train?' E.
'Oh. Dunno.' R.
'How much cash should we take?' E.
'No worry, got it covered.' R.
'BE CAREFUL!' E.

Thursday was just a few days away. Half a lifetime, it felt, as the hours ticked by with agonizing sluggishness. Her stomach lurched every time she tried to picture the events of that morning. Could she really go through with it? Douglas might change his mind too. What then?

'Where to meet?' E.
'Waterloo International. About 3.' R.
'OK.' E.
'Shit, do we need visas?' R.
'Don't think so. CR in EU now.' E.
'OK. How u doing?' R.
'Just want this to be over.' E.

How long would Douglas take to slip away? She felt sick at the thought of having to hurry it through, at having the additional pressure of a timetable. Every time she looked at him he seemed so cheerful in comparison, as if he were anticipating a longed-for holiday. But would his nerve hold, once the morphine drip was accelerating his passing? What if either of them panicked? They would both know, from experience, the point of no return when it arrived.

Monday night and no let-up from the drizzle. Douglas settled down for the night at ten as usual. He squeezed her hand and smiled, wordlessly. She smiled back without feeling it. *He must guess how I'm feeling.*

'I want you to promise me, Eva, that you will not fritter away your time afterwards. That you will focus on what you want to do and cherish every moment you do it. I will be very angry if you don't.'

'Don't you worry about that.'

'I mean it! I'll come back to haunt you!' His eyes danced.

There'll be enough haunting going on already, but she smiled back at him anyway. She had worn herself out cleaning the house all day, trying to keep her mind too busy to think. But the more mundane the task, the more her thoughts were free to wander and she found herself thinking about Prague and how it would be. In the evening she looked up images of the city online. But they couldn't tell her what it would be like to live there, how the people would be, how she would feel amongst them. She had never felt Czech, even when Baba had been alive and conversing with her daily in their mother tongue. Baba had not been a stickler for Czech customs anyway, apart from some of the food they ate. Memories of *guláš* with bread *knedlíky*, dark rye bread with caraway, chicken *řízek* with mashed potatoes – a tiny part of the culture. Eva would feel like a stranger in her own land. Would it be worth it? What if it all turned out to be an illusion, if she couldn't trace her family, where else would she go? Panic would set in with these thoughts until the breakthrough moment: *it wouldn't matter*. She could take it one day at a time. Just as long as she tried to live for each moment and not in the past.

She was asleep when Alex returned, deep in a dream where she wandered through sunlit squares of Gothic buildings and bullet-ridden walls, walking towards Baba and another woman whose face she couldn't quite make out.

Alex woke early on Tuesday morning, sensing something was wrong. Five-thirty, just after. Eva still slept beside him.

He hurried downstairs. In Douglas' room he could make out the shape in bed in the nightlight's dimness. There was an unsteadiness in Douglas' breathing rate that alerted him. He examined the breathing equipment – everything seemed in order. On the display screen the heart-rate was slower than usual at forty-three beats per minute, with some spaced-out dips. Blood pressure was a little higher than usual. He bent down to examine his father's face and at that point Douglas' eyes flew open and Alex saw fear there.

'I'm not ready yet! Tell her – oh!'
'It's all right, Dad. It's OK. Did you have a bad dream?'
'Dream? Oh, yes, a dream.'
'Do you want a drink?'
'No. No, I'll be fine. Just a wee while and - .' Douglas looked past him. 'Is Eva gone?'

'What? No, she's asleep. I can sort you out until she comes down.'

Douglas looked confused, then closed his eyes. Alex frowned and rubbed his chin. Bad dream, probably, he was just disorientated. Best to keep him under closer observation, though. He went upstairs to wake Eva.

'Don't worry, I'll sit with him longer this morning. But probably nothing. You can get off to work.'

'He asked if you were gone.'

'Really? He is a bit confused, then. I'll go down in a moment.'

As Alex drove to the hospital an hour later he mused about his father. Decline could happen any time, he knew that. Mini-strokes were also a possibility in these cases. He had asked Eva to double-check the oxygen tank. Alex had prepared himself months ago for his father's eventual death. Would he at least be able to say good-bye? That had helped with his mother's passing, at least. He should try and spend some more time at home, take the pressure off Eva, make things up to her somehow. He'd look at his week's schedule.

'I'm sorry, lassie. I didna know what I was saying.'

'It's all right. Alex hasn't guessed anything.'

'Close-run thing.'

'Don't worry now, Douglas.'

'I'm so tired, lassie. So very tired now.'

Eva knew it too. Since Sunday there had been a change, slight at first, but something different, slower now. Nature was perhaps starting her own countdown, easing them along the path they would be taking.

Roz spent Monday sorting through her clothes. What to pack? Evening wear? Which shoes? But how many suitcases could she afford to drag around with her? At least on a train there would be no baggage allowance to worry about. What could she bear to leave behind? She wanted everything. Howard didn't deserve to keep any of her stuff, even if it had been bought with his money. She had paid for them in full, plenty, well-earned over the years. She'd cram in all her jewelry for sure. Shame about the furniture. Why she couldn't just hire a removal van and – well, why not? Who would know where they had been taken, if she paid the guys to keep quiet?

If they had thought about this much earlier she and Eva could have looked for a house to rent there and she could have sent on some of her stuff. Could you arrange that, from here? She could have found someone in her network to help. But then, that would have left a trail to be followed. *It's not bloody fair, why did things have to get so complicated? Why am I having to scuttle away like a thief in the night, with so little to show for my life?*

Howard had stayed in the London flat since Saturday, no contact. She was left free to rattle around the house and estate with only the daily cleaner and Wanda, her assistant, for occasional company and gossip about what was going on in the village. Woodberrow was just half a mile away and Henley a few miles further, but Roz didn't venture out much anyway. This wasn't her world, the suffocating network of county ladies doing their bit for the community whilst they stabbed each other in the back. Howard liked to play his country squire role to perfection by hosting the annual summer village fete, a fundraiser for the church restorations, in the vast estate grounds and Roz would delegate the event's organization to a team of willing helpers who she paid well for their time and sweat. What would she miss about her life here? Nothing. Just the money, and a lot of that she had extracted from Howard's safe and from an ATM in preparation for Thursday. On Tuesday she packaged up the DVD and wrote the letter. She had hesitated when deciding where to send it. The Leader of the Opposition? It would get hushed up, for sure. So, straight to the police then. She should have had copies of the disk made - damn, too late now. She had to hope it would hit the right mark. She would post it Thursday morning, before she took the train from Henley to London.

Roz went for long walks around the estate in the pouring rain, marvelling at the autumnal shades in the trees as if seeing them for the first time. On Tuesday evening she flitted between TV channels, not seeing anything. No goodbye letters to write. No one would miss her. She drank nearly half a bottle of Howard's best single malt before passing out on the sofa with the TV still on, grateful that her mother had not lived to see this moment.

11

Wednesday 24 November 2004

Eva lay in the early-morning darkness and listened to the rise and fall of Alex's deep breathing next to her. Why had she let him make love to her last night? Because she had felt sorry for him, despite his betrayal with Camille. She could have carried on punishing him but his life was about to change forever too. This was to be a way of saying goodbye. She had felt nothing, not even bothering to fake an orgasm. He must have known. Silence throughout the act, mechanical movements, it had taken just a few minutes and then he had rolled off her, exhausted even by this small effort, and fallen asleep. She tried to remember the last time. Four months ago? Five? Not even a mercy fuck when she had come home with the news that something inside her brain would soon kill her. Not even a cuddle. Any of his patients might have at least have had his arm around their shoulders.

    She wanted him to go to work quickly today. There was so much to do. She had to think about what to pack. Tomorrow morning would find her mind too flaky to concentrate on the practicalities of leaving.

    'Eva,' murmured Alex and he moved his body closer to her.

    'Do you want some tea?' She was out of the bed in a flash before their bodies could touch.

    Whilst the kettle was boiling she peeked around the door to Douglas' room. Reassuring beeps from the machinery and snuffles from Douglas greeted her. She would go in soon. Alex was making tea when she returned to the kitchen. He moved towards her, arms outstretched. She dodged and grabbed her tea mug instead.

    He looked glum. 'Is this how you want it?'

She paused. 'It's so soon. I need time.' *Getting good at lying.*

'I'm trying,' he pleaded. 'I want to make things right.'

Last night over dinner at a local Chinese restaurant he had told her that Camille was going back to Lyon.

'And the baby?' Eva's tone had been calm. *No point in making a fuss now.*

'Don't know if she'll keep it.'

'Oh.' She wanted to say, *how convenient. No need to pay maintenance, then. Just dispose of the problem in an incinerator.*

And then he had talked about his work. Not about the two of them. Not how he was going to make things up to her, no questions about what she wanted or whether she would like to go away for a short break. All about him. It made her decision to leave even easier. In bed that night she prayed that maybe Douglas would slip away in the night, that her intervention would not be necessary. She prayed that she could leave the house at midday tomorrow with a clean soul.

After Alex had left for work, Roz started texting again.

'Packed yet?' R.

'Still doing it. Working out how much to take. Need to be light. How about u?' E.

'Tricky. Got cash sorted.' R.

'How much?' E.

'Don't ask!' R.

'Watch it. Security screens at station, etc.?' E.

'Stuff it down my knickers?' R.

'Gross!' E.

She knew she shouldn't be joking around. Things were different for Roz. No looking back, no what-ifs. What would Roz do when she was gone, one day? Could she stay in a foreign country alone? But Roz wouldn't be alone for long. Men still loved that wild red hair, the sultry green eyes, and her animal lust for life. Even the booze and coke hadn't destroyed her looks yet. Roz would surely find solace somewhere with someone else's fortune to enjoy. At thirty-six years, the two of them could not be more different. Each time Eva looked in the mirror more careworn lines seemed to appear, early grey hairs, and a hairstyle that needed updating.

A high wind had been up since the morning, with clouds of

fallen leaves whooshing high over hedges, causing the willow in the back garden to bend at precarious angles, with weaker branches and twigs snapping off like matchsticks. Eva couldn't settle. She buzzed from one room to another, not even sure what she was supposed to be checking. Douglas seemed to be sleepier today. When he spoke his voice was tremulous and her heart beat rapidly as she observed the display screen showing his own heart-rate was continuing to fall slightly. *Please God, just take him. Take him now. Why are you making him hang on like this?* Old prayers learned at Baba's knee but half-forgotten since then now crept back into her mind. *Forgive us our trespasses, as we forgive those who trespass against us.* It should be enough that Douglas would forgive her, surely?

Her empty stomach ached. Every mouthful she tried to force down tasted like cardboard. When she was sure that Douglas was asleep she quickly walked down the road to the shopping parade and took a full daily cash allowance from the ATM from her joint account with Alex and from her own nest-egg account. She had already done the same on Monday and Tuesday, and tomorrow she would take the final amount on the way to the Tube station. A small contribution in comparison with what Roz would bring, perhaps. But how long would it all last?

In her mind, Eva had rehearsed all the timings: the walk to Ealing Broadway station, how long the Tube train would take to reach Waterloo. Roz had the Eurostar train timetable sorted, she had assured Eva. They would be in Paris by six o'clock UK time. In Paris they would switch stations and take a train heading east, maybe a circuitous route via Germany to make their trail less obvious. How often would there be a passport check? Waterloo, definitely, Paris, too, but after that? How soon could their trail go cold? Eva didn't like the uncertainty. In her nursing work she had always known the plan, the risks, and the timings. This was different. This could go horribly wrong with one false move.

But once they were there, in Prague, these feelings would stop. She could start with a clean slate. It could even be an adventure. Douglas had begged her to cherish every moment, and she would. She would learn to live life for every day and with an urgency that would make everything fresh and exciting. It seemed so easy one minute. And yet, in a flash, the fear of uncertainty returned with the thought of the deed that she had to perform tomorrow driving out all her hopes and desires.

She had to wake Douglas for lunch and helped him feed himself. He was a little irritable and cursed himself when he dripped food onto the tray from his mouth.

'It's all right, you're doing fine. Just a bit sleepy, still?'

'Don't talk down to me, woman! I get enough of that from Alex and Miriam.'

'Sorry.'

'Aye, well, it's not your fault. I'm not quite the full biscuit today.'

Eva flushed.

'Don't worry, lassie. It'll be fine.' He gripped her hand, still surprisingly strong. 'Just don't lose your nerve.'

He brightened in the afternoon, started talking about Catherine and how she had always loved autumn colours and wild weather. *Brought out the beast in her*, his eyes twinkled. Eva remembered Catherine's vibrancy and how the thought of her light being extinguished forever had been so heart-wrenching for them all.

Douglas challenged Eva to a game of chess, which ended in a draw. 'You're getting better, lassie.'

'You've been a good teacher.'

When he dozed off again about four, she went upstairs, looked at her open suitcase and small holdall on the bed and finished packing within half an hour. What was the point in agonizing over what to wear? Baba's box was the last item to go in and she wrapped it lovingly inside an Indian cotton shawl. Her winter coat would probably not cope with the Czech weather in the next few months. That would be one of the first things to buy. Nothing expensive. *One winter's wear is probably be all I'll need.* That thought make her tremble.

She climbed the loft ladder carefully to stash the case and holdall just far enough in to be easy to retrieve. She checked her passport again. The photo, taken three years earlier, reflected confidence and ease, head held high. A lifetime ago, it seemed now. She and Alex had gone to Portugal, a short break to fit in with their hectic work schedules. She had been a Ward Sister, a high-flier in her domain, married to a handsome and dedicated consultant surgeon. Comfortably off, smugly secure with a predictably stable future, they had thought. Life had turned on a sixpence for them since then.

She didn't want Alex to come home tonight. She wanted at least to be asleep when he did. But Alex turned up earlier than usual at seven, buoyant, chatty, engaging Douglas in more games of chess when she could see that the old man wanted to rest. The games were not a success. Douglas became increasingly irritated by Alex's joviality and made some serious mistakes which lost him his key pieces too early in the game.

'You're slipping, Dad. Or are you just letting me win for a change?'

Douglas had harrumphed, pushed the board away impatiently, watched Alex put away the set with a mixture of annoyance and regret on his face. Eva sat in silence in the armchair, observing the father-son tableau, heavy with knowledge she could not share.

'Early night?' Alex suggested.

'I'm going to stay up a bit, stay with him. He's been a bit – not himself today.'

'I could do that.'

'You go up, Alex, you need your sleep more than I do.'

He pulled a face but nodded, planting a kiss on her cheek. 'Don't stay up too long.'

She wrapped a shawl around her, despite the heat, and settled into the armchair opposite Douglas' bed, watching. Thinking. Dreading.

12

Thursday 25 November 2004

'Tea, Mr. McKinley?'

Alex nodded and the nurse hurried off. He had already conducted a quick ward round, nine consultations in clinic and it was still only ten-forty-five. Starting early had its advantages; some of his colleagues didn't turn up till eight-thirty so there were fewer interruptions. Thursdays were treadmill-days. Getting through the clinic by midday was usually his goal, then he could move on to concentrating on research, paperwork, even the occasional surgery although he preferred to dedicate particular mornings for his operations in the knowledge that his brain and reflexes would be sharper. Pediatric surgery was a young man's game and he was in his mid-forties. Young by other standards, but getting towards middle age slowdown in this particular game. He had to make the most of his gifts whilst he was still on top form.

Getting enough sleep was also part of the requirements and last night he had tossed and turned, acutely aware that Eva was also awake beside him. 'I'll go to the spare room,' he had said.

'It's all right. Do what you need to do for yourself. I'll be fine.'

She would, indeed, be fine. She never made a fuss, never issued ultimatums. She was his friend and he had hurt her. For the first time in his life Alex felt ashamed of himself. He couldn't even look his father in the eye anymore. That old man wasting away still had more power and authority in his little finger than he could ever possess himself. If pushed, he would have to admit that he had become jealous of the bond between his father and Eva, relegated to the role of observer and feeling helpless to bring comfort to either of them.

Whilst he lay awake the previous night he thought back to Douglas' demeanour on Monday. A definite deterioration. Perhaps they would be counting just weeks now, or even days. The old man was sleeping more, irritable when awake as if in a hurry. Alex didn't doubt that his father wanted to re-join his late mother. His father was the last person he would have associated with a belief in the afterlife – never a topic they had discussed – but who knows what effect the prospect of your own impending death does to your beliefs? What would he do himself? He didn't believe at all. Faced with a similar diagnosis, he would find a way to hurry his own end, avoid the indignity of a slow painful exit. It wasn't a question that he had discussed with Eva about her own situation. After her initial shock and grief, she had drifted into a state of passive acceptance he could not understand. She kept every day to the same schedule of caring for his father, with the occasional respite from Miriam's services. The house had become her prison. And he hadn't even asked her what he could do to help. But maybe that could change now. If his father really was in slow decline, then she could look forward to a welcome release and perhaps they could start all over again.

By mid-morning he had reached a decision. He would insist that Miriam came more frequently. He would change his work schedule to see more of both Douglas and Eva. If she wouldn't go away on a short break then he would think of some other way for them to have personal time away from their lives' demands.

He could finish this clinic by eleven-thirty if he tried. It would take about forty minutes to get home. He'd ring Miriam now to book her in for a few hours so he could take Eva out to lunch, a first small step, get themselves used to being together again. He could always catch up on his research later in the day, if his on-call shift was quiet.

He drained his tea-mug and shuffled the pile of manila patient files on his desk, renewed and purposeful.

Miriam had told Alex she could be at the house by twelve-thirty. That would do. Eleven-twenty-two now. Alex switches on his car engine and drives out of the hospital car park. A sunny day after so much rain lifts his spirits. A good day to start over.

He switches on the car radio. A threatened Tube strike has been averted at the last minute. Thank God for not working in central London anymore, he thinks. Half an hour, on average, to drive under seven miles each way to work at Northwick Park Hospital, not a great burden. *There's a new Italian restaurant just opened near Ealing Broadway, I'll take Eva for lunch there. Won't be far from the house, then, if there's a problem with Dad.* Eleven-fifty-two and he is parked on his driveway. *Nice timing. Nice surprise for Eva.* The meal out the other night had been awkward. He is going to try harder today.

When he opens the front door, the first thing that strikes him is the silence. He can't hear the usual background hum of Douglas' nebulizer. Then his eye catches the sight of a suitcase and holdall outside Douglas' room further down the hall. A question is half-formed in his mind as he pushes the door open.

The curtains are closed. Eva is crouching by Douglas' bed, her face turned towards him as he enters, frozen in misery. Douglas is covered by a white bed sheet, from head to toe. The machinery is silent. The drip stands empty, bag removed. Eva gets up unsteadily. Her face is puffy and damp, she's breathing fast. She stares at him and then steps aside, her arms hugging herself as he approaches the bed. Taking a deep breath, he stretches out his hand and lifts the sheet to reveal his father's face. He swallows hard as he takes in the peace he reads there, the mouth slightly open, the pain lines erased. Alex's hand quivers slightly as he replaces the sheet.

He turns to face Eva.

'When? Why didn't you ring me?'

She is silent and looks away.

He spies the envelope on the bedside table, propped up against the lamp. No addressee. 'Is that for me?'

Eva whispers, 'it's for everyone.'

He picks up the envelope, hesitates, and then rips it open. Eva sinks into the armchair and buries her face in her hands.

He finds it hard to breathe as he reads the words. Words of exoneration for Eva. No apologies. No final words of comfort or love for him. His heart feels ready to burst. In a flash, he turns, picks up a syringe from the uncleared tray and hurls himself at Eva. She flings herself on the floor to avoid the stab and he stands over her, panting, hands clenched. She rolls away, scrambles up and runs to the door.

'How could you do this!' he screams, 'you bitch!' He sinks to the floor, bent double.

She stands at the door, looking down at him. 'It's what he wanted,' she says quietly.

'I don't fucking care! He didn't have long. Why couldn't you both wait? Why couldn't you let me say goodbye?'

'Because he knew what you'd be like, Alex. He knew I couldn't leave him with you.'

Alex hurls himself at her, grabbing her arms and they both fall on the floor. She kicks and squirms and throws him off her. He crashes his shoulder against the wall and cries out in pain. They stare at each other, both crying now, Eva edging towards the door.

'Don't go!'

She shakes her head.

'If you stay, this can all go away. Eva, please! I won't say anything. They'll know he was going soon.'

'Don't be a fool! They'll check it out, check what's in his bloodstream. Don't you think I've already thought about that?'

He wipes his face, takes deep breaths. He is calmer now. 'Planned this well, didn't you, the pair of you? So, where are you off to?'

She is silent.

'Don't think I won't find you. You'll have to pay.'

'I already have,' she says over her shoulder as she leaves the room and he hears the bags being dragged across the hall carpet, the front door opening and shutting with a hint of a click. Alex remains on the floor of the darkened room, his arms wrapped around his knees, rocking to and fro.

13

Roz slumped in her chair, sipping her third gin-and-tonic. The bar she had found was just a short distance from Waterloo station, down a quiet side street where she felt safe from prying eyes. Dark sunglasses obscured her bloodshot eyes. Her cut lip from the previous Saturday was healing, easy to disguise. Even so, she felt others' eyes on her, the few drinkers this time of day making it feel harder to disappear. *It's crazy to be this scared. Who's gonna know I'm here?*

She had left Woodberrow soon after midday. Wanda had been fussing around the house. Roz had snapped at her a few times and then apologized. It wasn't the girl's fault. She wasn't to know. Roz had spent half the night packing, filling and then emptying a couple of suitcases, realising it would be stupid to be loaded down with too much stuff. She wanted to wear the silver fox fur coat Howard had bought her two years earlier – a gift of apology, for bawling her out one time in front of some guests – but Eva had said they should be careful, neutral enough to blend into a crowd. It would take too much space in her suitcase. But she crammed it in, somehow. Other clothes could be replaced more easily, not this. She wanted something to make her feel good in the days when things weren't going so well.

She had asked Wanda to drive her to Henley station. A trip to visit her aunt in Manchester for a couple of weeks, she had lied. *Let them start looking for me there, then. If they'll bother at all.* Wanda had also been instructed to post the DVD package. Her eyes had widened when she had read the address of Scotland Yard. Roz had given her an envelope with one thousand pounds of Howard's cash from the safe – *'go on, enjoy yourself whilst I'm away!'* – and had waved away the girl's protests. She wanted to say, *thanks for everything and good luck,* but the less she talked to her the easier it would be for Wanda to protest her ignorance about everything. Howard would be merciless in any interrogation.

But Howard would pay. For everything. That DVD would blow open his web of lies.

Even that thought and the drinks at the Waterloo bar didn't make Roz feel any happier. The euphoria of that Sunday afternoon with Eva, planning their escape, was disintegrating. The pit of her stomach felt like molten lead. *No going back now. Howard deserves everything coming to him. Not gonna waste one more day.*

She had sent two texts to Eva since midday. No reply. Had Eva lost her nerve? Had Douglas begged her to stay? *Just do it, Eva. Hurry up. I can't do this on my own.*

She ought to go and buy the tickets. *No. Too early.* She didn't want to hang around the platform waiting. Maybe there would be CCTV cameras somewhere in the station? *No. Leave it till the last minute, grab tickets, jump on the train with loads of others around us. That's the best way. And just another small drink or two before I go......*

The beep of a text. '10 mins to Waterloo. Where u?' E.

'Nearby. U OK?' R.

A couple of minutes passed.

'Got tickets?' E.

'Not yet.' R.

'Do it now! Meet ticket office.' E.

So, Eva was coming, after all. And she was telling her what to do. Roz felt a momentary flash of anger. If it hadn't been for her own prodding last Sunday, for her own determination to break free, nothing would have changed. Eva would have ploughed on till she or Douglas hit the grave first. *How dare she boss me around now?*

By the time Roz walked into Waterloo mainline station her arms ached from carrying her cases as did her neck from craning around every few minutes to see if she was being followed. Th effects of the gin-and-tonics were kicking in, with a blinding headache starting to blur her vision. She just managed to negotiate the escalator down to the Eurostar terminal where she saw Eva in a corner, shrunken, and sitting on a small suitcase with a holdall beside her. In that moment, Roz knew there was no turning back.

'Why haven't you bought the tickets yet, Roz?'

Straight in. Just like nothing was happening. Just another

journey. 'You OK? Eva?'

'Come on. I'll do it. Christ, you stink of gin! How the hell are you going to manage if you're just going to get wasted all the time?'

'Not now, right? Just bloody well be grateful I'm here!'

They glared at each other for a few moments.

'Let's get on with it. Give me some cash for the tickets,' Eva said.

'We shouldn't be spending this yet. Use your card.'

'Don't be stupid, Roz – they'll trace us in no time! I don't know how much – look, don't open your bag like that, everyone can see!'

There were several ticket counters already open, two of them with no queue. Eva moved over quickly. 'Two tickets to Paris, please.'

Roz stood behind her, shielding her from the view of other travellers. The girl behind the counter looked too bright and sparkly for Roz's mood. 'Certainly. Travelling on which date, please?'

'Um, today. For the next train, whenever that is.'

The girl frowned slightly. 'I'm afraid it would have been much cheaper to book in advance, but I'll see what I can do. Single or return?'

'Sorry? Return – of course.' Eva mumbled.

'And your date of return?'

'We haven't actually decided for sure…' Eva began. Roz bristled behind her. 'Um, what's the best option?'

'I could give you the fully-flexible ticket but it still needs a return date. However, there are no cancellation charges if you change your mind about the date later.'

'We'll do that then – how much?'

'That'll be three hundred and nine pounds. Each.'

'What the fuck?' The words slipped out before Roz could stop herself. The girl smiled sympathetically and her gaze wandered past them for a moment. Roz turned and saw a queue forming. She leant on the counter, pushing Eva away. 'Actually, make that two singles. We won't be - .'

'No!' Eva pushed Roz back. 'Look, just give us return tickets. Put down third of January for the return date and we'll worry about any changes later.'

'OK. I'll just call up the screen.' The girl tapped away on her keyboard, a half-smile on her face. Roz tapped her manicured fingernails on the counter until Eva placed her hand over them.

'You have just less than fifty-five minutes till the next train to clear through security. I need both passports, please.'

'Why?'

'To know the names which will go on the tickets, of course.' Then she flashed that bright smile again.

Oh shit. Roz and Eva exchanged glances. Eva shrugged her shoulders and reached into her handbag. Roz copied her action, slapping her passport down hard. The girl's eyes widened slightly when Roz then placed bundles of tens and twenties in front of her. An elderly man at the next position was eyeing the pile of cash and Roz turned her back to block his view. The tickets and passports were pushed back under the glass screen.

'Have a good trip!' trilled the cashier.

'I want a triple espresso after that,' Roz muttered.

'You'll have to wait. And you need to do something with all that cash, Roz, or you won't get through security. Go buy traveller's cheques. Use more than one office or they'll ask questions with that much money.'

Twenty minutes later, they were queuing up for security. Roz felt like a bag lady, struggling with the two cases which now contained her whole world. Her hair flopped into her eyes as she hoisted the cases on to the conveyer belt for the X-ray machine, the newly-purchased travellers' cheques safely stored in her handbag. No beeps. *Thank God.* Eva's turn. A warning beep. A belt she should have taken off before the walk-through. Quick frisk. Enough of a delay. They hurried down the platform, Eva pausing every couple of minutes so that Roz could catch up as she tottered along in her high-heeled suede boots.

'Come on!' Eva hissed.

Roz collapsed into her seat and as the train slipped away smoothly she had to stifle a sob. *This isn't how it had meant to be.* When she turned to look at Eva beside her she saw her slumped, eyes closed, her face taut with pain. Maybe the other passengers would just think they had had a heavy night. *I don't have to go to Prague with Eva. Why can't I stay in Paris, enjoy myself? She can find her family on her own without dragging me along, and then come and join me. Who in their right minds would choose Central Europe over Paris, for God's sake?*

But she had made a promise to Eva, that drunken Sunday afternoon: *I'll look after you, chick. We're mates, right, and that's what mates do.* On her own, Eva could have a seizure, the last one, and no one would care, no one would be there who knew and loved her like she did, despite everything. *No one should die alone.*

Howard's money would insulate them, Roz reckoned, through the worst they would face. They would have an amazing time, in fact. It could be a blast. And Prague could be easier and cheaper for her to get her coke fixes.

But even as each mile separated them from their past, Roz wondered why she still felt such a sense of dread.

14

A biting wind greets them as they step out of the train at Paris Gard du Nord station just before seven local time. Eva reminds Roz to remove her sunglasses as they approach passport control. Her stomach does somersaults as their passport pages are flicked through by a surly dark-skinned woman who, after casting her eyes over Roz's lip scab for a moment, gestures them past. Eva breaks into a cold sweat and her head is throbbing. *First step done. Just keep going.*

'I'll go and find out about trains to Prague,' she says.

'Don't leave me here!' pleads Roz.

'Come with me then.'

Eva finds out they need to take a train from Gard de l'Est to Frankfurt, then an overnight sleeper to Prague. They stagger the ten-minute walk to the station where Roz finally sinks down on a banquette in a bar and refuses to move any further until she's had a strong shot of something. More of her money wasted, Roz grumbles, when Eva insists on buying return tickets to Prague to detract from any unwanted attention. At least the tickets are unnamed this time, argues Eva, our trail can go cold here. Roz wants to find a hotel in Paris for the night and to start the next leg of their journey in the morning.

'No, we should keep moving,' says Eva. She finds herself looking around her frequently, imagining every policeman on the station to be observing them, waiting, sending messages. *Is Alex speaking to police at home, even now? He's had a few hours for everything to sink in, to make a decision.* She wants to know, however bad it is. Anything but this nagging uncertainty. On the Eurostar, she had been watchful of people moving up and down the aisle, a stupid idea running through her mind of seeing someone from Alex's hospital who was maybe off on a long weekend to Paris, their eyes meeting, questions, lies...... *I'll sleep on the next train. I'll feel safer by then.*

But she doesn't. She can't sleep, for one thing, because Roz is full of questions: where will they find somewhere to live? Can she get by with just English? What's the food like? And how long will their money last in Prague? *How the hell am I supposed to know?* As the train speeds across the German plains Roz is unexpectedly chatty. It's as if she is obliterating her memory of everything she has abandoned in England, thinks Eva, and wishes she could banish her own internal images of Douglas and Alex so easily. As the hours pass with no views to distract them save distant lights of unknown towns flashing past, Roz's upbeat mood starts to dissolve. By the time they reach Frankfurt after midnight, she has sunk into silence again. She disappears to the station toilet and comes back a few minutes later, sniffing and wiping a smudge of white powder from her nostrils. Eva shakes her head in disbelief.

'How the hell did you get that past security? You idiot! You could have ruined everything!'

'Stop nagging, for fuck's sake. Tiny amount, that's all. It'll be fine. Oh God, that feels better!' Roz smiles and nods at two men leaning against a pillar on the platform who are watching them. Eva insists on moving to a quieter spot. The half-hour wait feels like an eternity. The sleeper train to Prague finally lurches into view, all hulking dark brown metal, brakes screeching so loud that Eva covers her ears and then also her nose to cut out the overpowering stench of diesel fumes. Once on board, they push and fumble their way through the narrow corridor looking for their couchette number, past closed grey curtains until they are there at last and Eva notes, gratefully, that the couchette is empty. No one else's snoring or inane conversations to endure.

'Isn't there an ensuite in here?' demands Roz.

'You were the one who wanted to save money – no. We passed a loo when we got on, remember?'

'But I want a shower!'

'Tough!'

Eva's body can't hold out any longer. As soon as she lies down on her bunk she falls asleep, rocked by the train's motion, dreaming…dreaming of Baba waiting for her, beckoning, Douglas hovering in the background and then…..she wakes with a start as the train lurches to a halt. *Surely we can't be there already?* Looking over at Roz she sees her eyes are open too, blinking fast. Then the train moves off again. Sleep now eludes Eva. Everything feels unreal. She will surely wake and find herself still at home with Douglas still living and needing to be cared for. But now there's just a yawning void. No schedule to follow now.

'Do you remember that school trip to Switzerland when we were fifteen?' asks Roz suddenly. 'Bit like these couchettes, it was - hey, d'you remember sharing with Lesley and Karen and how they kept us all awake with wolf-whistling the night-workers on the tracks? Remember?'

Of course, Eva remembers. Their first time abroad, complaining about the food, talking after lights out in the dormitory and paying inflated prices for gaudily-painted wooden cuckoo clocks to take home to their families as souvenirs. Innocent times. They talk and reminisce some more, egging each other on, Eva grateful for this distraction. But every mile further makes her realize the havoc she has left behind. As the train clunks on they fall into silence, lost inside their separate minds.

Eva goes to the toilet about six and runs a comb through her hair. *Should I dye it blonde to disguise myself?* She shakes her head at the thought. Whatever had made her think she could get away with this?

There is no sunrise to speak of. The sky simply changes slowly from one shade of grey to a lighter one. At seven they hear heavy footsteps coming down the corridor, a man's deep voice calling out in German and Czech that breakfast is available in the buffet car. Roz looks at Eva, who shakes her head. The thought of food makes her feel sick.

On and on, the train rolls and lurches. Still an hour or so to go. Now the names of stations they pass through are no longer German but distinctly Slavic. Despite herself, Eva feels a surge of excitement. Baba's homeland. Hers too, even if only at the time of her conception. She had dreamed for years of returning. But not like this.

'Isn't there a border we stop at?' asks Roz.

It seems not. The train is rolling slower now, frustratingly sluggish. Then the clouds start shedding their load of sleet.

'Shit! It's not even December yet!' says Roz, surveying the sky. 'You never said it would be like this!'

Run-down cottages the colour of mustard yellow with dull red roofs come into view, crouching against the embankment. Pylons rise up and piles of rusting metal tracks on the sidings are being gradually obscured with a thin blanket of sleet now turning to snow. The train clatters and swerves, ploughing its way eastwards. Eva urges it on silently, wanting desperately to get there now, after so long. *Why is it that the last leg of any journey always seems so slow?*

She spends the next hour trying to recall simple phrases in Czech but they elude her. When Baba died eighteen years ago, the habit of speaking Czech daily had been broken. Roz snorts that she'll buy a phrasebook.

'Praha Hlavní Nádraží, Praha Hlavní Nádraží.' The distant voice of the station announcer drifts in through their slightly-open window as Prague main station comes into view. The train's brakes squeal and it grinds to a halt with a huge shudder, as if equally relieved to have arrived. Eva's legs tremble as they clamber down off the train on to the white-dusted platform, hauling their cases down. They are swept along by the dense crowd, down steep stone steps and then along a corridor with a rough cement floor. Eyes of passers-by dart to their faces and then flick away their gaze as soon as eyes meet. *No passport control or security check here,* Eva notes with relief.

The corridor ends in a short flight of steps leading upwards. At the top, Eva dumps her case and holdall and takes stock of her surroundings. Roz stands by her side, puffing with exertion.

Eva didn't know what she had been expecting. Maybe a touch of nineteenth-century elegance, of colonnaded halls and uniformed porters? The walls, the ceiling – everything is a preponderance of dark browns and dirty reds, dull fluorescent lighting, a smell of stale beer and something else she cannot place. The concourse is heaving with people, wrapped up in thick coats or anoraks of similar fabrics and colours so that it looks as if they have all shopped at the same place for their clothing. Against a pillar leans a group of men in multiple layers of frayed clothes, gripping brown bottles and surrounded by a moat of empty ones on the concrete floor. One of the men breaks away from the group and seems to be heading towards Roz, eyes fixed on her expensive clothes, his grimy hand outstretched and his mouth half-open to reveal yellow stumps of gaping teeth. He's calling out something and then an elderly woman in a purple anorak and thick grey scarf suddenly appears between them, shooing him away with a practised flick of her hand. He veers off instead towards a group of young people carrying backpacks.

Roz sinks down on her case, looks around and then buries her face in her hands. Lifting it again she glares at Eva. Eva swallows hard. 'Don't say it,' Eva mutters. 'Not a word.'

15

Eva slumped back on a plastic chair near a snack booth while Roz stood over her, furiously sucking on a cigarette. What kind of fantasy had she been expecting? A welcoming committee of apple-cheeked Baba look-alikes bearing platters of chicken *řízek* and honey cake?

'Right,' Roz said, stamping out her cigarette butt. 'What do you want?' she nodded towards the booth.

'Anything, I don't care,' Eva muttered.

'Better change some money first. Stay here.'

She disappeared for a while and Eva huddled over the luggage. Every time she raised her head someone seemed to be staring at her but would then look away quickly. She couldn't look that odd, surely, a bit dishevelled perhaps, baggy-eyed definitely. What in hell's name had made her think of coming here? *'I can speak the language'?* Bullshit. She couldn't make out a single word from the buzz around her, but then Baba's speech had been so measured and precise.

'Here,' came Roz's voice again and she thrust a polystyrene cup of coffee and a cling film-wrapped baguette at Eva. Slices of ham, salami and cheese were protruding.

'How did you manage?' Eva asked.

Roz shrugged. 'Bit of sign language and stuff – like you do on holiday, really.'

Like on holiday. Maybe that's how we should be thinking. Just an extended holiday, that's all. Eva was starving by now and tore into the squelchy mass of soft bread and filling. Roz also took one mouthful of hers and pulled a face. 'Ugh!' she spluttered. 'This salami!'

'A bit greasy,' Eva conceded, though she was past caring. The coffee was bitter with granules floating on top.

Roz threw her food and drink in a nearby bin and wiped her mouth on a tissue. 'Tell me it's going to get better than this,' she muttered.

Eva looked around the concourse and near an exit spotted a kiosk marked *Accommodation, Unterkunft, Hotel.* Roz followed her gaze.

'I'll give it a try,' Eva offered.

They dragged their cases over the short distance, jostled by backpackers rushing towards the platforms downstairs. In the booth sat a young dark-haired girl, slender as a reed, chewing gum rapidly and reading a magazine. She didn't seem to notice them at first so Eva cleared her throat and managed a '*dobrý den.*'

The girl finally looked up, eyes sweeping over them. '*Dobrý den,*' she returned without expression.

'*Hledáme hotel na jeden týden, prosím Vás,*' Eva managed to stammer. A hotel for a week.

'*Co že?*' the girl screwed up her eyes and frowned at Eva.

Eva felt herself flush and then repeated the phrase. *Is my accent really so awful that the girl can't really understand me?*

'Oh, for God's sake,' exploded Roz behind Eva. She then started to speak loudly and slowly, using exaggerated hand gestures. 'Look, hotel, you know, we want a hotel. That's what you do here, isn't it?'

The girl glared at Roz, chewing even more quickly now and left her seat, calling someone's name through a door behind her.

'Roz,' Eva begged, 'don't start getting people's backs up.'

A balding man with a huge beer belly and droopy moustache shuffled out. He nodded to them whilst listening to the girl's rapid explanation. Eva couldn't follow a single word, and panic started to rise inside her. *How the hell am I ever going to cope in this strange new world?*

'Hotel?' he tilted his chin, speaking English and looking straight at Roz.

'Yes, if that's not too much trouble,' Roz spat out. 'One week. Good quality.'

'Good quality? Ah. Hilton? Radisson, yes?'

Roz started to smile. 'Yeah. Something like that.'

'Roz -?' Eva started to protest.
'OK, OK, I try,' he nodded.
'Wait a minute,' Eva interjected, 'how much?'
He stroked his chin. 'Five or six thousand crowns, maybe more.'
'What's that in English money?' Eva asked.
He consulted a chart beneath the counter top and tapped out something on a calculator. 'One hundred fifty sterling.'
'For the week?' Roz asked.
'No! One night!' he laughed.
'What?' they both chorused.
'Thought this place was supposed to be cheap!' Roz turned on Eva angrily.
'Look, how was I supposed to know?'
The man was staring at them, bemused. 'You want cheap?'
'Yes, but nice, not – you know -,' Eva faltered.
The man looked Roz over. Eva guessed he was taking in the expensive coat and boots. Then he looked at Eva and nodded. 'Wait. I phone,' he said, disappearing back through the door.
The young girl had gone back to reading her magazine, ignoring them. 'Busy, are you, chick?' Roz asked her, arching an immaculately groomed eyebrow.
'Shut up Roz,' Eva murmured. The girl acted as if she hadn't heard. After a couple of minutes the man returned, holding a slip of paper. 'Here,' he handed it to Eva. 'This good place, clean, not expensive. Two thousand crowns one night. You pay there. Take taxi,' he pointed to the exit door.
'*Děkuji moc, pane*,' Eva thanked him, much relieved.
His face lit up. '*Mluvíte hesky česky*,' he nodded, smiling now.
'What's he saying?' asked Roz.
'He said I speak Czech nicely.'
She snorted. 'Yeah, right.'
'*Na Shledanou*,' Eva bade him goodbye.
'*Na Shledanou*,' he inclined his head to her.
'Right, can we get going please?' Roz tugged at Eva's sleeve.
Eva smiled to herself. One small step. Maybe Douglas would be proud of her and suddenly the temporary lightness fled and she started trembling at the memory of what she had done. Roz glanced sideways at her, searching her face. 'Hey, we'll be OK.'

A row of white taxis was parked outside. Eva approached the first driver, who sported a haircut which, back in England, would have screamed *'skinhead'*. He took the slip of paper from her, read the address, nodded briefly after a moment and loaded their cases into his boot. Roz clutched her brown holdall to her chest, shaking her head when he offered to take it. He shrugged his shoulders in reply. He drove as quickly as the traffic would allow, switching lanes constantly, cutting up other drivers in defiance of their car-horns. Eva and Roz held on to the door handles on each swerve.

'We'll have to buy a map,' Eva said. 'I've no idea where we're going.'

Ten minutes later the car drew up in a residential street outside a terraced building painted mint green. An inset brass plate was inscribed *'Hotel U Andělů'*. The pavement was slippery with a coat of settled snow and Eva heard Roz cursing behind her. Eva pushed open the heavy wooden door of the hotel. Inside was a small square reception hall, its plain whitewashed walls hung with black-and-white sketches of old buildings and churches. A carpet in the middle of the floor was faded red but clean. The pine reception counter was stacked with colourful leaflets – *Prague tours, Prague by night*. A sign by a brass button invited them, in English, French, German and Czech, to ring for attention. Eva's hesitant touch of the button summoned into view a small stocky woman, mid-sixties she guessed, with wiry dyed-ginger hair and, she noticed with relief, a welcoming smile.

'*Dobrý den, dobrý den,*' she nodded to both of them. '*Máte přání?*' It was the kind of polite elegant greeting that Baba would have expected. *How may I help you?*

'*Dobrý den,*' Eva replied. 'Um, do you speak English please?' She ignored Roz's grunt behind her.

'Ah, *Angličanky?* Yes,' the woman smiled, 'you telephone from station, yes? I try a little. I have room for you. First, please, I need passports.'

'Oh.' Eva's momentary hesitation brought a slight cloud to the woman's face. *What's there to worry about now? What are the chances of anyone tracing us this far?* 'Of course,' Eva replied, rifling in her handbag and nodding to Roz to do the same.

The woman flicked to the back page of Eva's passport, transcribed some information onto her hotel registration form and then did the same with Roz's details. She frowned for a moment. 'No address,' she pointed to the passport pages.

Neither of them had ever filled in their emergency contact page. Roz and Eva exchanged glances. Without thinking, Eva offered their old address in Bloomsbury. The woman didn't question how they could prove it.

'Now, please pay for one night, rest tomorrow,' she was smiling again, her warm brown eyes looking into Eva's. If she had noticed Roz's cut lip she did not let it show.

After a few minutes they climbed a highly-polished wooden staircase to the second floor. The heavy bedroom door swung open to reveal a small bright room, again with whitewashed walls and a well-varnished parquet floor. Two single beds stood against one wall, separated by a bedside table with a single lamp. The beds were covered with spotless white duvets and pillows. On the opposite wall a small TV was fixed high on a metal bracket. To the side of this was a plain single wardrobe in orange-stained pine. Under the window there stood a narrow teak-effect table, half-covered by a white lace runner and with small armchairs placed at either side. The woman gestured to another door, just beside the entrance and Eva pushed it open to reveal a shower room and toilet. The total effect was fresh, spartan but strangely comforting. Eva looked longingly at the beds.

'Pěkně, děkuji moc,' Eva breathed.

'Ah, mluvíte česky, Paní,' the woman beamed at her.

'Only a little.'

She left them with a recommendation for the Café Marco Polo next door for lunch, wished them a pleasant stay and handed the key to Eva without a glance at Roz. An English landlady might have been more chatty and nosy. Eva was grateful for the woman's reserve.

As Eva sank on to one of the beds Roz spat out, 'it's like a bloody monk's cell! We should have gone for a proper hotel.'

'Actually, I quite like it,'

'You would.'

'What's that supposed to mean?'

'Well, you're used to....' Roz trailed off, gesturing around the room.

'Slumming it in suburban IKEA land, you mean? Not like

some bloody Country Living magazine? Yeah, that's right. I haven't lived like a spoiled brat for the last thirteen years like you, being waited on hand and foot. Well listen, you don't have to stay! Why don't you just sod off back to Howard - chances are he won't have even noticed his twenty grand is missing – or what do you think?'

Roz sat down heavily on the other bed and rubbed her eyes, wincing as she touched her mouth.

'I'm sorry. Let's not argue,' Eva sighed. 'We've got more important things to think about now.'

'Like what?'

'Like what the hell do we do when the money runs out?' *But it's not just about the money. How are we going to cope here? Is this the place I want to end my days, with Roz bitching every step of the way?*

16

Eva slept heavily and woke to find darkness settling. As she rolled over to face Roz's bed she saw that she was lying on her back, awake, her face wet.

'Couldn't you sleep?' Eva asked.

Roz shook her head. 'Can we get out of here, please? I'm feeling really cooped up. Aren't you?'

Eva's body yearned for more sleep but she agreed reluctantly. Down in reception she asked Pani Novotná, as she had told them her name was, about a city map and directions. Apparently, they were a short walk away from a metro station which would take them directly into the centre in about five minutes. She explained how to buy tickets for both the metro and tram systems and showed Eva a map of the three underground railway lines. In comparison to London's system it seemed dead simple. By five-thirty they reached Anděl station, darkness now upon them. It would have been quicker had they not been tiptoeing most of the way to avoid skidding on the now icy pavements. Past them strode young girls, confident even in their stiletto heels. Pani Novotná had already apologized on behalf of the inclement weather – *'too cold too soon, strange even for us Czechs'*.

As they waited on the platform Eva studied the city map. Prague seemed to be divided into numbered districts. Pani Novotná had explained that the historical city centre was covered by districts 1 and 2. Their hotel was located in Prague 5, in the southwest of the city. The station was clean and brightly-lit and the train looked new and was half-full of passengers more cosmopolitan in appearance than she had expected.

The end of November. Back home she would have already started thinking about Christmas. Eva folded up the map on her knees and closed her eyes, tears pricking the inside of her eyelids. *What now? Where's the daily routine? How do I learn to live a second life?* When she opened her eyes again she noticed an old lady opposite was staring, first at her boots and then her eyes travelled up Eva's body to her head. Instinctively Eva ran her fingers through her hair and then caught the sight of her distorted reflection in the dark window behind the old lady. Eva's hair appeared tangled, the parting askew. The woman continued to stare unsmilingly and Eva felt the colour rising in her cheeks. She turned to glance at Roz beside her. She, in turn, was staring at the old woman.

'I wonder,' said Roz in a loud voice, never taking her eyes off the woman, 'whether their mothers ever taught them that it's rude to stare?'

Several pairs of eyes around them swivelled to look at Roz. One teenage boy, dark-skinned, was grinning broadly. The old lady finally gave up her silent interrogation of Eva's appearance, flicked a disdainful look at Roz and went back to reading her newspaper. It suddenly occurred to Eva that this woman was probably the same age as Baba would have been, had she still been alive, and she had to suppress a ridiculous urge to scribble down Baba's name on her map and to show it to her — what would be the chances of them having known each other, even growing up together?

The train pulled into Můstek station which was the first interconnection on metro line C. 'This is it, come on,' Eva said, nudging Roz, who elbowed her way out of the packed carriage, clearing a pathway for them.

The escalator was smooth and silent. The number of exits from the station was bewildering. Finally, Eva suggested the exit for Václavské Náměstí - Wenceslas Square - as sounding the most promising and they followed close behind a group of excited Japanese, their heads constantly turning this way and that to take in their surroundings. Eva looked at them in envy — they were here to enjoy themselves, a break from their normal routine, creating memories upon which to reflect in their future. There would be no one to pass hers on to.

Outside, the pavement was thronged with pedestrians and the darkness was ablaze with blindingly-lit shop windows and neon signs. Sleet was driven into their faces and they clung to each other for warmth and stability on the slippery paving-stones. Václavské Náměstí turned out to be a long sloping street rather than a conventional square, rising up before them broad and steep. Roz groaned at the sight.

'I'm not gonna make it far up there in these boots.'

'Look! Over there!' Eva pointed further on to the right, a familiar name emblazoned on a jutting shop sign. *Bata shoes*. She remembered the shoe empire had started here.

They staggered and slithered over the fifty yards or so and entered the shop with relief. 'This is a bit more like it, chick,' exclaimed Roz as her eyes swept over the shelves and displays. 'Might not be Prada, but it'll do for now.'

They could have been back in London. Roz looked ecstatic. Eva pulled on a pair of fur-lined ankle boots, their inside lining soft, warm and comforting. The flat soles were fitted with the kind of deep tread which would grip the outside road surfaces well enough to make her feel more secure. Roz was indicating to a middle-aged assistant that she needed a larger size in the knee-high black boots she had chosen.

'Look, Eva, they even take Visa,' she said.

'No! I thought we had agreed – cash only from now on.'

Roz pulled a face but said nothing. She paid for both of them. Eva didn't like the feeling of being reliant on Roz's money, but wondered how else she was going to cope here. She turned towards the exit, now wearing her new flat boots, but Roz tugged at her elbow. 'I want to go upstairs, see what else they've got,' she nodded to the display panel of four floors on the wall.

'I'm not here to help you shop,' Eva retorted.

Roz hesitated, her mouth set.

'Do you want me to leave you here, then?' Eva asked.

'No!' Fear registered suddenly in Roz's eyes and she followed Eva out obediently. The boots were fine, but Eva's coat was not. She couldn't stop shivering. Something would have to be done about that as well, but not tonight. She didn't like the idea of going through their money – Roz's money, mostly – so quickly. The boots hadn't been as cheap as she had expected.

She turned her head to the right and looked up the street. Shops and bars lined both sides and the garish colours of their neon signs – with their insistent and strident chorus of *'look at me!'* - irritated her. Looking at the upper stories she saw tall elegant windows and elaborate carvings in the stonework. The clashing appearance of these buildings made her think of older women trying to recapture the looks of their youth by wearing too much makeup and dressing inappropriately for their age. Her gaze was next drawn upwards to the top of the street where the monolithic Museum towered over this modern retail invasion. Thirty-six years earlier it would have been looking down on a rolling convoy of Soviet tanks. That much she had learned from Baba and the history books. Somewhere, near here, blood would have been spilled; screams and protests would have filled the air. Her parents, grandfather, if she closed her eyes she could almost smell….

'Let's go eat,' Roz's voice cut through Eva's thoughts. 'Hey, I can see a McDonald's, look, over there.' She pointed across the street.

'You must be joking,' Eva snapped. 'We came all the way here and we end up in McDonald's?'

'So what?' Roz shrugged. 'At least you won't have to work out what you're eating.'

Passing through the familiar décor, the queue in front of them was slowed down by a family of Americans taking ages in making their choices, their teenage children wrapped up in colourful ski suits and jostling for position. Roz and Eva took a table by the window. Eva shook her head as she bit into her burger. This stuff must taste the same the whole world over, she thought, no allowance made for local preferences for different flavours. Maybe that was the secret of its success because this food didn't taste of anything at all. Over Roz's shoulder she had a good view of the street with its passers-by scurrying for shelter from the east wind.

'Got to find a decent bar,' said Roz with her mouth full, 'somewhere where we can hang out and find out more about this place. Maybe we'll find some other Brits living here, you know, get some info about finding a place to live and all that.'

We shouldn't be here, surrounded by other Brits or Americans or whatever, eating and drinking the same things we've been used to back home. Eva didn't want to live like a stereotypical expatriate, whinging about cultural differences or getting excited about finding shops where you could buy Marmite or Heinz baked beans. *We should be trying to integrate ourselves into the same patterns of life as local people. I don't want to stand out. I want to feel as if I truly belong here, to disappear from Alex's world and to evolve into someone new. Maybe finding Baba's origins will help me with that. American burgers will surely not be part of that picture.*

On the other hand, maybe Roz had a point, she conceded. It would be good to gain some local knowledge without the language barrier, at least for now. There would be questions to field – why were they here, where were they from – and so on. They would need to come up with an agreed storyline and stick to it.

As ideas drifted into her mind, Eva caught sight of a police car drawing up outside. Two policemen emerged dressed in black uniforms and caps, their gun holsters visible even from where she was sitting. They were chewing gum vigorously, turning their heads as they looked up and down the street. Then they looked towards the window and she saw one of them looking straight at her.

'What's up?' asked Roz. 'You look like you've seen a ghost.'

Eva jerked her chin towards the window and Roz turned her head to see. Both policemen had now lit up cigarettes and were leaning against their car, laughing, and seemingly oblivious to the sleet settling on their caps. Now they had turned sideways and one of them was pointing to something or someone further up the hill. Then they started laughing again.

'You're like a rabbit in the headlights,' Roz sneered at Eva, 'stop getting paranoid or we'll both be having heart attacks. It'll be fine, see?'

But Eva's hunger had disappeared and she pushed away the polystyrene container. 'I can't live like this,' she whispered, 'I'll be looking over my shoulder for the rest of my life, don't you see? I don't think -.'

'Then don't think! Just put it out of your mind.'

'You think I can just pretend nothing ever happened?'

'I didn't say that. But you can't beat yourself up forever. What's done is done. Look, let's get out of here and find somewhere better.'

Somewhere better turned out to be a bar in a shopping arcade called Černá Růže, Black Rose, on Na Příkopě. Roz's mouth formed a perfect O when they entered the mall and she gaped through the shop plate-glass windows at Dolce and Gabbana and a range of other designer outlets. 'Pity they're closed now,' she said, glancing at her watch. 'Still, now I know where I'll be going tomorrow.'

The bar was a chrome and glass affair with deep black leather sofas and armchairs to sink into and an attentive pair of dark-haired good-looking waiters hovering around the glass tables. Roz smiled broadly and raised her glass of vodka and tonic to Eva's white wine in a mock toast. 'Might not be so bad here after all,' she grinned, her eyes still on the taller of the two waiters as he stood behind the bar polishing glasses in slow rhythmic movements, his eyes occasionally darting over to their table. 'Hey, cheer up, it's Friday night and we're out on the piss, just like the old days! Come on, Eva, when was the last time you went out on a Friday?'

'Alex always seemed to be working on a Friday night. Douglas and I would play a bit of chess but he always beat me,' Eva said, the images suddenly pouring through her mind. 'what do you think Alex is doing now? There'll have to be a post-mortem, how's he going to explain…?'

'I've told you - stop it! Don't crucify yourself. Let's have another drink.'

And another. And then another. Alcohol wielded its power to anaesthetize them for a while. It was starting to taste so good and Eva's body felt light and relaxed. She recalled the years when they could drink each other under the table but still have a clear enough head for work the next day. The bar soon filled up with a mixture of people. Some were men in dark grey suits who talked loudly in English, with either a native or heavy local accent, mostly about real estate deals they were working on. Roz surveyed a group of well-dressed and heavily-made-up girls who glided past their table in short skirts defying the weather and swaying on improbably high heels. The girls settled in a corner spot and were soon greeted in familiar terms by the waiter Roz had been flirting with. She scowled.

'How do they manage to be so skinny and still have good tits?' Roz complained. Eva rolled her eyes.

In another corner a stout man of Middle Eastern appearance, his belly straining against his black linen shirt, was fingering a chunky gold bracelet on his left wrist and looking over at the group of young girls as they flicked their hair and sipped their drinks slowly, their eyes darting around the bar as if checking out the competition. The man was ignoring his delicate-looking companion, a girl of maybe no more than seventeen, who was clutching his arm and occasionally resting her head, with its curtain of flowing dark hair, on his fleshy shoulder. An ice bucket containing a bottle of champagne stood on the low table in front of them, glasses poured but not yet touched. Eva thought the girl's beautiful hair had been despoiled by a harsh shade of burgundy. *Why try to enhance her natural beauty at the risk of ruining the effect?* Hair dye should be for those who need it by virtue of the grey hairs which arrive uninvited. She turned to look at her own reflection in the window and felt ashamed at her negligence.

'What do you reckon, then?' Roz gestured towards the couple. 'Hooker?'

'No. I don't think so.'

'Then why else would she be with someone like that?'

'Desperate?'

'Why would someone with looks like that be desperate?'

'Then maybe she loves him,' Eva suggested. 'Look at how she's cuddled up. Her face isn't hard enough, I think, to be using him.'

Roz chortled. 'You're so naïve, Eva! It's obvious he must be loaded. She must make him feel like a stud. They've got a good deal from each other. What else could it be?'

'Does it always come down to money, Roz? Or sex?'

'What else is there?'

But this girl seemed like a child to Eva's eyes; there was hope in her face of perhaps a more comfortable life with a secure future. There was so much they would need to learn about life here, she felt, before they could make sound judgments about people and their choices.

'Do you know what I was doing last Friday night?' said Roz suddenly. 'I was sitting down with Wanda and we were drawing up a list of things to prepare for a dinner party Howard was planning for tomorrow night. Christ, I wonder what he's going to do now, especially if that DVD has been opened...' Roz started laughing now, a hysterical edge to her voice Eva didn't like, and she sensed they were attracting unwanted attention.

'Let's get out of here now. I think we've had enough,' Eva murmured, pulling at Roz's arm. 'I want to go back to the hotel.'

'What? Back to that monk's cell? No thanks! I'm just starting to enjoy myself.'

Roz squinted towards the bar. The waiters were whispering together, grinning, and watching her. Eva felt embarrassed. *Two drunken women on the pull? Is that what we look like?*

'Come on, Roz!'

'Fuck off!' She shook off Eva's arm.

'Look, it's our first day here, and we should be keeping our heads down.'

'Yeah, chick, I intend to,' she smirked, nodding to the waiter to come over. 'Here,' she said, thrusting a handful of Czech banknotes into Eva's hand, 'go have a good time somewhere else, if you must. Catch up with you later?' She raised her eyebrows and winked.

'Be careful,' Eva muttered.

Roz waved her away.

Outside the sharp wind cut through Eva and she hurried away back to Můstek station, flakes of new snow stinging her eyes, wishing she could rewind the last thirty-six hours and choose another path.

17

Roz stumbled around in the dark, hopping on one foot as she tried to take off her boots. She lost her balance and crashed down on her bed. *Shit*. She could see Eva's sleeping form stir and then the bedside light came on, blinding her.

'Turn it off, for fuck's sake,' Roz slurred.

Eva's eyes opened. Her eyes were brimming with unshed tears and Roz felt a pang of remorse. For a moment, anyway. She wasn't in the mood for a lecture. She belched loudly and rubbed her stomach.

'My head is killing me,' Eva whispered.

'Yeah, well, I'm not so bright either.'

'That's your own fault. You can hardly compare –.'

'Is that all I'm going to hear about now? You and your fucking headaches! Am I supposed to just sit around now, nursing you and waiting for you to die? Aren't you going to even try a little bit to live first? Why are you giving in –?'

'You've no bloody idea, have you –?'

'Oh, cut the crap, Eva! You've spent so long nursing dying buggers you've forgotten what real people are like! Look, you don't know, right? Could be years yet. You said the headaches come and go anyway and –.'

Eva was sitting bolt upright now. 'Do you what it's like to wake up and wonder if it going to be today? Tomorrow? Not knowing. Christ, not knowing when or how –.'

'Exactly! You don't know, chick. So what's the point in living in the future? Grab it now, just do it! C'mon, we can have a blast here –.'

'Just go away! Go on! Bugger off back to your bars and your one-night stands. What have you got to lose? Go buy yourself a good time. Not stopping you. Just get off my case.'

'Oh for God's sake!' Roz grunted and fell forward on to her pillow. There was no sense in continuing this argument. She needed sleep badly. Tomorrow would be better. Tomorrow they would......her breathing became slower and deeper, snuffling and snoring as she was drawn deeper into sleep.

The next morning the inside of Roz's mouth felt like a suede glove and her head throbbed. She lay quietly, looking through her lashes over at Eva who was still asleep. With a groan, Roz remembered snatches of their row. *Stupid, stupid cow!* Her tongue had run away with itself. But maybe some of those things she had said were true. Eva was counting the days, even the minutes, without stopping to notice them. This could be such a great way to end, go out on a high. She could make sure Eva was comfortable.....

'Hi.' Eva was sitting up.

Roz turned her head. 'Hiya. Sorry 'bout last night, chick.'

'That was the drink talking, I suppose?'

'Yeah.'

'Know what?'

'What?' replied Roz, cautiously.

'I think that, maybe....' Eva inclined her head. 'Maybe you're scared a bit too.'

'What? What am I supposed to be scared of?'

'Have you thought about – you know – what you'll do when I'm gone –.'

'Oh, don't start that again!'

'You could go back home. Not to Howard, but somewhere. What's to keep you here?'

'Oh, stop all the what-ifs, will you?' Roz turned over, her back towards Eva. Her stomach lurched as she thought, *what would keep me here? Where else to go?*

'Roz, I know you're awake. Stop pretending.'

'Hm? Wanna lie in a bit.'

She heard Eva sigh and get out of bed, then the sound of loud splashing in the shower. Roz lay with her eyes shut, trying to block out the image of the fumbling inebriated waiter who had tried unsuccessfully to penetrate her a few hours earlier in a store room behind the bar at Černá Růže. *For God's sake. What was I thinking? I can do better than that, can't I?*

'I'm going out,' Eva announced as she dried her hair vigorously with one of the hotel's thin towels.

'What for? It's snowing again.'

'I need a warmer coat.'

'Well, you know where the cash is, chick.'

'Thanks, but I'll take my own.'

'Please yourself.'

'Breakfast is downstairs in the dining room, if you're coming.'

'Don't they do room service?'

'Dream on, Roz.'

'I will. I'm gonna stay here and imagine I'm in the Radisson or somewhere. D'you think we should see if they're doing any cheap deals?'

'What we should do is start looking for a flat.'

Roz sighed. 'Well, you go and do some research, then.'

Eva finished getting dressed. 'Come on, get up, and stop being a slug.'

'Tomorrow. Promise. We'll get started then.'

Roz closed her eyes and remembered the softness of her own bed at home. *That's what I want. Western luxury at an East European price. Why not? Life could be made sweet here, it just needs a bit of time, the right connections. Not hard graft. Eva can do all that. She'll probably enjoy it, trailing round the real estate agencies. Let her get on with it. Maybe someone back at the Černá Růže bar could give me a shortcut to the right people to talk to. Yeah. Life was all about knowing the right people. Always worked for me before.* Roz drifted back into slumber dreaming of luxury apartments, indoor swimming pools and handsome wealthy strangers who had a thing for redheads.

Eight o'clock on the first Saturday morning of Eva's new life and she was alone. She had left Roz sleeping off her hangover. The hotel's breakfast room in the basement was empty as Eva helped herself to slices of dark rye bread, smoked ham and cheese. A metal flask of coffee on a side table was still warm enough to make its contents drinkable. There was no sign of Pani Novotná in reception as Eva left the hotel soon after nine.

The sun shone out of a brilliant blue sky and fallen snow crunched under her new boots as she strode down the narrow street. She was remembering the directions Pani Novotná had given them yesterday about a new shopping centre in the locality. This would not be a Roz-type expedition. No raiding of designer labels. Eva just needed a new winter coat and she could do that on her own. She realized that she would have to get used to doing things on her own from now on. Roz could become an albatross around her neck if her drinking and man-chasing took over her life. How would they live, flung together again after years of living in dead marriages, having to get used to each other again?

A sheer mountain of glass and concrete rose up before her as she stood in front of the Anděl shopping mall. In England this might not have merited any special attention, but here the new buildings stood uneasily amongst their older forebears as intruders on the landscape. She passed through the automatic doors and her senses were assaulted on all sides by brand labels – American, Italian, German and Czech. Money spoke in many languages. It had been many months since she had been shopping anywhere like this and she felt a rising sense of panic when confronted by so many choices. She had to make a quick choice or else nothing at all. She parted with eight thousand crowns for a black three-quarters-length German-brand wool coat, her mind calculating the equivalent of one hundred and eighty pounds. More than she had bargained for. *I better try to get more than one winter out of that*, and smiled at the irony.

Escalators glided up and down, carrying their human prey. People of all ages crowded the walkways and music blared from every outlet, Eurotrash pop competing with R&B and jazz for attention. Throughout this sea of humanity, hell-bent on its retail mission, a certain theme of uniform emerged – jeans or sweatpants, trainers, tracksuit tops and logo'd T-shirts. She couldn't tell who had money and who had not. It seemed to be the ultimate classless society. Occasionally, to break the mould, there appeared some lovely young women who were sporting something obviously very expensive to match their immaculately made-up faces.

On the first floor of the mall she found a range of cafes and restaurants, ranging from hamburger or Chinese fast food booths to an elegant restaurant with pristine white tablecloths and wicker chairs, the waiters dressed in black with white half-aprons, striding between tables with round metal trays held high. A group of stylish young women occupied one of the tables, stirring their coffees slowly and rhythmically, their eyes following female passers-by and focusing here and there on the details of their clothes. Eva sat down at a table close to the edge of the outside section which was bounded by a white-painted low wooden trellis. Looking at these women she found herself wishing she had bought more than this coat and ran her fingers through her wiry brown hair.

'*Dobrý den, máte přání?*' came a male voice above her and she looked up into the waiter's dull eyes, his jaws chewing gum rapidly.

'*Ano, cappuccino, prosím,*' she replied. She tried to smile but her gesture was not returned. His pen flicked over his notepad, and then he ripped off the page and slammed it down on the table, turning on his heel without another word. When the coffee arrived there was no familiar dusting of cocoa powder on top. *Should I ask?* She made the coffee last for twenty minutes, and then ordered another. There was nothing to hurry away for. Everyone else here was with someone. She couldn't make out much of what anyone was saying in the general hubbub and was starting to fear whether she would ever pick up the language again. Having stretched out the second coffee for longer than she could bear she wandered off into the comforting anonymity of the crowds again.

As she drifted from one shop to another, carelessly fingering items of clothing on the rails and shelves Eva's mind was elsewhere and she was conscious of a rising tide of anger inside her. This wasn't the Prague she had wanted to see. Change the people and the price tags and she could be anywhere in the Western world. *But what had I been expecting?* Baba had never described the city to her, after all. Had it been her own sentimental imagination that had conjured up visions of something from the 1930s or 1940s? Besides, didn't these people deserve something better after the grey drabness of the Communist era?

Every item of clothing she held up to her face seemed, in the unforgiving harsh lights and mirrors, to accentuate her dull hair and pale cosmetic-free face. She thought she could sense other younger women throwing her glances of pity, even contempt. *How did I get to become like this? Maybe Roz is right. I had become so immersed in caring for others that I had forgotten about myself.* She rifled through her handbag for more money. Thirty minutes later she emerged from the ladies' restroom in the new tailored black wool trousers and cream silky blouse she had bought, luxuriating in the unfamiliar feel of the expensive fabrics against her skin. *A good start, but not there yet.* As she paused at the door of the hair and beauty salon two shops down she took a deep breath before pushing it open. The receptionist scowled when Eva said she didn't have an appointment and jerked her head towards a chair whilst she conferred with two colleagues. Fifteen minutes later, amid much pointing and sign language, two stylists were frowning and tut-tutting over the colour and condition of Eva's hair and skin. She closed her eyes and let their skillful hands begin to work their magic. The toxic smell of hair colorant assaulted her nostrils, then her hair and scalp were massaged vigorously by an older assistant whose hands looked better equipped for kneading bread. Then came the haircut, after much pouting from the lovely young stylist with a beetroot-like tint in her own long dark hair. Scissors rose and fell rhythmically and tendrils of hair dropped to the floor, round hair wands twirled and tugged until Eva's head and neck ached with the pressure. Last of all, a make-up girl hovered over her, exfoliating, moisturizing, and smearing on one make-up base after another, plucking excess hairs from Eva's brows.

It was nearly two o'clock when she finally opened her eyes. Eva McKinley had disappeared. Eva Poláková was staring back at her in the hairdresser's mirror, or close enough to her anyway. The fine lines and shadows of the intervening thirteen years remained but were, at least, diminished. Even her colour-mismatched eyes no longer made her feel self-conscious. She felt a tide of idiotic hope rising in her chest. *Would Douglas be proud of my new start now?*

As Eva emerged into the mall's main parade she felt like beaming at her reflection every time she passed a mirror. When she arrived back at Hotel U Andělů Pani Novotná greeted her with a wide smile. 'You look very nice, Pani McKinley.'

Eva blushed, feeling like the child, years ago, complimented on her first party dress which Baba would have sewn for her. Everything seemed possible now. Every moment would be made to count. Roz could do as she pleased. Eva was going to discover her family history and nothing was going to beat that feeling when she would finally uncover the stories behind the photos in Baba's oak box.

18

Years ago, when Eva and Roz had shared the flat in Bloomsbury, they had used a signal between them. A carton of milk would be placed outside the flat door to indicate to whichever one of them was coming home to enter quietly – *Sex in Progress* was the meaning. So Eva found herself looking down instinctively as she approached their hotel room before turning the handle.

Roz's bed was a duvet-covered lump. Eva could see her mass of tangled red curls spread over the white pillowcase. A gentle snoring was just audible. Eva felt the urge to reach out and shake her. *But what's the point? Roz is Roz. Nothing over the years has changed her. It's just a reaction, the release of escaping Howard's control. She'll calm down.*

Eva sank into one of the armchairs and watched Roz sleeping, the occasional fidget and scratch. The curtains were still open as Eva had left them that morning and the outside light was fading fast even though it was only mid-afternoon. The white sky was pregnant with snow which would surely fall soon. Perhaps they would battle through the kind of white winter they had only dreamed of as children. *How will we be next spring? How much will have changed for us?* Part of her wanted to know, the part that desired the security of certainty. They had to find somewhere to live and work to support them. But, at the same time, they had to keep themselves hidden, under the radar, from whatever authorities would exist here that could identify them, and which would surely send them back to England to face the consequences of their actions. Eva's hands twisted and turned in her lap, considering all of the possibilities. She imagined Douglas' face, reassuring, smiling. But what if Alex had chosen to destroy his father's letter of exoneration? How spiteful could he be?

Roz started to stir. Her face emerged from beneath the duvet, mascara and eyeliner forming black smudges under her eyes. Even from the armchair Eva could smell the familiar odours from those distant years of their single lives – stale cigarette smoke, whisky, musky perfume mixed with the salty aroma of sex. She closed her eyes briefly and they were back in Bloomsbury, comparing notes on the men they had had from the night before, and then arguing about whose turn it was to go to the launderette with the semen-stained bed-sheets. It had never occurred to Eva to ask Roz about her sex life with Howard. She could only remember Roz's horror when she had found out, just a few months into their marriage, that he had swung both ways. She had told Eva how she threw up when she found the photographic evidence in his safe and after that – well, it was no longer her bed that Howard had shared. Roz hadn't dared to take a lover herself for fear that Howard could use that against her in a divorce plea which would have put an end to her lavish lifestyle. Too late. Locked in her gilded cage. Occasionally, she would join Alex and Eva for dinner. On one occasion, after too much wine, Eva had imagined she could see a flash of desire in Roz's eyes when she talked to Alex and a fleeting hint of a returned interest in his. Later, Eva had accused Alex of wanting to sleep with Roz. The disdain in his face, and his lack of denial, came back to haunt Eva now. Roz was Roz. She couldn't help herself. It was Alex who had cheated, in the end.

Roz finally rolled over and opened her eyes, squinting at the window and then focusing on Eva, scowling.

'Are you ever going to get up?' Eva asked coldly.

'What? Yeah,' Roz yawned. 'What time is it?' Roz pulled herself upright and screwed up her eyes. 'What the hell have you done to yourself?'

'Oh, just been shopping, that's all.'

A smile spread slowly across Roz's face. 'You've had your hair done! Bloody hell, and a makeover on your face – hey, not bad!'

Eva fiddled with her hair. 'Maybe I should have had it dyed blonde or something, make it more difficult to recognize me -.'

'Oh for God's sake, don't start that again!' Roz slid back down under the duvet. 'Pass me the painkillers, there's a good girl.'

'Get them yourself! You look like shit, by the way.' *How often has Roz said that to me in the past? No more from now on.*

'No chance of a coffee, then?' Roz farted loudly. 'Sorry.'

'You'll have to go out.'

Roz sat up again and Eva's eyes were drawn to the purple bruise of a love-bite on her shoulder. Roz saw the look and grinned. 'Like old times, eh?'

'Oh grow up, Roz. That was fine ten years ago, maybe.'

'You're just jealous -.'

'Do you think drinking and screwing around will help us to forget?'

Roz looked away, running her fingers through her matted hair. 'How could I forget with you jumping around like a rabbit in the headlights all the time, nagging, whining -.'

Eva stood up and started moving towards the door.

'Where are you going?' Roz asked.

'Out. Anywhere.'

'Wait! I'll come with you.'

'No thanks.' Eva seized the door handle.

'No, wait Eva! Hey, come on, chick!'

Eva could hear Roz scrambling out of bed as she left the room and hurried down the stairs. *Fuck you, Roz*, as she bent her head down against the snow. She glowered at anyone on the metro train who looked at her. *This is the way to be now. Stand up and stare straight back at them. Take no shit from anyone.* A close-shaven man was crammed up against her in the packed carriage and she thought she felt a hand, his hand, crawling up her thigh. She gave him a firm shove and he looked shocked, muttered something and turned his back to her. Maybe she had been wrong about him but she didn't care.

It was dark when Eva came out of Můstek station. At the bottom of Vāclavskē Nāmēsti she hovered around the newspaper booth, glimpsing copies of the previous day's editions of two British tabloids through a crowd of American tourists who were leafing through a rack of postcards and guidebooks. She stretched out to reach a copy of the Daily Mail, but then held back. *What if I'm in there? With a picture? How lurid would the headline be? But then, what if there's nothing in the paper, if the editors had considered it too small an incident to report?* She had to know. Her hand shook as she took the copy down from the rack and paid the middle-aged man in charge of the booth. She sped towards the safe anonymity of McDonald's and found a quiet corner upstairs. Gulping down a coffee she turned the pages quickly, her finger tracing every headline and column, back and forth, back and forth. *Nothing. But this is yesterday's copy, just twenty-four hours after the event. Or maybe they'll keep it until next week. I'll have to buy a paper every day to be certain. What about Roz and that DVD of Howard's she sent to the police?* Eva scanned the pages again but once more found no mention. They'd cover that one up perhaps or at least take time to check for evidence of Roz's claims. Should she buy all the papers next week, or....?

Her thoughts were in freefall, descending into the absurd. Maybe she should just go home, face reality and take her chances. In her handbag was the Eurostar return ticket. Just over a month to go until its expiry date of 3rd January. *I can wait out that time, can't I? But what if, by then, I find I don't want to leave? This was Baba's country and so it's mine too, in a way. And maybe this should be the place to see out my time.* She looked for a paper tissue in her bag and, as she pulled it out, an English pound coin rolled out. She stroked it, twisting it around in her fingers and let it spin on the table. *'Heads' to stay, 'tails' to leave.* The coin seemed to hover forever on its edge, the brass glinting in the fluorescent lighting overhead. Finally it toppled over, still spinning and clattering.

Heads.

The road down from Václavské Náměstí past Můstek station narrowed as it progressed, evolving into little more than an alley. On the left Eva passed a street market, the stalls laden with cheap ceramics and wooden toys which were attracting the attention of a large crowd of Oriental children. Shoals of people pressed against each other in both directions and she seemed to be walking against a tide of humanity drawn from all points of the globe. She was jostled and pushed from behind until the alley suddenly opened up into a huge square with room to breathe at last. She leaned up against a pillar and unfolded the map that Pani Novotná had given her. This was Staroměstské Náměstí, Old Town Square. Crowds of tourists were huddled at the foot of a giant clock tower, emitting oohs and aahs as the clock struck six and cameras flashed. Tour guides speaking in German, Italian and Japanese offered up their commentaries to anyone who would listen. Glowing street lamps were dotted around the cobbled square and brave souls endured the bitter wind on the outside terraces of restaurants lining the right-hand side of the square, aided by huge outdoor heaters blasting out jets of comforting warmth. Everyone seemed to be with someone else and she felt a pang of loneliness. *Maybe I should have waited for Roz after all.*

Eva walked through the square, crisscrossing the walkways between stalls selling hot dogs, mulled wine, and more tourist souvenirs that served no useful purpose other than to provide proof that one had been here. *What's the point? The stuff just sits on your shelf and gathers dust or else gets stuffed into your loft.* Two grey horses were tethered to a pole, stamping their hooves and pulling against the open carriages behind them. A man dressed in many layers looked up and down the crowds for customers. Had Eva been with someone she would have been tempted but somehow she felt that a solitary trip would simply heighten her sense of isolation. The horse attendant lit up a cigarette and cursed at one of the shivering animals as it backed into him and she wanted to shout at him and to slap his bloated face.

She hovered outside the restaurants, looking at their menus without seeing them. How many hours was she going to waste like this before going back to the hotel and admitting defeat? But she wasn't going to give Roz that satisfaction of thinking she couldn't hack it alone. *Why on earth did I waste that money on these clothes and the new hair?*

One drink. One small drink, maybe mulled wine to warm her through, and then she'd go back. She chose an Italian restaurant and, looking at the menu, wished she hadn't ruined her appetite already on another McDonald's burger. She took a small table, the last empty one with two chairs near one of the outdoor heaters and with a good view of the square to distract her. Couples passed by, craning their necks to read the menu on its brass stand and casting glances around for empty tables. The first sip of mulled wine she took added to the inner glow that the fire was already giving her. Maybe she'd stay for another one after this. For the lack of anything else to do she laid out the city map on her table. *Yeah, spot the tourist....*

'Excuse me?'

She started and looked up.

'Excuse me, but is this seat taken?'

The accent was softly American, she guessed, the tone polite, and smiling eyes. But she drew back instinctively.

'I'm sorry to have bothered you, I'll find somewhere else.' He was turning away. She could see now that all the other tables were full.

'I'm sorry,' she spluttered, 'no, please, that seat is free if you need it.' She moved her wineglass and map, nearly launching them off the table in her haste, and he caught the glass just in time.

'Thank you,' she murmured.

'No problem. You sure this is OK?'

She nodded without looking up, rustling the map.

The waiter approached. 'I'll have the same,' the man said in perfect Czech and gesturing towards Eva's glass. He turned towards the heater and stretched his hands towards it. In that brief moment she looked up at the back of his head, taking in dark blond hair nestling above a thick black scarf and found herself wondering about an American who could speak such perfectly-accented Czech. When he turned back she saw blue-grey eyes smiling at her and she dropped her gaze.

'Real cold, isn't it?' he said. 'Sorry to cut in on you, but everywhere seems full tonight.'

She nodded silently, then managed, 'it's a popular time of year for tourists, I suppose.'

He looked at her map. 'English, right?'

'Yes.'

'On holiday?'

She hesitated. 'Sort of. And you?'

'No, I live here.'

'Really?'

'Surprised? Yeah, really. I work here, just over the other side of the square, in fact.' He took a deep draught of his wine and then sighed. 'Oh, that feels better.'

'So,' she cleared her throat and kept her gaze over his shoulder, 'how long have you lived here, then?'

'Couple of years.'

'So, you're used to this,' she swept her arm out to indicate the snow-covered ground.

'Sure. But we have even more back home in Canada.'

'Canada?'

'Let me guess,' he laughed, 'you thought American, right?'

'Um, well…'

'It's OK, hard to tell us apart, I guess?' His mockery did not feel unkind.

'I suppose it's like every American thinks English people are all Londoners,' she ventured.

'You're not from London, then?'

'Well, actually, yes, I am.' They laughed together and she allowed herself to look over his face.

'Great city. I haven't been there for a while.'

'Do you go back to Canada often?'

'Every Christmas, to see my family. Actually, we're from here, originally, I mean, my parents were born here – got away when the Russians invaded in '68. Still got some cousins somewhere outside Prague.'

She had to resist the temptation to shout 'snap'. All she could manage was a weak, 'how interesting'. He turned his head away again to call the waiter. She fought the idiotic urge to reach out and touch that dark blond hair.

'*Zaplatím, prosím,*' he waved a two hundred crown note at the waiter. 'Nice to meet you, but I gotta go,' he said to her, draining the last of his mulled wine. He half-rose to leave and then turned back to face her. 'You like jazz?'

'Jazz?' Half a lifetime ago she could have reeled off a long list of her favourite musicians, but now she was struggling. 'Um, yes, I do, actually, very much.'

'There's a new jazz club just opened on Hanákova. It's called The Red Door.' He paused. 'Maybe see you there sometime?'

'Oh. OK. Yes, maybe.'

He held out his hand. 'I'm Will.'

'Eva,' she replied, allowing him to take her hand in a light shake.

'You take care, Eva.'

She watched him melt into the crowds, craning her neck until his form disappeared.

19

Roz leant back against the padded banquette and grinned as she saw Eva enter the Černā Růže bar. There was a half-empty wineglass in front of her, with the ashtray well-filled and a glazed expression in her eyes.

'Looks like this could become our regular,' she gestured around the room. 'Might start getting the odd free drink, you never know. Where did you go then?'

'Just out and around,' Eva replied. 'I see your waiter's not here, then? Planning to do the others next, are you?'

Roz waved her hand at Eva impatiently through the cloud of cigarette smoke.

'I mean it, Roz, you disappear again like that one more time and we split up. I didn't come here to waste my time worrying about you. Listen, we've got to start thinking about getting a flat to rent or something. On Monday I'm going to check out some estate agents and get the local papers.'

Roz shrugged her shoulders. Finally she nodded. 'OK. By the way, next time you go shopping I'll come with you. You need a better hair colour shade than that and more clothes. So, what's with this new look, then? Trying to pull as well, are you?' Her eyes widened as she saw a blush spreading over Eva's face.

'Oh what? Eva? Jeez! You wouldn't have gone out on the pull – you've forgotten how!'

'It's nothing like that, Roz.'

'Really?' Roz leaned forward. 'Oh, come on!'

'Look, there's nothing to tell, OK? A guy just came up and shared my table. We talked a bit and then he left. That's it.'

'Name? Colour of hair and eyes? Shag factor? You going to meet him again?'

'No. So drop it.'

Roz grunted. 'So, Saturday night and we don't have a date. No husbands to bother us, no kids to put to bed, no one for you to nurse. Free to roam this fab city. Do you know how many women would envy us right now?'

'Maybe. But how many of them would have chosen our way of getting here?'

'Shit happens, chick. Do you seriously want to go back to how things were?'

Eva opened her mouth to answer and then shook her head.

'That's right, chick,' Roz continued with a wide grin. 'We can deal the cards now any which way we please. Waiter!'

Roz indicated a refill of her glass but Eva waved the waiter away. 'Forget that, Roz. Let's go eat some proper food.'

Eva took Roz to Staroměstské Náměstí. Roz meandered through the stalls, browsing idly through the piles of knick-knacks and then they wandered through some of the narrow streets and alleys nearby, clinging together for warmth. The second street they passed on the right was marked Hanákova.

'Let's try down here,' Eva suggested.

Roz squinted in the darkness. 'Doesn't look all that promising.'

'Just come on.' Halfway down the street Eva turned her head and Roz followed her gaze.

'What's that, then?' Roz demanded. She pointed to a door with scuffed red paint and a picture of a saxophone in the window next to it. Even from across the road Roz could hear a low hum of bass instruments.

'No idea,' said Eva, steering Roz away and peering further down the street. 'Looks like a Greek restaurant down there, let's check it out.'

After a passable first course washed down with a Moravian white wine that even Roz was impressed with, they settled back for a cigarette break. 'You going back on these, then?' asked Roz as

Eva reached out for the pack.

'What the hell, why not? Listen, Roz, I bought a newspaper today. An English one, I mean.'

'Great,' said Roz airily, 'we can keep ourselves up to date with what Howard's doing back home to save the country – Eva, for fuck's sake, what's the point of reading the news?'

'You don't understand – I had to see, whether it's been in the papers yet.'

'You think they'll print something about him, then?'

'Oh, stop thinking about bloody Howard – I'm talking about me!'

'Oh! And was it?'

'No.'

Roz sighed. 'Well, that's all right then, chick, isn't it?'

'Not necessarily. Could be in another paper. Or maybe next week.'

'C'mon Eva, what the hell could they do to you, anyway? Douglas left the letter and, then, you've got your own problems to give you some justification....you could say your own situation clouded your judgment or something.'

Eva was staring at her in fury. 'I'm not playing that card, having everyone say, oh poor woman, she's dying anyway and she must have been desperate - .'

'OK, OK, you've made your point!'

The waitress brought their main course. This was the first decent meal Roz had had in days and yet she couldn't taste a thing. Her eyes followed the young waitress as she hurried between the tables. The girl was dark-haired with soft brown eyes, not as thin as the other girls they had seen around. When she smiled Roz noticed a dimple in her right cheek which gave her an air of childlike innocence.

'Something not quite right about her accent,' murmured Eva.

When the waitress brought the dessert menu Eva asked her where she was from. She looked taken aback by the question.

'Limassol,' she replied. 'Cyprus. My father is Czech but he met my mother there when he worked in a bar there many years ago.'

'Why did you come here?'

The girl shrugged. 'My father said he was homesick and he wanted to be near his parents again.'

Eva translated for Roz, who had kept her eyes fixed on the girl. 'Ask her if she likes it here,' said Roz. When Eva posed the question the waitress shrugged with a sad smile.

'I do not like the cold,' she replied, before excusing herself.

'Poor cow,' muttered Roz.

'How many people are here, do you think, who don't want to be?'

'Well, I can think of better places, but hey, you're the one with the family tree to trace.'

An icy blast of air cut their faces as they emerged back on to Hanákova and they instinctively linked arms. Walking back the way they had come Roz saw that a small crowd had formed outside the Red Door. Eva scanned the group and checked her watch.

'Why do you keep looking at that place? What is it, anyway?' came Roz's muffled voice through her thick scarf.

'Some kind of club, I think.'

'Let's go in, then, get warm at least.' As the door opened briefly the sound of a saxophone wafted out.

'Let's try it some other time,' Eva said.

'Why wait? Look, I'm half-bloody-frozen, what's there to think about?'

Roz steered her over and through the door. It was cramped and dark inside. Roz had pushed through the crowd, ignoring protests and grabbed a corner table just before a young couple reached it. 'Sorted!' she announced, surveying the dense crowd around them. 'Where's the waiter, then?'

The girls around them were dressed as if for summer – a uniform of short skirts and skimpy tops prevailed and Roz wondered whether a lifetime of this kind of winter had somehow inured them to the cold. She felt suddenly old, shivering inside her coat. The atmosphere was hot and smoky and the girls' cleavages glistened with a soft sheen of moisture. It was a while before a harassed-looking waiter found them. Roz ordered two drinks each for them, on the basis that it would save time.

'Two Black Velvets for me and two Tequila Sunrises for her.' She lit a cigarette. 'Remember,' she whispered to Eva, 'the night we drank eight of those without getting pissed?' Roz smiled as she reminisced. She had been twenty-three years old with a bright future and a cast-iron constitution. She used to make homemade cocktails that could fell a horse.

'This isn't a competition,' Eva replied testily.

'Course not, chick. Whatever gave you that idea?' smirked Roz.

People around them were pressed up against each other like fish in a net, squirming to get through to get a glimpse of the live band. The lighting was low, making it hard to see the details of people's faces. Each time the door opened Eva's eyes were drawn towards it.

'Looking for someone?' asked Roz, a smile playing around her lips.

'No.'

'Told you about this place, did he?'

'Oh, all right, yes, he did.'

'Hmm, now let me guess.' Roz craned her neck to get a better view of the incoming group. 'That one, maybe? No, not your type.'

'You don't know my type!' Eva snapped. 'Forget about it – let's just drink up and go.'

'You're such a fuckin' misery, d'you know that?' Roz spilled some of the Black Velvet over her long skirt and started to rub at the stain with her sleeve. 'Sod it! Got to go to the loo. Don't elope whilst I'm away.'

Roz had been gone for only a couple of minutes when a voice behind Eva said, 'Can I join you?' He was short and broad, with fair hair cut too close to his scalp. The English he spoke was heavily-accented.

'No,' Eva replied in Czech. 'I'm with a friend.'

'Ah, but I heard you speaking English! But your Czech is quite good for a foreigner.'

'Actually, I'm not a foreigner.'

'Excuse me?'

'Never mind –.' Roz had pushed her way back through the crowd and now looked the man up and down and then over at Eva, raising her eyebrows. Eva shook her head.

'Can we help you?' Roz asked him.

He looked her over. 'I don't think so,' he laughed before moving away into the throng.

'Fucking cheek!' Roz hissed at his departing back. 'Christ, Eva, for one moment I thought you really were desperate. Still, after Alex....'

Eva wasn't counting the drinks. The waiter just kept coming over, that's all. The music anchored her, flooding through her like warm water. She closed her eyes and remembered the student dives in London she and Roz used to haunt and the occasional treat of a trip to somewhere like Ronnie Scott's. The men with soulful eyes and beautiful bodies....

'What's wrong now?' asked Roz, as Eva wiped away a tear.

'Nothing. Just remembering another time.'

Roz didn't protest when Eva suggested leaving. The effect of the Black Velvets was kicking in and she slithered on the pavements as they walked slowly, arm in arm, in silence back to Můstek station. When they got back to the hotel room Roz lay on her bed and flicked through the TV channels. Czech quiz shows, a dubbed episode of Dallas from the 1980s, one German channel and Sky news.

'We should watch the Czech channels, it might help you to pick up a bit of the language,' Eva said.

'Don't think I'll need to bother, at this rate.'

'But how can you understand how people think unless you learn their language and culture?'

'Why the fuck should I care about how they think?'

'Well, when it comes to looking for a job, you'll have to.'

'Can't we think about that later? Let's just chill out for now.' Roz yawned and fell asleep with the TV remote still in her hand.

20

After having spent Sunday dragging Roz around the tourist sights, relying on a written guide in English for orientation and historical notes, Eva was fed up of her whinging. *You should get to know this place properly, Roz, so you can get around on your own without me.* But Roz had only been happy when she found some clothes shops open, even though she had moaned that the best items only seemed to be stocked in tiny sizes. Eva tossed and turned all that night, grateful for the new dawn, her years in nursing having created a habit of early waking she could not break now.

She left Roz a note - *Gone walkabout. Meet you Černá Růže 5 pm* - and skipped breakfast to get out as soon as possible. Having scanned the English papers once more, hardly breathing while turning the pages, she set off down Nārodnī Třída and after ten minutes reached the River Vltava. She leaned against the stone balustrade, watching the grey water swirling around the pillars of Charles Bridge a little distance further up the river, and enjoyed the feel of strong early-winter sunshine on the back of her head as a counterbalance to the chill seeping up through her boots from the snow underneath. In England, sunshine as strong as this would have turned any vestige of snow into grey slush by mid-morning. But the crisp white blanket under her boots felt as firm as before. A large boat restaurant was moored on the nearside bank, its name picked out in gold italic script against the dark green wood.

Two middle-aged men in smart grey buttoned-up coats passed her by, their laptop computer cases slung over their shoulders. *Has Alex gone to work today? Will there be a post-mortem for Douglas? When will the funeral be held?* The thoughts chilled her even more than the wind which whipped up off the water. She moved on as her feet were beginning to feel numb from cold. Within a few minutes she had turned on to Charles Bridge. Passing through the growing crowds of tourists she hung around on the edge of one group, listening to an English-speaking guide who was pointing at all the statues lining the bridge and giving a succinct description of their history and symbolism. Further on, an old man was standing behind an easel, with samples of sketches laid in a pile at his feet. A pretty young Oriental girl was perched on a stool too high for her legs as his charcoal-stained fingers swept over the white paper, his eyes darting from the sheet to her face and then back again. Eva stepped behind him to watch his craft. *How many of these does he have to do a day to scrape a living? Does he never tire of the need to enhance people's features to create a more flattering image than Nature had intended?* He looked around at her at one point, smiling and gesturing for her to wait her turn. Eva had forgotten to apply any make-up before leaving the hotel, so unused was she to the ritual after so many years, but suddenly she felt naked without it and shook her head.

She continued walking along the bridge to the end, looking up at the ruined medieval tower-gate beyond which the road rose sharply. She was curious to explore further but this was not the day to play the tourist role. *There'll be other times. Or will there? Shouldn't I just live in the moment?* Living with uncertainty was something she had been grappling with for the last couple of months and now she craved the predictability and security of her life long ago, however dull it had been. Then the sun came out again and the glow it brought to her face lifted the gloom and swept away her dark thoughts. Exuberant crowds of youngsters rushing past filled her with shame for her hesitation. *There are all kinds of prisons, some of which we create for ourselves.*

She walked purposefully back on to the main road, crossed it and headed back downriver to Nārodnī Třīda. Halfway down on the right she spotted an estate agent's office with display boards outside. Roz should have been with her, taking joint responsibility for making these arrangements. It felt just like back in the days at the Bloomsbury flat – *Eva, the loo's not flushing, can you call the plumber, Eva, I'm too tired to go to the launderette, Eva, the landlord says our rent is overdue, Eva, Eva....*

With her dictionary in one hand and a city map in the other Eva squinted up at the display board. Most of the flats seemed to be for sale only, but then she found a small section at the bottom which listed a few apartments for rental. 'Prague 6 – Nebušice, forty thousand crowns a month for a 3 + 1 nadstandardní,' she read aloud. *What does that mean?* Thirty thousand crowns for a 2 + 1 in Prague 4 – *Nusle*, which was closer to the centre. She pushed open the office door.

'*Dobrý den*,' intoned the girl behind the desk without looking up.

'*Dobrý den*,' Eva replied. 'Um, do you speak English?'

'A little,' the girl murmured, still keeping her eyes on her computer screen. 'You want something?'

'I'm looking for a flat to rent. Two bedrooms.'

'How much?'

'Well, I don't know, but not expensive.'

'Which area?'

'Quite central, but I don't know Prague and, well, I need some advice.'

The girl sighed heavily, opened a drawer in her desk and thrust three sheets of paper at Eva. She then pointed to a city map on the wall and went back to her PC screen. Eva sat down on a chair beneath the wall map and flicked through the pages.

'Excuse me, but what does *2 + 1* mean?'

'Two rooms and kitchen.'

'You mean two bedrooms, living room and kitchen?'

The girl frowned. 'I said two rooms. That is all.'

Eva shuffled the papers. 'It seems expensive.'

'For us, yes, but for you, maybe not.' She looked over Eva's clothes and Eva felt her face starting to burn.

'Look, I want to see someone else!' Eva snapped. The girl shrugged but then called out someone's name. A man in his late twenties emerged from a back office. The girl muttered something in a low voice. He nodded towards Eva, managing a salesman's broad smile.

'May I help you?' he asked in beautifully-accented English, his eyes travelling up and down Eva's figure.

'Yes, well, I hope so. I'm looking to rent a flat with my friend – maybe long-term - and I need advice about the best locations and how to compare prices. These properties - ,' Eva pointed to the papers, 'look like a lot of money. I thought it would be cheap here.'

He smiled broadly. 'Ah, you see, Prague is not like the rest of the Czech Republic. We have – how you say – new market forces here. Many foreigners come and the prices go up.'

Oh, our fault is it, then? Right. Well, hooray for bloody capitalism. You lot must be raking it in.

'Of course,' he went on, 'you can find something cheaper in newspapers but maybe not good standard. Maybe only *panelāky*. These,' he waved to the display boards, 'all very nice, some *luxusní*. Top of range, you say?'

Nadstandardní. Luxusní. These were words which would make Roz happy but not their wallets. The agent's commission would rely on such prices. The girl's beautiful shoes, Eva noticed, surely would too. What were *panelāky*? She didn't want to show her ignorance.

'I understand,' she said. 'Could you please explain how the process works?'

'We make legal agreement with landlord. You have permits?'

'What permits?'

'Foreigner's visa, work permit.'

'Surely we don't need that? We're all part of the EU now?'

His mouth smiled but not his eyes. 'Czech government still has many rules. First, you must go to Foreigners Police and get document to say you have no criminal record in your country and then…'

Eva's heart was sinking as he droned on about the raft of paperwork she had to obtain. *Christ, we were supposed to be able to disappear here without a trace. Roz will go ballistic.* She carried on nodding but without listening, thanked him and left hurriedly. Maybe Roz could turn to her barman boyfriend for advice. There had to be a way around this.

Baba had once told Eva of a grand café near the river where, as a young girl, she would gaze up at the tall windows and wish her mother could afford to take her there for *palačinky* and ice cream.

'Was it a very expensive place, then?' Eva had asked.

'For us, yes,' Baba had replied, 'but for some others, no.'

'So, who could afford to go there, then?

'Communist party members, the senior ones. But they didn't go there so much. It was really the place to meet people who were the life blood of our country.'

'What, you mean politicians?'

Eva had not understood then why that had made Baba laugh so much. 'No, no, Eva! I mean the thinkers. Intellectuals, writers, poets. The people who can teach you how to think about life, and how to dream of building a better future.'

But Baba had never struck Eva as being much of a dreamer. She had always been too busy, feeding and clothing them on the little money that she had earned working in a bakery. Eva's image of Baba had been of flour up to her elbows in the kitchen, not poring over a book in an armchair.

'What was this place called?' Eva had asked.

'Kavárna Slavia.'

'Do you suppose it's still there? Wouldn't the Russians have closed it down?'

Baba had thought for a moment, and then replied softly, 'they could not close it down, even if they have locked up all the writers and poets.' Which they had.

'One day, Baba, I will take you there and buy you the biggest pile of pancakes and ice cream they've got.' Eva had promised with the endless optimism of a twelve-year-old. Baba had laughed and ruffled Eva's hair.

There it was now, across the road from Eva, on a corner site. *'Kavárna Slavia'* inscribed in sloping copper-plated script flowing across tall wide windows which looked out on to the river on one side and the National Theatre on the other. She stood for a moment at the foot of the stone steps, taking it all in before climbing them up to the double doors. Inside, the décor was a clash of dark cherry-wood, onyx and Art Deco lighting, with long neat rows of round tables running the length of the room. Somehow she was disappointed. The age of the building had suggested to her that rich nineteenth-century furnishings would have provided a better setting, something warmer and more comforting than these hard materials. There was no background classical music to soothe her either, just a low murmur of dozens of voices blending as one. Old ladies were bundled up in thick knitted cardigans; some wearing crushed velvet hats in plum or forest green, stroking tall glasses of clear tea in front of them. These were women of Baba's generation. Without exception, their attire was neat and controlled, irrespective of their build. They held their bodies stiffly and spoke in low measured tones that helped Eva to pick out individual words and sentences. She took a table just inside the entrance door to get the best view, wishing she had brought a notebook to record it all.

It was only eleven-forty-five by now, but early lunches were already being served. A little girl, maybe three or four, was working her way through a mound of off-white ice cream in a tall glass, the spoon too long for her fingers to handle competently. Eva ordered a plain white coffee and settled down to watch. Where were Baba's writers and poets now? No one here seemed to fit that category. Ordinary humanity, both local and visiting, had expanded to take their seats, to exchange family gossip and pore over maps and brochures. Maybe no one felt the need to discuss the value of man's existence anymore. The Revolution was past. Judging by what she could grasp of conversations around her, the daily battle was no longer for one's political soul but for the latest brand of TV or car. The ghosts of the nation's conscience would have to congregate elsewhere. Perhaps she should order *palačinky* and ice cream as an offering to Baba's spirit.

The sheaf of real estate details was bulging in Eva's pocket, demanding further perusal. It had to be done. A breeze stirred the papers on her table as the entrance door opened again. A tall slender lady stood there, clutching the arm of a shorter woman whose dumpiness made her companion look even taller. The shorter woman cast her gaze around the room before finally steering the tall lady carefully over to an empty table by the window about two yards away. The lady was dressed from head to toe in a swirling hooded cape of dove-grey and her silvery hair tied back in a chignon. Her face was angular without being too hard, the eyes obscured behind dark glasses. She slid gracefully on to the chair which an eager young waiter had held out for her. Looking around the room she nodded and smiled briefly at some of the other customers. She removed her gloves with a delicate precision and laid them neatly on the table. The waiter murmured something, she nodded and he disappeared, returning almost instantly with two tall glasses of cloudy liquid. No one else, Eva noticed, had been served so quickly. The lady gazed out of the window for a while whilst her dumpy companion drank quickly, her eyes darting around the other tables. She briefly glanced at Eva, frowned slightly and then flicked her attention to the lady, murmuring a few words. Eva stirred her coffee and went back to reading the estate agents' lists.

Within a couple of minutes two men entered noisily and heads were turned. Both looked to be in their seventies. They carried with them a strong whiff of tobacco and a hint of stale sweat from the shorter of the two. They settled at the table next to Eva. The taller man had thick-lensed glasses perched on his long hooked nose. His companion removed a small tape recorder from his pocket and placed it on the table between them. The interviewee, if he was such, looked around the room over the top of his glasses, scratching his short grey beard. The bored expression on his face suddenly disappeared when his gaze fell on the tall lady by the window. Muttering something to his companion, he rose and strode over to her table, bowed slightly and raised her hand to his lips. Her smile of recognition lit up her face and imbued it with the vitality of a much younger woman. They spoke softly together for a few moments, heads lowered, and then he gestured back to his own table, murmuring something and with his facial expression almost regretful. She nodded and a smile played around her lips, as if savouring a private joke. Her companion waited silently throughout this exchange and, on the man's departure, spoke swiftly and low into the lady's ear. It was the lady's turn to frown, a shadow erasing the beauty of a moment ago.

The man returned to his table and waited patiently for his interviewer to stop fiddling with the tape recorder's controls. It was then that the interviewer addressed the other man as *Pan Senator*, who inclined his head in acknowledgment of this title. Eva stared at her papers to avoid the impression of being an eavesdropper. The interviewer's tone was respectful, his words coming at a measured pace with precise pronunciation in sharp contrast to the half-swallowed guttural babble she had been struggling to understand around her these past couple of days. Whilst there were many words she could not recognize the gist of their conversation was quite clear. It seemed that the tall man, the Senator, was being interviewed for his political memoirs. The delicate and respectful tone of the questions was unfamiliar to her ears, being more used to the savage and staccato style of a John Humphrys or Jeremy Paxman. The interviewer's questions felt more like a search for confirmation than a challenge.

As Eva looked up into the middle distance to consider this, the corner of her eye caught a glimpse of the dumpy woman who was looking at her again. *No, she must have been observing the men. She seems to know the Senator, after all.* The Senator was droning on. Eva's interest was now turning to irritation. The interviewer should be probing more, cutting through the flow of excess information and challenging the self-satisfied tone. *Stop nodding at him, you wimp, and take control. And why does that woman keep looking over at me?*

The click-click of the tape recorder was soft but insistent. Whatever else the Senator had to say would have to wait for another time. The tape was finished and the interviewer rose, scraped back his chair and performed a clumsy half-bow to his subject. The Senator jerked his head in weary acknowledgement. The audience was over, for now. The interviewer made his way out, bundling his tape recorder back into his jacket as he went. The Senator snapped his fingers at a passing waitress and ordered a *slivovice*.

Eva felt there seemed little point in staying. The magic of the place Baba had described had eluded her. As she rose to leave she caught the dumpy woman's quizzical gaze, her head inclined to one side. *Roz was right – they should be told it's rude to stare.* The tall lady sat beside her companion, silent and expressionless. Eva wondered whether the Senator would join their table now and whether this would be another encounter worthy of observation but none of them made a move.

21

As Eva walked back down Nārodnī Třída and turned into a narrow alleyway with the thought of flat-hunting still troubling her, the idea of turning to Will flashed into her mind. Someone like him, who lived and worked here and understood the language and customs, seemed to be the obvious source of help. He could help them negotiate their way through the bureaucracy and he might know the right people to talk to. She and Roz would need to concoct a script of half-truths but the words 'criminal record' were burned into her mind. Would there be something saying they were being looked for? No, there had to be some backroom dodges. Baba had always said that, in Communist times, there had been the official price and then the real one. That was the way things had worked, through a trusted network. The question was whether Eva wanted to drag Will into this when she hardly knew him. No strings attached – no relationship to manipulate as a bargaining tool. She didn't want to use anyone.

With the afternoon to kill before she would meet up with Roz again Eva spent an hour in a cheap Chinese restaurant nearby and then wandered aimlessly through intertwining streets and alleys, peering into dimly-lit grocer's windows with their lacklustre displays of piles of tinned sardines, jars filled with pickled cabbage or beetroot and packets of *knedlíky* mix. These shops were sprinkled liberally amongst the side streets and she wondered how they all managed to survive. She would need to learn to negotiate her way through them without the comforting anonymity of a supermarket. She came across the welcoming sight of an Italian delicatessen with a small range of goods but at least offering some things that Roz would be prepared to try. Eva caught herself. *Why am I suddenly worried about what Roz is prepared to eat? We haven't lived together for years so why should I assume any responsibility for her?* But Eva wondered whether Roz would have forgotten how to cook and clean after the years of privilege.

These shops were in stark contrast to the futuristic cornucopia of the shopping mall at Anděl. They radiated a sense of stubborn resistance to the onslaught of global consumerism so evident on the main thoroughfares with their Western brands, a cinema showing American blockbusters and branches of international companies in banking and property development. Eva felt she could get lost in these myriad tiny alleys and be on a different planet. Here the real voice of Prague seemed to be speaking to her, the Prague that Baba had known, loved and lost.

As Eva strolled past yet another musty antique shop the dark alley opened into a square bursting with sunshine. She blinked in the unexpected light and let her gaze wander around the surrounding buildings which were clearly much older and ornate than the ones she had just been passing. The external plaster walls were all painted in the same shade of buttery cream, topped by either grey slates or ridged tiles in reddish-brown hues, uneven with age. A church to the right had an almost pristine exterior compared to the pockmarked walls of neighbouring buildings, standing like a bride outshining her attendants. She wondered at their age, maybe a couple of hundred years or more. Some walls carried a tide mark about ten feet off the ground with the plaster below being more discoloured and damaged. Then Eva remembered reading about the floods of 2002. They had meant nothing to her at the time. But here she was now. She noted the name of the square. Josefová. An elegant name, she thought, to match the buildings.

'So come on then, what about these flats you've found?' Černá Růže was quiet tonight. Roz lit two cigarettes and passed one to Eva.

'Forget it. Too pricey.' Eva blew smoke above her head. She told Roz what the estate agent had said about visa documents and criminal record checks. Roz's face darkened.

'Shit!' she muttered. 'Thought this was gonna be easy.'

'How was I supposed to know? Look, I was thinking we could

do with some help to get around it. Do you think your barman friend,' Eva nodded to the bar where he was polishing glasses, 'could give us any ideas?'

Roz sighed. 'Jiří could be worth a try, I suppose.'

'I'll leave you to work your charms then, shall I?' Eva smiled ruefully, heading for the ladies' toilet.

I've done my bit for the day. Roz can put in some effort now for a change. When Eva left the toilet she turned left instead of right, passing through the glass-roofed dining area and out of an automatic door which led to a paved garden, dotted with tall bare trees through which strings of small white fairy lights had been threaded to throw out a soft spangled light which lifted the darkening gloom. The garden was ringed on three sides by small retail outlets selling more of the modern comforts which she was beginning to find prevailed in this area – Italian designer shoes, and minimalist Swedish furniture and décor at prices that surely only the expatriate businessmen who frequented this bar could afford, with the subliminal calls to flex their credit cards. She returned to the table to find Roz grinning broadly.

'Done deal,' Roz said, raising her glass.

'Well?'

'His uncle's got a place in Prague 4 we can look at. Two bedrooms at twenty-five thousand crowns a month. We can see it tomorrow.'

'Still a lot of money, isn't it?'

'Got any better ideas?'

They ate at a Czech restaurant where they were served huge slabs of peppered steak done to perfection. Roz poked at her salad garnish of grated carrot and white cabbage which she complained tasted of sugared water. Later she persuaded Eva to go back to The Red Door again. Eva's feet ached from all the walking she had done during the day and she was glad to rest them for a couple of hours. The club was half-empty. Perhaps this was normal for a Monday night. Will wasn't there. *But then, why should I expect him to be?*

They were to meet Jiří at five-thirty the next evening at his uncle's flat in Prague 4. His instructions were to take the metro to

I.P. Pavlová station, and then the number eleven tram for five stops. Jiří was waiting for them at the tram stop and they all walked together for about ten minutes, reaching an estate of six tower blocks ringing a central wasteland through which a sharp wind whistled. Eva looked up at the block they were approaching, most of the floors ablaze with light radiating from dozens of windows above them. Jiri called the block a *panelák*. Now she understood. *The estate agent would be laughing his head off if he could see me now.* Jiří had a key to the front door but used the buzzer. A crackling voice could just be heard in response to his greeting, and then they passed through into the hall. A welcoming wall of heat struck Eva in the face, accompanied by the unmistakable smells of fried meat and garlic. Roz wrinkled her nose and threw Eva a look. The lift door's grill-gate clanged behind them and Jiří jabbed the number seven button. Eva noticed there were fourteen buttons in all, a real tower block. The lift creaked slowly upwards, the three of them crammed up against each other. As they emerged on to the seventh floor Eva saw three doors, one to the left and right, and the third straight in front. At the base of each door lay the same kind of rough woven doormat beside which occupants had lined up outdoor shoes in varying shades of scuffed brown or grey. The uniformity of all this made Eva think of an army barracks or school dormitory. All the beech veneer doors had spy-holes inserted just at eye level. The corridor walls were covered in flaking pale blue paint. She felt Roz behind her shifting nervously.

Jiří pressed the doorbell of the flat to the left of them but then used his key anyway. The door opened to reveal a narrow corridor with a worn parquet floor. Standing there was a stooped man with wispy tufts of grey hair and sunken blue eyes, his walnut-coloured skin deeply lined.

'*Dobrý den*,' he said. No smile of greeting.

'*Dobrý den*,' Jiří inclined his head in response and swept out his arm to introduce Eva and Roz. The man nodded and gestured for them to enter, shuffling ahead. Still in the corridor he opened a door on the right and pulled on a cord. The light revealed a small bathroom and toilet with panelled Formica walls in mottled blue, the white sanitary fittings stained with age. Eva could hear Roz's sharp intake of breath behind her. Moving on there was another door on the same side which led them into a small kitchen. Simple white melamine cupboards lined one wall. A wooden square table with two stools stood against a net-curtained window and a small fridge hummed in the corner. The gas stove reminded Eva of the ancient chipped contraption of her childhood home. Eva smiled politely at the old man but he ignored her, steering them instead into a longer narrow room with the same worn parquet floor as in the corridor but with a square of faded orange and blue carpet in the centre. Against the far wall stood a black glass-fronted cabinet containing some paperbacks and a set of short tumblers with tarnished gilt rims. A backless beige sofa with a couple of brown hessian-covered cushions took up most of the nearside wall. Lastly, they were ushered into a bedroom containing a double bed and a varnished pine wardrobe on each side.

'You said there were two bedrooms?' Roz looked up enquiringly at Jiři.

He shrugged. 'Yes. One here and there,' he pointed back into the living room at the sofa, 'that is bed too.'

'You mean that one of us has to sleep in the sitting room?' Her tone was incredulous.

'You share this bed, then?' He smiled and winked at Eva. 'Keep warm, yes?'

'It's very – clean,' Eva managed.

Jiři frowned. 'Of course.'

The old man spoke rapidly to Jiři but Eva couldn't catch the gist of it, nor Jiři's reply. Then Jiři turned to Roz. 'My uncle ask when you want to move in?'

Eva held up a warning hand to Roz and replied quickly, 'thank you very much, Jiři. It's very kind of you. Roz and I will talk about this and let you know tomorrow.'

Jiři frowned again and he muttered something to his uncle who looked downcast. 'No need for papers, OK?' said Jiři, his expression hopeful again.

'Yes, well, thank you, we'll – we'll let you know.' Eva replied.

She thanked Jiři's uncle in Czech and received a curt goodbye in return. Eva gripped Roz's arm tightly, steering her gently but firmly out of the flat, thanking Jiři again but leaving him behind. Once in the safety of the lift she let Roz give vent to her feelings.

'Jesus Christ!' Roz exploded. 'What a dump! No way am I living there. How the hell do people expect -?'

'Roz, you have to remember – this is probably how most Czechs live. We've just seen the glitzy parts of town, that's all. This, here, this is the reality. And, anyway, we wouldn't need to get any papers, you heard Jiří. I mean, what choice do we have?'

'Eva, I didn't drag myself out of a shit-hole in Moss Side to end up living the rest of my life somewhere like this! Don't be so cheap, girl!'

Their return journey on the tram was full of resentful silence. They arrived back at I.P. Pavlova station and Roz pulled Eva into the Peking House Chinese restaurant above it.

'Look, we could make the flat look nice,' Eva urged. 'Once it's tarted up a bit it'll be fine. We can make do until we get a chance to settle. Now we've got to think about the next step.'

'Which is?'

'Find some kind of job, of course. How else are we going to pay for all this?'

'You think we're gonna get jobs here? What the hell are you thinking of – teaching English or something?'

'Could be a start.'

Roz sighed heavily. 'There's got to be an easier way.'

'No, Roz. Easy is what you've been used to. We're on our own now.' Eva watched in alarm as tears started to trickle from Roz's eyes.

'How the fuck did we come to be like this? It's not fair!' Roz wiped her face with her napkin. 'I mean, look at that girl over there,' she pointed behind Eva who turned to see a beautiful blonde, maybe in her early twenties, with the kind of manicured appearance that suggested a life of ease. 'And look at the guy with her. Why not, eh? Why does it have to be so hard?'

Eva reached out and squeezed her friend's hand. 'We'll be all right.' She raised her glass. 'We'll find a way, OK?'

22

The next morning found Roz outside a phone booth whilst Eva was ringing the telephone numbers from several real estate adverts in a newspaper called *Annonce*. She shuffled around, her coat wrapped up against the wind. After a few minutes Eva came out.
'Well?'

Eva shook her head. 'Two people hung up on me almost straightaway. On the third call they told me the flat was already gone. The next two numbers didn't answer.'

They walked arm in arm to Kavárna Slavia. 'This is hopeless,' said Roz as Eva ordered cakes and coffee.

'Maybe we should get back to Jiri,' Eva suggested.

Roz shuddered. 'No way. Let's look at that agent's list again.'

'It's not just about the cost. Going through the agent will guarantee having to get permits – and we can't, right?' They had managed to secure a window table and, amongst the plates and coffee cups, spread out the agent's lists. Eva stared out of the window as Roz's finger followed the words Eva had highlighted. Eva seemed to rouse herself from her torpor and fixed her gaze on two women entering.

'Who are you looking at?' Roz turned her head and saw a tall woman swathed in a long dove-grey cloak, eyes hidden behind large dark glasses, and a shorter broader companion whose plum-coloured velvet hat was covered in fine snow. Roz turned back to the table and read the curiosity in Eva's face.

'They came in yesterday.'

'So?' asked Roz.

'The waiters made a big fuss of them.'

'Celebrities?'

'Don't know.'

'Whatever.' Roz turned her attention back to the papers, alternating between the adverts and the map.

Eva's eyes followed the women who were heading for the table behind them. Once again, a waiter appeared as if from nowhere and began to fuss around the two incomers. The young waitress who was serving Eva and Roz asked whether they wanted anything else.

'Don't suppose you've got an uncle with a flat to let?' asked Roz.

'*Prosím?*' The girl looked puzzled.

Eva smiled at the girl and said haltingly in Czech, 'we're looking for a flat to rent. It's difficult.' The girl nodded sympathetically, looking over Roz's shoulder at the copy of *Annonce* before she moved off to another table.

'Maybe you're right about Jiří,' sighed Roz as she closed the newspaper. 'Where's the loo here?'

Eva pointed to the stairs at the back of the café.

'See you in a minute,' said Roz.

In the privacy of the cubicle, Roz unwrapped the small folded piece of greaseproof paper carefully, rolled a thousand-crown note up and snorted the short line of white powder with practised efficiency. *Nice stuff. And cheaper than back home.* Jiří had proved to be useful in more ways than one. She closed her eyes for a few minutes and leant back against the wall. *Just a little help to get through another day.*

When she returned upstairs she found Eva sitting with the two women. Roz scowled, her newly-enhanced mood dented by the prospect of engaging in polite conversation with two old biddies who would probably ask questions she would rather not field. Roz stood close to the table, surveying the scene and taking in Eva's smiling face and the look of interest in the short woman's eyes. There was something about those eyes that made Roz uncomfortable. The tall woman remained mysterious behind her dark glasses. A faint hint of lilies and fresh linen wafted from her clothes and Roz noticed the hand resting on the table had slender tapering fingers, with a single ring on her left hand's third finger made of delicately twisted strands of silver. *Nice piece, worth a bit, probably.* Roz looked over the woman's face. The complexion had a faint sheen of powder but was otherwise bare.

Then the tall woman spoke. 'Ah, your friend has returned! Please join us.'

Roz was taken aback by her flawless and unaccented English. The woman smiled. 'Angela Winstanley.' The graceful hand was extended to Roz who hesitated and then sat down next to the woman's companion. 'And may I present my dear friend Pani Havlová?' Roz and Pani Havlová nodded to each other. Roz's defiant gaze was returned in full.

Angela continued. 'And may I apologize for my appearance? My eyes are a little fragile at the moment, and even this light is difficult for me. I hope you don't find it too strange. One always feels more comfortable when one can see the eyes, but alas….'

'Sure. Fine. Whatever.'

Eva turned to Roz, who was sitting with folded arms. 'Mrs. Winstanley overheard our conversation about flat-hunting. She may be able to help.'

'Great.' Roz screwed up her eyes. *Something's not right here.*

'Oh, it's Angela, please, let's not be so formal! Eva told me you're on an extended trip, Roz? Doing some research into Czech culture?'

Roz stifled a laugh. *Nice one, Eva.* She nodded briefly and drew out a cigarette. Pani Havlová scowled and placed her hand on Roz's wrist, shaking her head and pointing to Angela's eyes. Roz pulled a face.

'We were talking about how hard it is to find a good quality flat without paying the earth,' Eva said.

'Were you now?' said Roz flatly, her eyes never leaving Angela's face.

Angela's mouth twitched.

'I think we're going to need all the help we can get, aren't we, Roz?' Eva babbled on.

Angela smiled at Roz. 'Tell me, my dear, what is your interest in this country?'

'Fancied a change. Thought it would be nice to have a white Christmas,' replied Roz, her expression deadpan.

An unexpectedly deep laugh erupted from Angela's delicate

throat. 'Very well, my dear. I apologize for my nosiness.' She turned to Eva and her look was suddenly serious. 'Let me know if I can help you in any way. I know how difficult it can be to settle in a new country.'

'Oh, so you live here too?'

'Since 1946, in fact.'

'Wow! You stuck it out for this long?' Roz interrupted, her jaw slack.

Pani Havlová grunted. Angela frowned suddenly and her tone was icy. 'My dear girl, this country has been my chosen home for most of my adult life. You will need some time to come to understand this new world. If you decide to stay, that is.'

'I'm sorry, Angela,' Eva said quickly, throwing an angry look at Roz, 'I'm sure she doesn't mean to -.'

Angela raised her long hand. 'There is no need to apologize. So, how can I be of assistance?'

'Well,' Eva replied, 'there are so many things – but right now we just need to find a flat. We're in a hotel this week, near Anděl. We're not fussy, honestly, but we need a two-bedroomed place, quite central and not overpriced.'

'Do you have residency permits yet?'

'No.'

'So, you came with nothing planned?' Angela drummed her fingers on the table.

'We want to keep things simple, if you know what I mean,' said Roz curtly.

'Quite,' came the brisk reply. Then Angela's face seemed to soften again as she turned to Eva. 'I may be able to help you.' She lifted up her small grey handbag, extracted a pen and wrote quickly on their newspaper. 'I have to leave now. Come tomorrow afternoon, around three. This is my address. Josefová. Number twelve.'

Eva's face was flushed with excitement. Roz leaned back in her chair, pursing her lips and stirring her coffee slowly.

23

'It's just a coincidence,' said Roz.

'I don't know, but it's spooky, isn't it? I mean, to live there, of all places?' Eva mused.

They lay on their respective beds back in Hotel U Andělů, Roz leafing through an English version of Vogue she had bought in a kiosk.

'So, what did you think of Angela?' Eva continued.

'Bit batty, I thought. Reminded me a bit of one of Howard's old aunts. Now, the other one, Havlová. She's one to watch.'

'Why?'

'Doesn't she make you think of one of those old women in spy novels, the sort you think are past it but they turn out to be in the secret police, or something?'

'She never spoke,' Eva murmured. 'What is she to Angela? And why has Angela lived here so long?'

'Who cares?'

'Do you think Angela can help us, though? Hope so, or we're going to run up a hell of a hotel bill at this rate.'

'She couldn't take her eyes off you, though, could she? What's she after?' Roz grinned suddenly. 'Reckon she's gay, then?'

'Don't be stupid! She was being kind, that's all. Isn't that what Brits abroad maybe do – stick together and help each other out?'

'Yeah, well, we'll see.'

'Thing is, though,' Eva went on, 'She doesn't know us - why would you offer to help someone you'd only just met?'

''Cos we've got honest faces? Look, what's the point of worrying about it now? We'll check it out tomorrow, right?'

'I don't want to lie to her, Roz.'

'Well, you can hardly tell her the truth, can you? We'll just do half-truths, if that makes you feel better.'

As the light outside faded they switched on the bedside lamp but kept the curtains open, watching the steady fall of snow settling on the rooftops. Eva tried to focus on the beauty of the scene but found herself wondering whether Roz, like her, was thinking back to last Thursday. The day after tomorrow, it would be just one week since when they had turned off the lights of their previous lives. Eva had done more than that. She had snuffed out the life-light of another human being. Douglas had begged her to do it. *But that doesn't necessarily make it right. Will I be asking Roz to do the same for me, whenever the time comes?*

Just before three o'clock the next day they were in Josefová, facing a heavy oak door, to the left of which was a panel of door buzzers with faded script on white cardboard labels, six in total. Eva ran her finger down the list. *Vondráčková. Oborná. Týnovský. Winstanley. Hanákovī.* Then a blank label. A dark blue plaque with the number twelve in white was fixed to the wall.

'Go on, then,' snapped Roz, stamping her feet and blowing on her hands.

It took a few minutes after Eva pressed the Winstanley button, but a crackle came from the intercom.

'It's Eva and Roz,' said Eva loudly, her mouth close to the grille.

'Push the door hard and come to the first floor,' came Angela's distant voice.

The entrance hall seemed barely warmer than outside. The floor was made up of uneven worn flagstones and before them rose a stone staircase. The walls were a faded shade of mustard. The high ceiling was covered in cracked plaster with ornate cornices running around the edges and a heavy iron-framed light hung down.

'No lift, then,' grunted Roz.

To the right and left of them were panelled double doors of dark oak. As they walked up the stairs their boots echoed up the stairwell, each step with a slight dip in the middle, perhaps worn smooth by many other feet over a couple of hundred years. On the first floor the double door on the right carried a small brass plaque with Angela's name. Almost as soon as Eva touched the buzzer one of the huge doors opened and Angela stood there with a broad smile on her face.

'I'm so glad you decided to come!' she ushered them in.

'Did you think we wouldn't?' asked Roz before Eva could stop her.

'Well, after such a brief meeting – I wasn't sure. Please, let me take your coats. Do come through.'

The warmth of the interior matched Angela's welcome. The parquet floor in this wide corridor was, in stark contrast to the one in Jiří's uncle's flat, highly polished and covered with a runner thick and soft under their feet, the colours picked out in terracotta and teal. The ceiling was as high as the one on the stairs but unadorned. As they entered the large square living room Eva gasped at its brightness as a massive window running almost the whole side of the front wall allowed the remainder of mid-afternoon winter sunlight to pour in. The walls were whitewashed and dotted with watercolours and a few small oil paintings, all pictures abstract in nature. The room was simply furnished with a few pieces in dark oak. Two doors, closed, led off the room.

'It's beautiful!' Eva breathed. 'Are all the flats this large?'

'This is what is known as a family house. I'm not sure of the exact age of the building – 1700s, I think - but it would have housed two or three generations of each family, usually with the oldest generation on the ground floor to help their mobility. Convenient, don't you think? Living together, but separately on each floor. They would have been wealthy merchants, perhaps, over the years until – well, the Communist era did introduce many changes, of course. May I offer you coffee or tea?'

'Whatever is easier for you,' Eva replied.

'Coffee, please. Double strength,' said Roz. 'So, what do you reckon, then?' she whispered in Eva's ear when Angela had gone into the kitchen.

'Wish we could have somewhere like this,' Eva replied.

When Angela returned carrying a laden tray she said, 'But, of course, you'll be wanting to know why I invited you. I have another flat like this one upstairs. The lady who lived there died last month and I've been wondering what to do with it. I knew her for years, you see, and the thought of having new people in – but then, life has to move on, doesn't it?'

'So, you own all this?' asked Roz incredulously.

'Yes.'

Roz nodded, looked over at Eva and winked.

'Could we take a look?' Eva asked.

'Of course. Do help yourself to biscuits. A poor selection, I'm afraid. I don't entertain much these days. So, Eva, we had so little time yesterday to talk about your Czech background.' Her dark glasses glinted from the last of the sun's rays to penetrate the room.

'Well, there's not much I can tell you. My grandmother said the family came from Prague. She didn't want to talk about the past and ever since she died, well, I want to know more.'

'Understandable. Difficult, of course, to trace one's family sometimes. It can take a great deal of time and effort. And you,' Angela turned her face to Roz, 'do you have any connection with Prague?'

Roz was silent for a moment, and then said simply, 'I'm with her.'

'We've been friends for years,' Eva interjected, 'we thought we'd make a sort of fresh start here. We'll be looking for work here too.' She saw Angela's gaze rest on their hands. Perhaps the faint indentation of their now-discarded wedding rings was still visible, but Angela said nothing.

'Well, perhaps I can offer you some advice from time to time, although I have very limited knowledge of the job market here. There may be some contacts at the University where I still teach occasionally.'

'What do you teach?' Eva asked.

'History of Art,' Angela waved at the pictures on the wall, 'although my own tastes are eclectic, as you can see. I also paint a little myself.'

'Is this your own work?' Roz asked, looking around the walls.

'Yes. I sell some pieces from time to time, a few exhibitions, that sort of thing. Do you know anything about art, then, Roz?'

'Went to Art College, years ago.'

'How wonderful! We must talk about it sometime. Do you still work in that area?'

Roz looked away. 'No.'

'And you, Eva, what kind of work do you do, if I may ask?'

'I used to be a nurse.'

'A very worthwhile profession, much undervalued, I think. Well, I mustn't keep you too long. I expect you'll be wanting to see the flat now?'

Angela rose and from a drawer in the sideboard extracted a bunch of keys. Eva and Roz followed her to the floor above. The door label here was blank. Inside the flat the bare parquet floor echoed beneath their feet. The layout of the flat was identical to Angela's. There was a vaguely musty smell in the air mixed with the heavy scent of floor-wax. The walls in the living room were bare and only a couple of worn armchairs stood around a small carpet square.

'You'll need to buy some furniture, of course. I can recommend some places to look, if you like. Here are the bedrooms. The second one is quite small, I'm afraid, and again you'll need to buy furniture. Mrs. Nováková's family took everything after she died.'

'Just as well, I guess,' joked Roz, 'wouldn't wanna sleep in a bed someone may have died in.'

Eva nudged Roz furiously. Angela's face betrayed no emotion. 'Quite. Please feel free to look around.'

Eva went into the kitchen which was simply furnished but spotless. Through the window she could see down into a small courtyard at the back of the building. She and Roz stood there for a moment, looking at each other. Roz pursed her lips but finally nodded.

'We'd love to take it,' Eva said to Angela when they re-entered the living room. 'How much would it be?'

'Oh, I do so hate talking about money! Shall we say, fifteen thousand crowns a month? You'll need to pay for electricity, gas and water on top of that as all the flats have separate meters.'

'Thank you,' Eva looked back to Roz. 'I'm sure that will be fine.'

'Do you need any, er, paperwork?' Roz watched Angela closely.

Angela looked down for a moment and then smiled. 'I don't feel there's any need for that.'

'But you don't know us!' The words burst out of Eva and Roz glared at her.

'I feel that I can trust you. One uses one's instinct in these matters, does one not?' said Angela softly. 'You can move in any day you choose. I'll only ask that you pay the first month's rent in advance, if you don't mind.'

'What about the neighbours?' Roz asked

Angela's mouth twitched slightly. 'Oh, you won't need to worry about loud music or parties, my dear. They're all as old as me and twice as deaf.'

24

'You know what, Baba once told me that you're only as lucky as the number of people you meet who are prepared to help you.' Eva cuddled her pillow. 'If I had a superstitious bone in my body, I could swear that Baba's giving us a helping hand right now. Does that sound crazy?'

Roz stared at her friend. 'You're reading far too much into this, chick. I'm not sure about this at all. But what the hell, we need somewhere to live right now.'

'And with no strings attached. Isn't that brilliant?'

*She sounds likes she's eighteen again. She's forgotten the shit we're both in and that any day…..*Roz smiled briefly. 'Yeah, chick, sure, it's great news.'

They had agreed with Angela that they would move in on Saturday and confirmed their departure date with Pani Novotná at the hotel, who asked them if they had enjoyed their week in Prague and whether they would be returning one day. Roz asked Eva to translate that she had found it an eye-opening experience and Pani Novotná had beamed at both of them, the irony passing over her head completely, and wished them a safe journey.

'What if we bump into her one day in town?' Eva fretted.

'Doubt if she'd remember us. She must see hundreds of people each year. Anyway, so what? Don't be so jumpy.'

They had two days to buy furniture for the flat, or at least beds to avoid sleeping on the floor. Angela had scribbled down the names of a couple of shops – 'give them my name and they'll offer you a fair price' – but Roz had insisted on visiting some of the upmarket modern showrooms in the city centre. As they wandered around, with Roz sniffing at any attempt by the salespeople to be drawn into conversation, Eva complained about the prices.

'Maybe there's an IKEA somewhere,' she urged.

Roz glowered at her. 'Do you think I'm going to live with that kind of tat again? Jesus, Eva, listen to yourself. Suburbia really has scrambled your brain.'

'Oh don't be such a snob! We can't afford this, that's all I'm saying.'

'We? *We?* I'm the one who's paying, remember?'

'Well, you won't be paying for long, at this rate. I mean, that sofa comes to the equivalent of about a thousand quid for a start. Look, we can trade up later, once we have a steady income coming in.'

'Doing what, exactly?'

Everything comes down to money, in the end. It may not make you happy but it bloody well helps, thought Roz as she extracted a compromise out of the situation. *I'll get some more money somehow.*

Two suitcases for Eva and two for Roz, plus her holdall. This was the sum of all of their possessions that Saturday morning. They splashed out on a taxi to Josefová 12 and sat in the creaky armchairs of their new flat waiting for the succession of deliveries which would bring beds, wardrobes, sofa, a coffee table and a couple of new chairs for the fitted kitchen table. Those were all the items they had agreed on, for now. Angela had handed over their keys in exchange for an envelope containing their first month's rent.

'Come downstairs for tea later, if you like,' she had offered, smiling at Eva.

Their voices echoed in the empty flat. Sitting by the window, Eva knew they had made the right choice. Even in its current stark condition this place felt like the warm cocoon of security that she craved and its simplicity added to that sensation. Roz was talking about all the extra things she wanted – a flat-screen TV, top-of-the-range music system, satellite channels, new mobile phones – but Eva was only listening with half an ear. These objects were what Roz needed to anchor herself and Eva couldn't deny that she would enjoy them too, but she didn't feel as if she needed them as badly as Roz did. Books, yes, and music too. Most of all, just a space to be, to please herself only. *When was the last time I experienced that luxury?* By mid-morning Eva was getting fed up of Roz's endless pacing around the room and sent her out to buy bedding and a few basic items for the kitchen.

'What kind of stuff do you want?' Roz asked.

'I'll trust your superior taste, shall I? Like you said, you're the one paying.'

Roz stuck out her tongue and Eva was relieved to be left in peace for a couple of hours. As she waited in between deliveries she stood at the living room window which overlooked the square. *There must be dozens of squares around town like this and now this one will be my new home, for however long.* She went to her bedroom and opened her suitcase, lifting out Baba's oak box and placing it on the windowsill. *Welcome home, Baba.* Eva shivered, wiping away a stray tear.

By late afternoon everything had arrived and the smell of new furniture was, she had to admit, wonderful. She stroked the smooth teak of the coffee table and the leather fabric of the deep sofa. Alex had been so frugal, she couldn't remember the last time they had bought new furniture. The sense of a hopeful, fresh beginning had kicked in finally. Time to celebrate properly, Roz had urged. The feel of the house keys between Eva's fingers in her coat pocket as they walked through Josefová was reassuring. She would have somewhere to return that night that she could proudly call home. Even Roz had looked around approvingly, proclaiming it to be a good start.

They found an Indian restaurant called Bombay Brasserie on Pařížska, a smart street radiating off Staroměstské Náměstí. 'To a week of luck,' Roz raised her glass, 'and many more to come.' Her voice grew louder over the next hour or so, as she described with glee the fallout she believed would surely come now for Howard after the DVD and letter she had sent to the police.

'I wouldn't be so sure about that,' Eva said. 'The Tory party machine may well continue to protect him yet. Remember, he's got connections that help to fill the party coffers.'

Roz looked crestfallen. 'So, you don't think - .'

'All I'm saying is, it may take a lot more than that. Look, I'm sure that one day he'll get his comeuppance.'

A couple of men had taken a table near them and Eva noticed how one of them kept glancing over. He was speaking in a low voice to his companion. German? Swedish? She couldn't make it out. The men ordered their meal in English.

'Did you ever love Howard for himself?' Eva asked Roz suddenly.

'Thassa funny question,' Roz slurred, looking taken aback. 'Dunno.'

'You don't know? Can't you remember? I mean, in comparison with the others before?'

'Don't think I ever loved any of them - I mean, I fancied them and all that, but, well – how would I know?'

'That you loved them?' Eva found herself scrabbling around for an answer. 'I suppose – well, if you couldn't imagine being without them, couldn't bear the thought of…'

'Nope. Nothing like that.'

'You poor cow,' Eva said softly. She thought enviously of Douglas, yearning to re-join Catherine.

Roz shrugged. 'Nothing but trouble there, chick. Look what that bastard Alex did to you.' But it wasn't Alex that Eva had been thinking about.

'Hello, ladies.'

Eva was jolted out of her daydream. The two men who had been dining nearby were now hovering over her. The taller of them who spoke was greying with thick glasses which distorted his pale blue eyes. He looked between Eva and Roz as if trying to decide something. Instinctively, Eva shuddered. His companion was shorter and dark-haired, with a belly that strained his shirt buttons.

'May we buy you a drink?' The tall man rasped.

'No thanks,' Eva replied quickly.

Roz shot her a look. 'Sure,' she smiled up at him. 'Cheers.'

He pulled up two chairs from a nearby table and gestured to the waiter. 'I am Lars and this is my friend Olaf. We are on a business trip from Sweden. You are English, yes?'

'Yeah, I'm Roz.'

'And your friend?'

Eva remained silent.

'That's Eva - .'

'Who's leaving, by the way.' Eva scraped her chair back and stood up. 'Roz, don't you think it's time to go?'

'Nope. It's only half-past nine.'

'Roz, I really do think - .'

'I think your friend would like to stay,' said Lars quietly. He and Roz were looking each other over. Roz, Eva thought, was probably wondering how much he was worth. His suit was well-cut, at least.

'Can't we change your mind?' Olaf was leering at Eva.

Eva looked between the three of them and then leant down to whisper in Roz's ear, 'this is really not a good idea.'

'Lay off, will ya?'

Eva straightened up. 'You're going do it again, aren't you?'

'What?'

'You know perfectly well. I thought we'd agreed - .'

'Whassa your problem, Eva?'

'Roz, you've had too much to drink and I can't keep worrying about you, wondering where you are!'

'Look, you're not my bloody mother, right? Now, sit down and have a drink, for fuck's sake, and stop making a prat of yourself.'

'Hey, Eva, don't be scared of us,' smiled Lars. 'You're new to Prague?'

'Have you got your keys?' Eva hissed to Roz, ignoring him.

'Yep. Don't wait up for me, mum.' Roz giggled and lit a cigarette with an unsteady hand. Lars leant over to help her.

'Don't worry, Eva, we'll look after her,' said Olaf. Roz was twirling a strand of her wiry red hair around her fingers, gazing directly at Lars who was ordering brandies. Eva hesitated. Her instinct was to stay and make sure Roz was OK.

'Roz - ,' she started.

'Don't spoil it, Eva. If you're going, then just go, right?' Roz's eyes were cold and distant.

Is this how it's going to be? Well, if this is the life she wants to lead then I want no part of it. I don't want to pretend we're nineteen again, drinking and shagging ourselves into a stupor. What's the point? Who are we trying to fool? I'm alone now, really alone.

In order to get back to Josefová Eva had to head west and found herself taking a short cut through Hanákova. A few minutes later she was standing outside The Red Door.

All the tables were taken - no surprise, given that it was Saturday night. There was the option of sharing a table with a young couple busy with their tongues down each other's throats, but that prospect didn't exactly tempt Eva. A couple of bar stools were still free and so she perched herself on one of them and ordered a glass of *svařák*, mulled red wine. The mirror behind the bar afforded her the unwelcome view of the petting couple and she shifted her body to avoid it. The saxophonist was good tonight. *Just one drink and that will be enough. Just one and I'll go home.*

'Well, hello again.'

Eva turned and saw the same Czech guy who had come on to her when she and Roz had come here the previous Saturday.

'On your own tonight? Your friend, she's not here?'

'I'll send her your love,' Eva replied curtly.

He looked puzzled. 'Excuse me?'

'Look, I'm – I'm waiting for someone,' she lied.

'Ah, but they are not here yet, are they?' he mocked, 'so, we can –.'

'Well, they're here now.'

Eva turned and looked into Will's smiling face. 'Oh! Hello.' Her throat tightened.

'Hi, Eva. Sorry I'm late. Excuse us,' he nodded to the man who backed away, murmuring an apology.

'Thank you for that,' Eva said to Will, unable to meet his eyes.

'No problem. So you found this place OK, then?'

'Yes. We've been a couple of times. Me and my friend Roz, I mean.'

'Oh? Like it that much?'

'Yes, I mean, the music is great,' she stuttered.

'Were you really waiting for someone?'

'Um, no.'

'So, is it OK if I join you for a little while, then?'

'Yes. Please.' *God, did I say that too quickly?* She caught herself checking her reflection in the mirror whilst Will ordered a beer. He could have come in with some gorgeous nineteen-year old blonde on his arm, but he hadn't. He was asking to join her instead. At least Roz wasn't here to spoil things.

'There are more jazz clubs in Prague, of course,' Will was saying now, 'but this one is better, more authentic, I think.'

She kept nodding, drinking him in. *Just let him talk. Try and look like you see these places every day. Try and remember the kind of music you used to like and have something neutral to talk about. Have a chance to just look at him…..*

'Have you eaten yet?' Will asked.

'Yes. Roz and I went to an Indian restaurant in Pařížská.'

'Let me guess - Bombay Brasserie, right? Yeah, I know it. Great lamb curry. Where's Roz now?'

Eva suddenly felt a pang of conscience. 'She decided to stay. She found some new company to amuse her.'

'Oh, OK. And what about you? You're happy to leave her there?'

Eva shook her head. 'No, but she's stubborn so what can I do?'

'Well, at least you've made a friend out here.'

'No, you see, we came out here together. We've found a place to live now, not far from here.'

'Does that mean you're gonna stay a while?'

Eva fiddled with her glass. 'We're starting over, you might say. It's – it's complicated.' She caught Will glancing briefly at her left hand and she wondered whether he could see the indentation on her ring finger. Her hand suddenly felt naked, as did the rest of her.

'Complicated,' he repeated. 'Well, I know how that feels. Were you married, back home? I was married too, once, long time ago.'

'Not now. You?'

'No, not now.'

If he keeps looking at me like that, it's all going to tumble out of me and then I'll ruin everything. Eva chewed her lip.

'Hey, Will, how's it going?' A thickset bearded man appeared at Will's shoulder and they shook hands.

'Hey, man, great to see you!' said Will. 'Eva, this is Nick. We used to work at the same law firm till he got headhunted by the competition. Nick, this is Eva. She's just moved here.'

'Hi, Eva, nice to meet you.' Nick's handshake was warm and vigorous. He turned back to Will. 'You gonna play tomorrow?'

'Sure thing. Hey Eva, we play ice hockey on Sundays, would you like to come and watch?'

'Yes, why not?' *Why not indeed. Roz can occupy herself now.*

'You can bring your friend Roz, if you like?'

Eva felt a sudden stab of jealousy. 'No. It's not her kind of thing.' *Nor mine, if I'm being honest.* She didn't want them to meet. Roz could make anyone fall for her if she wanted to, and play with them like a cat with its prey. Eva had seen her do it, years ago, and Roz hadn't lost her touch if this week was anything to go by.

Will scribbled down an address on the back of his beer mat. 'This is the winter stadium, it's in Prague 5. See you there at ten?'

'Oh, are you going now?' She tried not to sound disappointed.

'I need all the sleep I can get to keep up with the other guys. Getting old,' he laughed, his eyes crinkling.

'But you're younger than me,' she said suddenly and instantly regretted her outburst.

'Am I? How d'you know? Anyway, is that a problem?' he looked at her quizzically.

She shook her head but kept her mouth shut.

'You going home my way?' asked Nick, finishing his beer.

'Yeah,' replied Will, then nodded to Eva, 'you gonna be OK here?'

'Oh, I'll be going now too,' she said briskly. 'I was only planning to stay for one drink anyway.' The three of them pushed their way back through the dense clutch of bodies and the outside temperature was a shock to Eva after the huddled warmth of the club's interior. Nick and Will turned to go right, and then Will stopped.

'You sure you'll be OK walking home on your own?'

If Douglas could only see me now – would he give this situation his blessing? 'I'll be fine, thanks anyway. Good night.' Eva turned to the left and hurried up the road. *Don't look back. This isn't what you came here for.*

25

It was after two a.m. when Eva heard the key turn in the apartment door. She heard Roz cursing as she stumbled through the darkness, sounding as if she had tripped over something. *Drunk again! Sod it, she can sleep it off by herself.* Eva tried to slip back into her dream, a confusing blur between Will and Douglas, a feeling of being held, the warmth of two bodies clinging together. But sleep wouldn't come and the density of the enveloping darkness in her bedroom was pierced by a sliver of light coming through the partially-opened door from the living room. Then she heard the sound of retching coming from the bathroom and got out of bed reluctantly.

'Roz?' Eva called. 'If you've made a mess in there you'd better clean it up yourself. Roz?'

Then there came a keening from the bathroom that raised the hair on the back of her neck. 'Roz? What's up – oh, Jesus!'

Eva stood in the bathroom doorway. The bruises on Roz's face, neck, and arms were livid. There was a bleeding cut just above her left eyebrow and her dress was torn and soiled. She was whimpering, kneeling on the floor in front of the toilet, her face turned towards Eva with a look of utter wretchedness.

'Bloody hell, Roz, what happened? Have you been mugged, or something?'

Roz stood up shakily and Eva moved forward to catch her swaying body. Roz started to sob loudly now, the whole of her body shuddering in Eva's arms.

'Roz, talk to me – what's happened?'

Between sobs Roz spat out the words. 'They – they – wanted to play games.'

'Who did? What are you talking about?'

'They held me down and tried to – oh God!'

'Who? Who, for God's sake?'

'Those guys –.'

'The guys? In the restaurant? You're telling me that that those guys we met – oh Roz, Roz! Why did you go with them? After everything I've said - .'

'Don't you fucking lecture me!' Roz suddenly screamed at Eva. 'Don't you dare!'

'I'm sorry, I'm sorry,' Eva said, 'but you shouldn't have gone on your own.'

'You wouldn't come, remember? It's as much your bloody fault as mine!'

'Did they –?'

Roz winced and touched her crotch. 'They tried.'

'Oh, sweet Jesus, no!' Eva started to cry as Roz clung to her. Eva led her into the sitting room and cradled her head as she sobbed. Roz winced again as she sat down and rolled over on to her side.

'We have to go to the police,' Eva said.

'No!'

'Roz, you've been assaulted, for God's sake! They can't get away with this!'

'We can't go! There'll be questions and – and – you know how these cases can go. I couldn't bear to go through all of that. What good would it do?'

'There has to be something we can do. They might do it to someone else – how can we let them get away with it?'

'Drop it, Eva. I just want to forget about it. Get me my sleeping pills, will you?'

'And what about tomorrow? Will you be able to forget about it then?'

'I said, drop it, all right?' She burst into tears again, shuddering violently.

Eva hugged her close. 'How did you manage to get away?'

'I kneed one of them in the balls and threw vodka in the other's eyes. There was a taxi driver, outside their hotel. He wanted to call the police when he saw the state of me. I said no.'

'Hotel? So, didn't the staff see you?'

'It was a crappy place. Empty. And I had thought it would be smarter — you know, they looked like they had money. They had wanted you to come along too, and then they wanted to have me at the same time - .' She shuddered. 'At first I thought, yeah, why not, it'll be fun like a real fantasy, having two at once, but then — oh, Jesus! Even a real hooker wouldn't have wanted to - .' She clammed up, a vein throbbing in her bruised temple.

'It's not your fault, Roz. No one deserves this. Come on. I'll help you clean up and I'll get some stuff from a pharmacy tomorrow.'

Eva managed to help Roz to bed and lay beside her for the rest of the night. Towards dawn Roz finally fell asleep whilst Eva was still wakeful, angry at herself, Howard, and for all the reasons that had brought them to this place. *Our first week of freedom. Completely screwed up now.*

'You can't leave me!' Roz shrieked.

'But I promised him. Look, you'll be all right, it's just for a few hours and then I'll be right back, I promise. Just get some rest.'

'And what am I supposed to do? Stare at the four walls and pretend nothing happened? You should be looking after me — isn't that what you've been saying all along, that we should stick together?'

'Don't throw that back in my face, you were the one who chose to go off with strangers.'

'So, you're saying now that this is all my fault? That I asked for it?'

'Roz, don't go twisting my words. You know what I meant — anyway, you should get more sleep. Go and take another pill.'

'You're a heartless bitch, do you that? One sniff of another prick - .'

'Don't you dare start, Roz!'

'Thought you'd said you weren't looking.'

'I'm not starting anything. He might just be a good friend that we both need, that's all.' *Am I being heartless? I'm not trying to get back at her. Frankly, I shouldn't have mentioned Will. I should have just said I was going shopping for us both. But it's out there now, hanging between us and she'll give me no mercy. Who's the hypocrite now?*

'Are you really going to come back?' Roz's eyes were pleading now. 'Promise you won't go and spend the night with him?'

'I promise,' Eva replied, but caught herself thinking about what she should wear. On the way downstairs Eva passed Angela's door and prayed that she hadn't heard the commotion last night or that she would call in and see Roz's face. It might be none of her business - this was just a commercial relationship, after all - but Eva wanted to avoid the embarrassment. Perhaps Angela would have been too delicate to ask questions but it might have occurred to her to wonder what kind of people she had trusted to share her house with. Would she have insisted they go to the police or questioned their motives for not doing so?

The combination of a fragmented night's sleep and the argument with Roz meant Eva was running late and so she took a taxi to the winter stadium. When she arrived she was nearly an hour later than planned. She took a seat at the back and watched the game without really seeing it, just a blur of figures gliding around and the intermittent cries of encouragement, the thwacking of the ball and the swish of the skates on ice. Will didn't appear to have noticed her arrival, so intent did he appear on the game he was playing. *There was no point in coming. I'll go in a minute.* Then he raised his head and gave her a brief wave and smile before ploughing on. She was ashamed at the way her heart leapt at that moment.

'So you made it, finally,' he said half an hour later as the game finished and the group drifted away, calling their goodbyes to each other.

'Sorry I was late. But Roz isn't well.'

'Oh?'

'She, um, had a heavy night.'

'Oh, OK. Hope she had a good time to make it worthwhile,' he grinned and then looked concerned. 'Everything all right?'

'Not really.' Eva bit her lip hard. 'But we'll sort it out.'

'Anything I can do?'

Eva shook her head. It would have been as foolish to assume that he would understand as much as Angela might have.

'So, are you free for lunch?' Will asked.

She hesitated and looked at her watch. She had promised Roz to return soon. Roz would never let her hear the end of it otherwise. *But what would Roz do in my place?*

'Sure, I'd like that,' Eva replied.

Will drove them to Malá Strana which turned out to be the district just beyond the tower-gate end of Charles Bridge that Eva had been to on Monday. It had a quaint village atmosphere not unlike some of the upmarket parts of London but, she thought, with more interesting architecture.

'This is expat territory,' said Will waving his arm around the crowds as they approached a café situated in the square. 'A lot of the foreign embassies are located around here, too. The British one is just a couple of streets away on Thunovská. Useful to know if you ever need their help,' he added smiling.

'Hopefully not,' she muttered under her breath. 'So, how come you don't live around here?'

He laughed. 'I don't get paid *that* much.'

She looked at her watch.

'Do you need to get back to your friend?' Will asked.

She hesitated. 'I'll be OK for a while.'

'Don't feel you have to stay with me.'

She closed her eyes briefly and then when she opened them again saw he was looking straight at her.

'I'd like to stay,' she smiled.

After lunch they walked around the side streets whilst Will pointed out some of the buildings with blue plaques commemorating a previous occupant of note. He had something interesting to tell about all of them. 'You certainly know your Czech history,' she remarked.

'Well, I've had a lot of time to spend walking around the city on my own, when I'm not working.'

'On your own? I find that hard to believe,' she said, and then cursed silently for the clumsiness of the remark.

'Why do you say that?' his blue-grey eyes danced with amusement and she felt even more foolish.

'So, you said you had some family connection to this place.'

He looked at her for a moment and then said, 'Yeah. My family was from Prague. My parents and grandparents got away in 1968, like I told you, but I still have cousins here.'

'So, why have you come back?'

'I'm not really coming back. I mean, I was born in Toronto a couple of years after my folks arrived there. But when I joined this law firm they were spreading out into Europe and when they decided to open an office here I thought, why not? So here I am.'

'How long do you think you'll stay? I mean, it must feel very different from home.'

'Yes and no. It was tough at first, but you adapt. You'll find out – if you stay, that is. And will you, d'you think?'

Eva toyed with her cutlery. 'It's complicated.'

'See how it goes. So, why did you pick this place anyway, if that's not being too personal?'

'I have my own connections through my family. They came from Prague too. My grandmother and mother escaped in 1968. I was born on the run to England, somewhere in Austria, I was told. My mother died a few days after I was born, so it was just me and Baba in England.' Eva's fingernail drew patterns on the tablecloth and tears pricked the back of her eyes.

'I'm so sorry. Sounds like quite a story. So, what does your grandmother think of you coming here?'

She opened her mouth to reply but stopped in time. *One word would lead to another. This isn't the time to spill it all out.* 'I really should be getting back,' she said. 'Roz will be mad at me.'

'Maybe she should think herself lucky to have a friend who cares. Do you do everything together, then?'

She looked up at him but there was no sign of mockery in his eyes. 'She's my best friend.'

'Well, if she can bear to let you go, how about going back to The Red Door next Friday night? That's if you're not sick of the place by now.' He stretched out his hand to touch her arm briefly.

She had a date. She felt like eighteen again, but with a darker soul.

26

Roz heard the key turn in the front door as Eva returned. Through her half-open bedroom door she could see Eva tiptoeing across the living room. Roz turned over and moaned at her own aches and pains. She waited for Eva for enter her room, maybe to apologize for her delay, to offer her some comfort. Roz waited a few minutes, then realized it wasn't going to happen. Slowly and painfully, she rose from her bed and moved to the doorway. Eva had her back turned and was gazing out of the huge living room window. Behind her, Roz watched the skyline as it evolved from shades of pink and peach through to indigo and then inky blackness. *What's Eva thinking about? Is there something she's starting with this Will guy? It's not fair, we're in this together, she wouldn't be here if I hadn't pushed her to leave, she owes me big time. I'm not gonna play gooseberry to her relationship.*

'Had a nice time?' Roz snapped. Eva turned suddenly to face her. *Ha, there's a guilty look.*

'Oh, you're awake. How are you feeling?' Eva asked.

'Just dandy. What the hell do you care?'

'I only asked.'

'At least you came back, I suppose.'

'I said I would, didn't I?'

'Where did you go?'

'If you must know, we had lunch in Malá Strana. Near where the British Embassy is.'

'Lovely! Must remember to ask the Ambassador to send Howard my love.'

'Stop it, Roz.'

Roz rubbed her eyes, wincing. 'So, got another date?'

'Yes, actually.'

'When?'

'Next Friday.'

'Oh.' Roz scratched her nose. 'Can I come?'

'You are joking, aren't you?'

'So what am I supposed to do, then?'

'I'll give you a Czech dictionary to pass the time usefully.'

'Bitch.' Roz went into the kitchen and started clattering around with cups and then came back carrying two cups of coffee. 'Listen, chick, you're not gonna do something stupid, are you?'

'Like what?'

'Like move in with this guy.'

'Don't be daft, he's just a friend, that's all. Anyway, it's none of your bloody business.'

'So you're just gonna leave me here alone - .'

Eva sighed. 'Roz, at this rate you're more likely to abandon me.'

'That's not fair!'

'Look, there's no point in arguing about something that will never happen. We have to figure out how we're going to get by without anyone else getting involved. There's enough for us to cope with, as it is.'

'So, why are you going to see this guy again?'

'Just drop it, OK?'

Eva stood up and took her coffee cup over to the window and Roz shuffled over to join her. In the light of the street lamps in the square outside they could see people strolling around, some stopping to peer at the menus fixed to the outside of the two restaurants on the opposite side. Roz sniffed. *That's where we should be, be part of a group of Saturday night friends laughing and enjoying each other's company. No strings.* 'C'mon, let's go out, I could always put on extra make-up, I suppose,' she mumbled.

'Don't be ridiculous. You'd stand out a mile. I'll go and get some pizzas from somewhere.'

The pizzas turned out to be greasy with a miserly layer of topping. They managed what they could and then Eva told Roz she was going to have an early night. Roz sat beside a full ashtray, not listening, just flicking leisurely through her copy of Vogue.

'Roz?' Eva started.

'What is it now?'

'Maybe you should see a doctor.'

'I'll live.'

'Look, I'll stay in tomorrow – look after you.'

'How thoughtful of you, Eva.'

Eva sighed in exasperation. 'I still care about what happens to you, you know.'

Roz put down her magazine, her eyes brilliant with unshed tears. 'Just go and live your life, chick, that's what you came out here for, isn't it?'

'Roz - .'

'Just forget it – OK?' Roz fled to her bedroom, slamming the door behind her.

That bloody pizza, Eva thought, as she nursed her aching gut the next morning in-between bouts of vomiting. Roz seemed fine but then she had the constitution of an ox when it came to food and drink. She got up briefly to join Eva for coffee and then went back to her bedroom, closing the door. Eva assumed Roz was still mad at her from yesterday. After her third trip to the toilet before nine Eva noticed a piece of paper had been slipped under the main door. '*Come for tea, if you're free, at 3. Angela.*'

Eva sat at the table by the kitchen window, nursing a glass of water. The buildings opposite had occasional balconies to break up the monotony of the exterior. The state of the external plasterwork at the rear was in direct contrast to the walls of their house which fronted the square. These rear walls were dirty grey and badly cracked, perhaps unpainted for decades. *Had they run out of money or did it simply not matter if the only viewers were the residents themselves?* One window on the ground floor on the opposite side suddenly opened and an elderly woman fed a pink bed-sheet through the window. She gripped the sheet firmly with both hands and started to flap it vigorously. After a minute or so she turned it around and proceeded to repeat the process. She disappeared briefly with the sheet, only to return with a thin-looking duvet. The same exercise was replicated, causing the flesh on her withered arms to quiver with the effort. Finally she brought out the pillows which she slapped rhythmically, turning them this way and that. Eva felt she was witnessing a daily ritual. Baba would have approved of airing the bedding like this. She used to say that English housewives were sloppy and that they spent more time gossiping on street corners than cleaning their houses. The brass doorstep of their front door had always gleamed bright and shiny whatever the weather. Roz, on her first visit to the house during their schooldays, had brought in mud on her shoes and Baba had shooed her outside, telling her to leave the offending articles on the doormat. Roz had never returned after that.

Eva went back to bed briefly, wishing she had a radio to listen to. She could buy some books and that would be a way of starting to recall and improve her Czech although at that moment it all felt like a monumental effort. By eleven, she felt the need for fresh air to clear her head and now it seemed her stomach was starting to settle again. She found a small grocer's that was open in a nearby street and made a mental note of its opening times – six-thirty a.m. to eleven-thirty a.m. on Sundays and till five-thirty p.m. on other days. As she wandered down the aisles, missing desperately the supermarkets of home and resenting the presence of two young female assistants who seemed bent on following her every movement, she eventually chose some light rye bread, butter, smoked cheese, tomatoes and orange juice. On returning to the flat she laid them out on the kitchen table but found she could not face the prospect of eating any of it. Roz's door was still closed.

The hours dragged on. At half-past two Eva started to smarten herself up, left Roz a note, and arrived at Angela's door on the dot of three.

When Angela opened the door Eva saw she was dressed in black wool trousers and sweater, with a brightening multi-coloured silk scarf draped around her neck and shoulders. The dark glasses were still in place. Eva sensed a brief hesitancy but Angela then smiled shyly.

'I'm so glad you could make it, do come in,' Angela said at last. 'Will Roz not be joining us?'

'She's feeling a bit poorly,' Eva replied.

'You look a little tired yourself, Eva, if you don't mind my saying so. The onset of winter always brings some kind of virus and

I'm afraid this cold weather has arrived rather too early, even for us. You look surprised, my dear. This isn't quite Siberia, you know. Now, how are you settling in?' Angela poured tea and handed Eva a plate of cream cakes. 'Try one of these. They're one of my few vices, I'm afraid. I buy them in Maruška's on Betlēmskā.'

'The flat is wonderful. Thank you so much. I don't know what we would have done if we hadn't met you.'

Angela smiled briefly. 'Ah well. That is how life turns out sometimes.' She stirred her tea and turned her face to the window. 'Is there anything else you need?'

'A job?' Eva laughed nervously. 'No, the flat is lovely and we'll get on with sorting out other things next week.'

'Would you go back to nursing? I'm afraid it's poorly-paid here and the facilities may not be up to the standard you are used to.'

'I don't know. My Czech is slowly coming back to me already, but it needs a lot of work. Frankly, I'd do anything just to start earning some money of my own again.'

She saw Angela look down at her bare ring finger. 'Thought I may as well take it off,' Eva mumbled, stroking the finger mindlessly.

'It's none of my business, I know,' said Angela, 'but I imagine it must be very difficult for you.'

'It's very complicated, but it's better this way.' *Keep it simple, she doesn't need to know the rest.*

'I wish you luck,' Angela murmured. 'I have never been married but I did lose someone very special.'

'Oh, I'm not a widow!' Eva exclaimed.

'Even so,' Angela said firmly, 'it is loss of a kind. Being on one's own again requires a certain adjustment, does it not? Particularly if one does not have the comfort and support of family.'

Eva thought of Baba and wondered how she would have reacted to her predicament. *I'm glad that she had not lived to see me like this.* The brief touch of Angela's hand on her arm woke her from her thoughts.

'So, Eva, how do you plan to start tracing your family? As I said the other day, it can be very difficult here.'

'I don't know where to start. All I know is that I was born on the way to England, somewhere in Austria, I think. My mother died a couple of days after I was born when infection set in and they couldn't afford a doctor. I don't know much about it at all. My father and grandfather died in the Prague uprising. So, it was just me and Baba left. She did the best she could when we got to England. She didn't like talking about the past, she was a very private person. She died eighteen years ago. I was just eighteen, on my way to study nursing. I thought there would be years to find out, that somehow I'd get her to open up, but life just got in the way. And now – well, there are so many questions. I don't even know where to start. But now I'm here, at least I may be able to find out some answers.'

'That depends on the questions you want to ask,' said Angela, her head bowed.

'Sorry?'

'Nothing. What was your family name?'

'My maiden name was Poláková. My mother's name was Tereza. My father – Václav, I think. Baba's married name was Ludmila Šimková. I don't know about her maiden name. Isn't that terrible? I don't even know that.'

Angela put down her tea cup and drew her scarf around her more tightly. She fiddled briefly with her dark glasses but then left them in place. After a moment she said, 'there will be public record offices you could consult, of course, but it may be very difficult even then. We'll see. Anyway, if you like, I may be able to find a small job for you teaching English, until you can find your own feet.'

'You're very kind, thank you.'

Angela waved a hand, almost dismissively. Eva thought her face appeared to be paler now. 'I'm sorry, Angela, I should probably go now, if you're tired.'

'No – please stay and have some more tea. Now, what do you think of these pictures?' She rose and pulled a couple of small canvases from behind one of the armchairs.

'They're lovely.' Warm shades of terracotta and burgundy shot through with duck-egg blue splashes. Eva wished she understood abstract art but maybe there was nothing to understand – you just felt something, or not, about it.

'Would you like me to frame them so that you can start to cover the bare walls in your flat?'

'Well, that would be very kind – but I should pay you for them.'

'Not at all,' Angela shushed her. 'Just an old artist's vanity, that's all.'

'So, you painted these yourself?'

'Yes. I dabble a little. I find it quite therapeutic. In fact, there will be a small exhibition of my work tomorrow night at a gallery – that sounds grander than it really is, but it helps to supplement my income if I can sell a few paintings from time to time. Would you like to come? Some of the usual crowd are terrible bores, I'm afraid, but there are others who may amuse you.'

'Well, I know nothing about art, but it sounds like fun. I'd love to come. Thank you.'

Angela smiled briefly and poured more tea into her cup, her heavily-veined hand shaking with the effort. 'It's one of the few social occasions I attend these days, and it would be good to have some younger company for a change. As you grow older, my dear, you find your friends start dying out and you have to work hard at replacing them. Though some, of course, are irreplaceable.'

'After so many years of living here you must know half of the city.'

'Indeed. Indeed. That was how it once seemed. Believe me, there were some I wished I had never known – but listen to me, rambling on!'

She must have seen it all too. Where had she been in 1968? Had she been standing in Václavské Náměstí along with the thousands of others or, as a foreigner, had it all seemed unimportant to her? 'We all have things we'd rather not remember,' murmured Eva and then felt the strong need to leave before she said too much.

27

Today is Tuesday 7 December and I'm starting a diary. Every day is bringing new experiences and feelings and I want some way to hang on to them. Maybe this will be the first of many pages, or maybe my illness will cut me off tomorrow. Strange, but I'm not scared anymore but I can't say why. And who will read all this when I'm gone? Who's going to care about anything I record? 'This was what Roz said and this was how Angela helped me and how dour ordinary people in the street appeared to be. How I met Will. Whatever happened to him?' Maybe that's how it is going to be. He may end up being nothing important in my life and perhaps that shouldn't matter for he is not the reason I am here or why I choose to stay.

I feel like shit again this morning. Food poisoning can linger for days. I wanted to stay in bed today but Roz was up early and being all light and breezy again. I can't understand how she can bounce back so quickly after what happened to her on Saturday night. I would have been devastated. She says she doesn't want to talk about it. That's the only way she may be able to deal with it. I just hope she's learned her lesson. Things could have turned out much worse. She told me to fuck off so I guess she must be feeling better.

Roz is still going on about getting a TV and I've caved in. She even offered to get on the case herself today and slapped on thick makeup before she went out half an hour ago. She also promised to look at new mobile phones. I don't want to think about how much cash must be left in that holdall of hers. I said nothing to her about it, it'll only lead to another row about money. We must sound like an old married couple sometimes. I think she was pissed off that I went to Angela's yesterday afternoon but I was only gone an hour, if that. At least I managed to get Angela off the subject of me and my past. God, I came that close to saying stuff I shouldn't. Instead, I managed to get her talking about Czech politics. She seemed very well informed and I didn't like to think how she knew so many of the sordid details. She told me not to blame the

Czechs for the dourness they often show at first meeting. She said I had to understand what they had been through. For many Czechs life has been full of unfulfilled promises, apparently. New wealth has come into the hands of a minority and many of those beneficiaries still have connections to the old Communist regime. Prices have risen all round but wages and pensions have, by and large, not kept up. Unemployment is a new and unwelcome phenomenon. She said to give them time, and some Czechs can become friends for life. I did say that English people were friendlier on first encounter but she dismissed this opinion. Superficial, she said; they smile and then ignore you when you really need them. There was fire in her belly when she spoke about these things but she has revealed nothing about her own life. But then, why should she? Maybe I'll get to find out more, over time. Maybe she needs to trust me too.

I don't want to think about Christmas. Who should I be buying presents for? It's not how I had imagined spending it this year. Will Alex visit Douglas's grave? I want there to be flowers, lots of them. I think he'd like Angela. Has Alex forgiven me? Did he cover up for me, somehow? I don't care if they come looking. Just give me some time here to find what I'm looking for and have a bit of fun on the way. If they take me away after that – well, I'll worry about that when the time comes.

'Ta-dah!' Roz was beaming when she came home late afternoon. 'All the stuff's coming tomorrow morning!'

'What stuff?' Eva asked suspiciously.

'You know – what we agreed – TV, DVD player, hi-fi, satellite dish - .'

'What? We didn't agree anything of the sort! And you can't have a dish stuck on this building – Angela will go nuts!'

'Tough! I've already ordered it, chick.'

'How the hell did you manage all this in Czech?'

Roz tapped the side of her nose. 'Dropped off to see Jiří at the bar – now, there's a guy in the know. Paid him something for his help, of course.'

'I can imagine how!'

'I'm talking cash, you stupid cow, not a blow-job in the loo. Actually, maybe that would have been enough.' Roz's tone was wistful. 'What have you been up to, then?'

'Nothing. Just doing a bit of writing.'

'What about?'

'Just keeping a diary.'

Roz stared. 'What's the point of that? Actually, you'd better watch that. I mean, watch what you write about and, if you can't, then for God's sake keep it safe.'

'I hardly think anyone we know will want to read it.'

'Am I in it?'

'Why should you be? Look, I'm going out with Angela tonight. Should I get you some dinner before I go?'

'What? You're going out with her? Gone off men that much, have you?'

'She's invited me to an exhibition at an art gallery, that's all. They're showing some of her paintings apparently.' Eva hesitated. 'Would you like to join us?'

'No thanks. Weird old bird. Still thinks she's got a thing about you – what d'you reckon?'

'I'm not even going to answer that.'

At around seven-thirty in the evening Eva rang Angela's door buzzer. Angela was dressed again in the dove-grey outfit of before but instead of her cloak she wore a thick black fur coat and hat. Eva felt scruffy by comparison.

'Is Roz feeling better?' Angela asked as they descended the stairs.

'Oh, she's back to normal, thank you.'

'I must say you still look peaky, my dear.'

'I'll be fine.' Eva's hands went instinctively to her stomach which was still growling occasionally for lack of food.

'Have you eaten?'

'A bit. I'm not that hungry.'

'Then take care with the wine tonight. I'm afraid that they do tend to refill one's glass without asking.'

'Roz would love that!' Eva laughed and Angela smiled and touched her hand briefly.

They walked for about fifteen minutes, the snow muffling the sounds of the city and the night air mercifully still without the biting wind of the previous week. As they passed various shops, now closed, Angela pointed out recommendations – here a good café, there a shoe shop with reasonable prices. The art gallery, when they reached it, was in a basement in a street close to the river. Stepping carefully down the snow-covered steps Eva was met by a haze of soft lights and the warmth of many overdressed bodies in a room smaller than she had expected. The whitewashed walls provided a stark background to the dozen or so richly-coloured paintings fixed on to their surfaces. An old man in a dark brown shiny suit which may have last fitted him a decade ago bowed deeply over Angela's hand. Eva heard the murmur of the word *'Hraběnka'* in his greeting and she glanced at Angela, puzzled, watching her accept his words with a gracious tilt of her head. Soon everyone was turning to look at them. Not them. Angela. All eyes were on her. People were pushing their way through the crowd to add their own greetings. Eva heard the same word *'Hraběnka'* repeated each time.

A young man took their coats and soon the glasses of wine started to come their way, a slightly dry red wine which Angela said was made in Moravia. She seemed to be scanning the room, an anxious expression on her face, and then there were the constant interruptions and the flow of compliments – how many were genuine, Eva couldn't guess – about her latest works.

'Ah, there you are!' Angela pounced on a blond man in his thirties who entered the room. They greeted each other warmly. 'Patrick! I'm so glad you could come!'

He kissed her hand in an elaborate display of courtesy. *'Hraběnka* – how could I keep away?'

'Oh, Patrick, do stop teasing! I'd like you to meet Eva McKinley who has just arrived in Prague. She and her friend are renting Pani Nováková's old flat. Eva, this is Patrick Jennings who is Second Secretary at the British Embassy here and the right man to know if you lose your passport and any other help you may need.'

'Oh Angela – don't you understand that my work is of great political importance?' He winked at Eva and she liked him instantly. 'Angela, how are you feeling? Are you still having trouble with your eye infection?'

'It's a bother but I hope things will get back to normal soon. These dark glasses are very irritating and I can't paint properly with them on. Now then, Patrick, your job tonight is to keep Eva amused and stop her drinking too much on an empty stomach whilst I circulate, as I must. Don't worry, Eva, you'll be in very safe hands,' Angela smiled at her and then turned back to Patrick. 'Where is David tonight?'

'He's stuck in bed with flu,' replied Patrick. 'Or at least, that's what he told me.' He winked again. 'So you see, Eva, you will be very safe with me, as Angela says.'

'You are a dreadful boy!' Angela called over her shoulder as she made her way to the other side of the room.

'So, Eva, what brings you to Prague?' Patrick enquired.

'Um, well, I thought I'd see what it would be like to live here, new start and all that.'

'Oh? New start? Do tell.'

'It's really not that interesting,' Eva replied quickly. 'So, what about you?'

'Oh, same as you, really. And the lure of cheap fags, perhaps!' He roared with laughter at his own double-entendre and some of the older people around them looked over disapprovingly. 'So, my secret is out. Still, Czechs seem to be quite tolerant about people like me. Am I shocking you?'

'No, I was just thinking you'd get along well with my friend Roz.'

'Is she very wicked too?'

'She'd win an Olympic gold medal for it, believe me.'

'Well you must both come over for dinner one evening. David is a marvellous cook.' Patrick's easy conversation wafted over Eva like a warm summer breeze and she didn't want the evening to end. Eventually, about ten o'clock, the crowded room started to thin out as people bade each other slightly drunken farewells and there was much bowing and kissing on both cheeks.

'*S dovolením, prosím Vás,*' grunted a familiar voice and Eva turned round to see Pani Havlová as she struggled to push past them to reach the young man holding out her coat.

'Ah, Pani Havlová, how delightful to see you! You are looking ravishing tonight as usual!' slurred Patrick in Czech.

'Pan Jennings, as charming as usual,' she sniffed. She stared at Eva.

'May I introduce Eva McKinley who has come to live in our beautiful city?'

'We've already met,' Eva murmured.

'*Ano, ano,*' Pani Havlová nodded. She continued to stare at Eva unblinkingly and Eva started to feel queasy again. Then, feeling a hand on her arm, Eva turned to face Angela, whose face was slightly flushed.

'We must be going, Eva,' she said sharply. 'Thank you so much, Patrick. I hope we'll see you soon.' Angela steered Eva to the door, then turned to face Pani Havlová. They exchanged hurried words in low voices. Patrick leant against a pillar, eyebrows slightly raised, observing them.

'Come, Eva.' Angela's hand was tugging at her, half-pulling her up the stairs as Eva called goodbye to Patrick.

'Angela, is everything all right?' Eva asked breathlessly, trying to keep up with her long strides.

'It's late. We should be heading home.'

They walked in silence for a while. The streets were quiet with the occasional swoosh of a taxi driving too fast on the icy roads. After about ten minutes Eva found she could not contain her curiosity any longer. 'Angela, I heard people calling you *Hraběnka*.'

Angela seemed to stiffen beside her but her pace then slowed down to match Eva's. 'Yes. It means countess.'

'Oh.'

Angela stopped and turned to face her. Eva could smell the wine on her breath but Angela's voice seemed steady. 'You could call it a small vanity of mine, I suppose.'

'I don't understand.'

'Eva, I am not a countess or anything quite as grand as that. But when I arrived in Prague after the war - well, many Czechs seemed to be fascinated by anyone with any apparently elevated status, having lost most of their own aristocracy during wars in the seventeenth century, you see, and so it was easy to be accepted if – you must think I'm a terrible fraud, don't you?'

'I'm not in a position to pass judgment.'

Angela sighed and said, 'let's walk on.' They were half-way back to Josefová when Angela said, 'My family was not grand, in the sense of possessing titles that pass for aristocracy but in previous generations we had played an important role in our county. The estates we had once owned had dwindled with the impact of mismanagement, debt and death duties by the time I was born in the mid-1920s but my father was a proud man, proud of his ancestry and determined that his children should succeed in society. My brother was older than I and would inherit most of the wealth that was left to us, as little as that was. I was expected to marry well, preferably combining money with a title in whoever I should pursue. But that was not what I wanted and my father and I had many bitter arguments over our differences. I thought it was such a waste of life, you see, to be shackled to a husband just for material comforts and social position.' She threw Eva a sideways glance.

'And what about your mother?'

'She was on my side, for what that was worth – sadly, not very much. My father never heeded her opinions. Her views were too bohemian for his liking. I wanted an education and a profession, to establish a role for myself independent of anyone I would marry. I had a little talent as an artist – though not so much, as you will have seen for yourself tonight – and I had dreams. Such dreams.'

'What happened?'

'What happened was that I met Štefan.' Angela paused to wrap her coat collar around her neck more tightly. 'During the war there were pilots from Czechoslovakia who came to England to join the Allies. In our community we saw it as our role to welcome these young men and to teach them English to help in their work. We wanted to make some kind of contribution, you see. The men in our villages had gone to fight. My brother managed to return without any physical injuries but his mind was never the same again. He would wake in the night screaming. My mother nursed him as well as she could but she took his transformation badly and she died from nervous exhaustion a year later. Our house was, therefore, not a happy place. So, helping the Czech pilots came as some form of light relief for me. Štefan let me sketch him in his uniform. He was not particularly handsome but he carried himself proudly. He told me about his family in Prague. He had left a young wife behind at home.' She paused. 'But that didn't prevent us from falling in love. Does that sound selfish to you?'

'No, not at all.'

'I could blame my youth and inexperience,' Angela went on, 'but inside I knew the game I was playing. When my father found out there was the most almighty row. And then I discovered that I was carrying Štefan's child.'

Eva's hand flew to Angela's arm but she shrugged it off. 'I'm not looking for sympathy.'

'So, then...?'

'We could not marry. Štefan said his wife was a strict Catholic and would never grant him a divorce. My father ordered me to leave. The hypocrite! I knew how he had made my mother so unhappy with his own string of dalliances. With the help of my mother's money which she had left to me, Štefan and I moved to London. The war was over by then. But life was hard. We tried to pass ourselves off as a married couple but with no documents - ,' she shook her head.

'Look, Angela, you don't have to tell me any more if this is difficult.'

Angela went on as if she hadn't heard, her voice rising. 'Our daughter was born early. Too early. There weren't the medical facilities we have today, you see, and she didn't have the strength to pull through.' Eva wanted to hug her but Angela seemed more distant than ever. She wondered how many other people in Angela's life had heard this story.

Angela regained her composure and went on, her speech slowing down now. 'Štefan was homesick and I thought that if we started a new life in Prague it would help me to forget…and that, maybe, another child would come to replace our beautiful Ilona. But he never gave me another child. His health was poor, maybe that's why. These things aren't always meant to be.'

'And did it help? Moving here?'

Angela paused for a moment and then continued. 'Up to a point, yes. I found a new purpose in life. The Communists took power in 1948, supposedly with wide public support but not everyone was happy about it. Štefan and I were both idealists, you see. Foolish, some might say, but we could not compromise our own beliefs about human rights. Did you know that many of those Czech pilots, when they returned home, were imprisoned? They were considered a political threat to the new regime, idealists who had tasted true democracy in England. Can you imagine that?'

Eva shook her head, embarrassed at her ignorance of her own country's history. *'What people do to each other, their fellow countrymen, Eva, you cannot begin to understand.'* Baba's words now came back to her, from one of the few times she would talk about what had happened in the 1950s and 1960s.

Angela sighed. 'So you see, Štefan was in danger and we ended up fleeing to Austria, staying nearly ten years until we felt it safe to return. We managed to get work as teachers and I painted in my spare time. When Štefan's father died he inherited the house I now live in. We carried on with our involvement in underground political movements when we moved back. And, yes, I chose to pass myself off as an English aristocrat to gain some form of respect.'

'And did you ever marry?'

Angela laughed bitterly. 'His wife outlived him. Štefan died seventeen years ago. Without being able to give me his name. Without seeing the Velvet Revolution. Can you understand what that would have meant to someone like him? No, how could I expect you to? I'm sorry. I've been rambling on for too long.'

They had reached Josefová. As they climbed the stairs in silence Eva said, 'thank you.'

'For what?'

'Well, for confiding in me, and for inspiring me to go ahead and find out more about my own family. I wish I could find out everything about them.'

Angela shook her head and Eva wondered whether she would regret her outpourings in the cold light of morning.

28

'So, she's an old aristo, is she? Thought she was a bit of a snob,' mused Roz as she flicked through the TV channels.

'You haven't been listening to a word I've said, have you? That's exactly what she isn't. It's a hell of a story, though, isn't it?'

Roz yawned. 'Too melodramatic for my tastes, chick.'

'But think of how she had to defy the conventions of her day. How many women then had the guts to do that? You know, I was wondering…'

'What?'

'She must be about the same age as Baba. Would they have known each other?'

'Why should she have? Sounds like they were from very different worlds, doesn't it? Make me another coffee?'

'Get it yourself.'

Eva didn't want to admit that perhaps Roz was right and she was reading too much into this. She had spent the night wondering about Angela's story and had then spent this morning grovelling to Angela about Roz's proposal of the satellite dish. Angela had seemed more distant this morning and had grimaced at the prospect of the dish defacing the front of her building. But she had agreed, however reluctantly, and the technician had come at eleven and so had the separate delivery of all the equipment Roz had bought. Now here she was, in her element, surfing the channels and jabbing at the remote control like a toddler with a new toy.

'Honestly, Roz, it's all crap anyway. I bet you didn't watch half of it back in England. Why couldn't we do without it for a while?'

It seemed to Eva that the one consolation of the following days was that they weren't going out each evening to get blind drunk and she didn't have to worry about what Roz was getting up to. Eva was beginning to wonder how Roz had been coping these last couple of weeks without the crutch of cocaine. Then on Thursday Eva found the packet in the bathroom and they had a huge row.

'For Christ's sake, Roz! Where the hell did you get this stuff?'

'It's none of your business!'

'Well, someone's making money out of you – who is it?'

'I said -.'

'Is it Jiří?'

Roz sighed and nodded.

'Roz, how do you know it's safe? I mean if you don't really know the supplier – Jesus, it could be laced with something! Why take the risk?'

'Just shut up about it, OK? I can handle it.'

'Really? And how do you propose to carry on paying for it?'

'God, Eva, you're so naïve, aren't you? Anyway, it's cheaper out here.'

'If Angela were to find out about it we'd be out of here in no time. Think about that.'

'Gonna grass on me, are you?'

'No. Of course not. Just – just be careful, Roz, that's all.'

'Don't know how I've managed to get through life without you to look out for me,' Roz sneered.

'That's not fair. Anyway, things are different now, aren't they? We look after each other?' Eva reached out to stroke Roz's arm but she pulled away.

When the weather closed in Eva had to admit she was grateful for the injection of twenty-first century materialism that had turned their flat into a haven of comforts and distractions. Watching mindless TV helped her stop thinking about her troubles for a while, acting like a temporary anaesthetic. Angela's paintings, now framed, were delivered to them that afternoon. Angela had looked around their flat and had, Eva thought, looked both disapproving and amused in equal measure. But she issued no further invitation for tea or anything else to Eva and she felt disappointed. Maybe Angela's outpourings on Tuesday night had left her feeling exposed to someone she hardly knew. Eva had traded no secrets of her own so far. Maybe Angela was now expecting her to, and Eva fretted about what to do. Confiding in Roz would have brought no answers or reassurance. Roz neither understood nor cared. They were like two people living together but alone, each wrapped up in their own internal worlds. Eva wrote about it in her diary but found no particular comfort in setting her thoughts to paper.

Any sense of domestic harmony, however superficial, was dispelled by Friday morning. Eva was starting to feel like a skivvy again, always the one who cooked, emptied the ashtrays and cleaned the bathroom and toilet. Exasperated, she finally wrote out a list of chores and told Roz they had to decide how to divide them up. Eva endured the predicted verbal abuse but stood her ground. Then, in the afternoon, she announced she was going out.

'Thought you weren't seeing him till tonight,' Roz scowled.

'He has a name, you know. Anyway, I want to find something else to wear.'

Roz rolled her eyes. 'Oh yeah, *Will*, that's right. Your new date.' She made a mock swooning gesture which Eva ignored. 'What's his last name, then?'

'Um, I don't know, actually.'

'Address? Name of the law firm?'

'Um, no.'

'And you have the cheek to tell me *I'm* taking risks?'

'It's different.'

'How, exactly?'

'Just is, that's all,' Eva replied lamely.

'It'll be over by Christmas, at the latest, I bet. You'll see.'

Roz's words echoed in Eva's mind later as she browsed through one clothes shop after another. *Anyway, I should be dressing for myself, not him. What about this short skirt, perhaps? Who am I trying to kid? I couldn't get away with that. Put me next to one of those nubile twentysomethings in a similar outfit and – well, what would you think? Who would you choose?* And then there were Roz's last words which echoed in Eva's mind – it could all be over by Christmas. It wasn't just about Will. *How could I have guessed, this time last year, how my life would be turned upside down?* In the end she came home empty-handed and furious at herself.

Roz raised her eyebrows when Eva changed into her old clothes. 'Not looking to get laid, then?'

'Drop it.'

'Ask him if he's got a hot friend for me,' Roz cackled before settling down in front of the TV again.

Will was late.

Eva sat nursing her mulled red wine and grew increasingly fed-up of trying to look like she was really waiting for someone, even if it were true on this occasion. Mercifully, the pest of the previous Friday night was not here and she was not attracting anyone else's attention. *Maybe I really do look too dowdy tonight. Should have tried harder,* she cursed herself as she waited at the bar trying to ignore her reflection in the mirrored wall.

'I am so sorry!' Will's flustered face appeared in the mirror next to hers and she turned to see him scrabbling at his thick scarf as he removed it from his neck. 'I really am – got held up in a meeting at work, and then I realized I didn't have an address or number for you to let you know I would be late. Have you been waiting long?'

'No,' she lied, breathing in the smell of cold crisp air which lingered around him. Snowflakes were still clinging to his dark blond hair. She wanted to reach out and brush them off, just to feel its texture, to feel its thickness between her fingers.

'*Pivo, prosím.*' He ordered a beer from the waiter and then turned his full gaze and broad smile on her. 'Are you OK with staying here for a little while?'

'Of course.'

She wondered where else he had in mind, and suddenly had a horrible vision of Roz barging in on them – *surely Roz won't put up with staying in on a Friday night on her own?*

'Is everything OK, Eva?'

'Yes. I was – it's nothing.'

'How's your friend Roz now?'

Why does he have to ask about her? 'Fine, thanks,' she replied crisply, looking around the crowd.

'Look, Eva, if you had other plans, then - .'

'No. I don't. I'm sorry. I've just had a lot on my mind.'

'Oh? Are you working here now?'

That's right. If it's not about work, then what do I have to worry about? Are all guys just wrapped up in their work? 'No. Not yet. That's something I have to think about.'

'What kind of thing are you looking for?'

'Whatever I can get. I used to be a nurse but –,' she stroked her glass, 'I think I've had enough of looking after someone else.' She looked down at her hands, the hands that had fed Douglas' morphine drip. *How could I go back to that work, after what I've done? What if I was tempted to do it again, for someone else?*

Will drank deeply. 'So, what else do you want to do? What dreams did you have as a kid?'

He's asking me about my dreams. Who else has ever done that? 'Can't remember now. I once thought of being a journalist. I'm interested in politics. But I guess it's too late now.'

'Too late? Hey, you're making yourself sound old! You're not exactly running out of time, are you? Anyway, there's plenty to write about here, if you're brave enough.'

'What do you mean? They surely don't lock up people anymore for that kind of thing, do they?'

'No. But the editors are way too passive here. And there are still ways to keep people quiet, even now.'

Her curiosity was roused now as he went on to talk about the standards of press reporting and then she thought – *is this what I want to talk about all evening with him? Is this going to turn out to be a friendly chat about the state of the world?* She could almost hear Roz's derisory laughs. Some hot date that was, she'd say. *He said, 'you're not exactly running out of time, are you?' Maybe I should stop living as if this was all going to end tomorrow?*

'I'm sorry, am I boring you?' he asked suddenly.

'No. Not at all. It's, um, useful to understand how things work here.'

'But not what you were expecting to talk about on a Friday evening, right?'

She laughed nervously and he joined in. 'Another drink?' he offered.

Soon she found herself telling him about leaving Alex – but not about Douglas – and then how she wanted to find out more about Baba. He never interrupted and his gaze never left her face, though it didn't feel like an uncomfortable stare. Eva couldn't look at him, though, as she was speaking. She found herself addressing a point just beyond his shoulder and didn't realize how long she had been talking until he looked at his watch.

'Oh, I'm so sorry, I've been gabbling all evening,' she apologized.

'No, it's fine. I was just wondering about going somewhere to eat. They finish early in this town. Where would you like to go?'

'Don't mind. You'll know more places than me, anyway.'

It was Will's turn to talk when they sat down in the Greek restaurant across the road. She recalled how she and Roz had sat here - on a different table – on their first Saturday night in the city and the shy half-Cypriot waitress whom she had questioned. It felt like months had elapsed since then. Will talked a little about his work and then about his family. And then about his brief marriage. They had been too young, he said. There was no one to blame. He didn't tell Eva her name and she didn't want to know.

I'm not trying to get back at Roz for her dismissive words, honestly I'm not. But I'm not going back to Josefová tonight.

I remember what it's like to wake up in a strange place – maybe the first night in a hotel on holiday – and it takes a few seconds for the brain to kick in and recall where I am, which day it is and, more importantly, why I'm here?

I could lie about it, but I can hardly say that I'm being seduced or made to feel that I should do this. Will makes it so easy, with such a natural progression of intimacy throughout the evening. A look, a touch. There's no need to spell it out. I'm not drunk, either. The fusing of our bodies into one is gradual, gentle and deeply satisfying. We don't talk much. He strokes me continually all over, sure of his touch.

I block out images of everyone else. Of Douglas, who urged me to cherish every moment of my new life. Of a grieving and bewildered Alex, left hunched on the floor of the hall in our house back in London. Of Baba, who would have disapproved of this hastiness. Truth is, I don't care what anyone thinks. It's wonderful.

29

Eva returned to Josefová just after eleven-forty the next morning. Will had wanted her to stay and he had even skipped his usual Sunday morning ice hockey game. *I would have stayed, I really would but....*It would have been too easy for her to stay. She knew she wasn't playing with Will or being deliberately cruel. Making up a story about promising to attend another of Angela's art exhibitions seemed simple to lie about. But Eva feared she was too comfortable with him now, too much at risk of something slipping out, inadvertently, about what she had done. The closer their bodies became, the more she felt tempted to confide, to have this weight lifted from her soul. 'You don't even know his last name,' Roz had said, 'or where he lives.' The answers to those questions might now have been revealed, but that didn't mean Eva knew him.

But her resolve wasn't strong enough to refuse to see Will again that evening. He wasn't begging – that would have been a real turn-off – but his desire seemed genuine. When she passed a mirror reflection in a shop-window on the way home she thought, with a brief frisson of triumph, *someone wants me again.* Her footsteps echoed on the stone stairs of Josefová 12 as she climbed to the second floor and fumbled for her key.

Outside their flat door stood a carton of milk. As soon as Eva saw it, the significance of the symbol was clear. She closed her eyes. Roz was bound to have retaliated for her own overnight absence.

Eva opened the door as quietly as possible and paused for a moment, her ears straining for sounds. What came to them was a rhythmic cadence of heavy breathing broken by snuffles. Not Roz's. As Eva peered into the living room the noise grew louder and she saw Jiří's naked form sprawled on their new leather sofa. His face was squashed into a cushion, his eyes closed and his right arm dangled over the sofa's edge, as if reaching for something before he had fallen asleep. His limp penis lay slumped on his thigh.

Eva marched past into Roz's bedroom and shouted at the bulge under the duvet. 'Get the fuck up and get him out of here!'

Roz sat bolt upright, her eyes staring wildly. 'What's going on?'

'You heard me! Keep him in your own room or go somewhere else. That's always been the deal – remember?'

Behind her, Eva could hear scrambling and she turned to see Jiří scampering into the bathroom, his hands covering his genitals.

'Oh yeah,' Roz scratched her head vigorously. 'Sorry about that.' She groaned, clutching her head, falling back on her pillows. 'What time is it?'

'Nearly midday. Get him out, Roz. Now.'

'For God's sake, Eva, stop shouting. Anyway, so what? You didn't come back last night, did you? Weren't you doing the same thing to Will or were you just drinking tea all night?'

Eva ignored her. 'I don't want Angela to see Jiří - .'

'I'm sick and tired of hearing about fucking Angela, all right? She's taking good money from us for renting this place but she's not our mother, so I don't give a shit what she thinks, or anyone else! Get it? Now bugger off to your own room. I'll sort Jiří out.'

Eva sat in her own bedroom, fuming. This flat was supposed to be their haven. Roz had defiled it. All right, so they had never said that neither of them was to bring anyone home at night but Eva thought it was understood. Anyway, why hadn't he been sleeping in Roz's room, at least? Eva could hear hushed snatches of broken English and then the slam of the front door.

'Want a coffee?' Roz's voice, now subdued, came through Eva's bedroom door.

Eva sighed. 'All right, then.' They sat in the old armchairs. Eva didn't fancy sitting on that leather sofa.

'I'll clean it up later,' Roz muttered, nodding to it.

'You'd better. Jesus, Roz, why couldn't you have kept him in your own room?'

She shrugged. 'Got lost in the heat of the moment, you could say. Anyway, how was what's-his-name?'

Eva didn't reply but stirred her coffee.

'That good, or that bad?' Roz persisted.

'Don't want to talk about it.'

'Why not?'

Eva wanted to say, *this feels different*. But she remained silent.

Roz groaned. 'Don't tell me – you're in love!'

Eva bristled. 'Just leave me alone! You've been on at me ever since I met him and - .'

'You're looking for a new Mr. Right, chick, I can tell! So, you don't need old Rozzie anymore, got yourself a new fella, he'll look after you, right, 'cos, Rozzie, well, she's just an old lush and –.'

'Listen to yourself! All self-pity! Just sort yourself out, Roz.'

'Hey, you were the one who said we would look after each other now.'

'That doesn't mean we're, you know, joined at the hip, or something. We can still be together, even if we're with - .'

'Oh no. I know you. Once you've got a guy then, that's it, girlfriend, bye-bye.'

'Oh really? Well, as I recall, it was you who dumped me when Howard came along, so don't give me that crap - !'

The door buzzer cut through their shouting. Eva went to open the door, trying to shield the view of the messy living room. It was Angela with a newspaper in her hand, looking slightly flustered but smiling. 'I don't want to intrude,' she said, 'but if you have time, come and see me later. I may have found a job for you. Is everything all right?'

'Yes, yes, of course. Thank you. I'll be down in an hour, if that's all right.'

'Splendid! I'll see you then.'

Eva prayed Angela hadn't seen Jiří scuttling out down the stairs a few minutes earlier.

'I don't think I meet the criteria,' said Eva. She and Angela sat together reading the advert for an English-speaking obstetric nurse in a private American-run hospital that Angela said was favoured by expats.

'But surely it's worth making further enquiries, Eva? They may be flexible and with your experience -.'

'You're very kind but my background was rather different. I specialized in pediatrics and then palliative care, not obstetrics. Still,' Eva noted Angela's crestfallen expression, 'you're right, it may be worth a meeting to see what could develop. I'll ring them tomorrow.'

'Good. It will give you something to focus on. Now, I have made some soup, very nourishing. You look as if you could do with feeding up. Is your stomach still troubling you?'

'I do still feel a little strange.'

'I'm sure you must be very tired after everything you've been through in the last couple of weeks. You need someone to look after you.' Eva looked up sharply but Angela had disappeared into the kitchen. 'Do come through,' she called. They ate the beef and vegetable broth in silence. Angela then said quietly, 'I'm sorry I burdened you with my troubles the other night.'

'No, not at all. I'm sorry if I asked too many questions. It was very nosy of me. After all, you've only just met me and – well, I'm sorry if I intruded on your memories.'

'It was my choice to tell you. I hope that we will become good enough friends to help each other from time to time. You may think that people of my generation are easily shocked but I have seen enough of the world to understand that people behave out of character sometimes for the strangest of reasons. Now, if you still feel under the weather by the end of the week, go and see this lady.' Angela passed a note over. 'She has been my doctor for several years and she is very kind. She also speaks some English, although I'm sure you'll manage very well.'

'Thanks. By the way, this soup – it reminds me of the kind Baba used to make when I was little. It always made me feel better.'

'Then that's a wonderful memory to have of a grandmother. Something to hold on to in later years when life looks bleak and we wonder where to draw our comfort from.'

Eva wondered whether Angela was hinting at some distress of her own. 'Angela, have you ever been back to England?'

'No. There was nothing to return to. I kept in touch with an old friend in my village who wrote to me to say that my father died soon after I left and my brother later killed himself with drink so you see…' she waved her slender hand. 'This is truly my world. I have seen terrible things here too, but this city is in my blood and I have had the comfort of many friends over the years and work that I love. What else can one ask of life?'

Eva would have liked to ask whether she missed not having any more children but wished to spare her that pain. She wondered what Angela would have been like as a mother. She could have been a grandmother too by now. 'Do you still have many photos from England?'

'A few. Perhaps one day I can show them to you.'

'I'd like that very much. I wish I had more photos - from here, I mean, to fill in the gaps of my family. There's so little I know.'

'Don't be disappointed, my dear, if you can't find out very much. It is the future you should be thinking of inhabiting, not the past. You may find, after all, that you want to return to England.' Angela paused, and then said, 'now, if you'll excuse me, I have arranged to meet a friend in town. Do let me know how your phone call goes tomorrow, won't you? And don't forget to ring that doctor, if you need to.'

30

'I didn't know if you'd come,' said Will as Eva stood in his doorway several hours later. 'You left in such a hurry this morning. I wondered if I'd said or done something wrong.'

She knew she should have been happy to hear that, to know that he didn't want to treat last night as a one-off event, and that he cared about how she might be feeling. She smiled faintly and followed him inside. They stood there, in the hall, and she wanted to reach out and touch his face.

'Is anything wrong?' he asked.

'No. It's nothing you've done. It's just me, how I am at the moment.'

'Oh. Don't people usually say that when they're trying to back out of something?'

She sat down on the sofa and cradled a cushion in her lap, taking occasional sips of the wine he had poured. 'That's not what I mean, but, well…'

'If you're saying last night was a mistake then…' he ran his hand through his hair and grinned sheepishly, 'I'm sorry if you think I moved in on you too soon - .'

'I don't think that. We're not kids, after all. But you see, you don't really know me.'

'Isn't that how it usually starts out?' he laughed.

'Yes, but….' Her voice trailed off. *What version of the truth can I share with him? How can we have a relationship with my secrets hanging between us?*

'If you're thinking it's a big risk so soon after your marriage has ended, well, let's just take things one step at a time. What else is there?' he grinned. 'You're not an axe murderer, I can tell!'

Her face felt hot. 'Will, you don't understand -.'

'What's there to understand? I'm not good at playing guessing games, Eva, and if that's what you want then you've got the wrong guy.'

Immediately it felt as if the temperature in the room had plummeted. *What the hell am I doing? He must think I'm playing hard to get.*

'Will, I'm sorry. I don't really know what I'm saying really. I'm just - .'

'Scared?' He sat down, taking her hand. Her body went rigid and she didn't know how to respond to the way he was squeezing her hand. 'Look, if you've just walked out of a bad marriage, like you told me, then maybe it's normal to feel scared. I'm not gonna push you. You have to decide. So, let's just take it easy.' His hand now released hers and he reached up and touched the nape of her neck. She remembered those strokes last night and her eyes started to close. *It would be so easy to open up to him now, to be reassured that what I've done to Douglas won't come between us.* But then she moved away, just a little, but enough to bring a frown to his face.

'If it feels better then don't stay the night, if you're not sure,' he said.

I shouldn't have come. Then I wouldn't be torn now in this decision. I should have just put last night down to a lovely but isolated experience. She let him kiss her before saying, 'I think I should go.'

He bent his head and replied, 'I thought you might say that.'

'I just need more time to think, that's all.'

'OK. If you change your mind then – look, I have an invitation to join some friends at their place in the mountains next weekend. It's beautiful up there. If you want, we can do it just as friends, there are plenty of rooms. Just think about it. No pressure, honest.'

'OK. Look, I'm sorry if - .'

'It's no big deal. Take it easy, Eva. It's no big deal.' He was looking the other way as Eva rose and headed for the door, feeling utterly stupid.

'Playing hard to get, are you? Good for you,' Roz said when Eva told her later.

'I'm not playing anything. I'm just worried, that's all.'

'What's there to be worried about? People keep secrets from each other all the time. Doesn't have to be a big thing. Look at Howard,' she laughed bitterly, 'we had a great time till I found out about what he was really like. Just keep it simple. Keep it light, have fun whilst you can.'

'I'm not eighteen anymore, Roz. I don't want to just screw around like we did back then.'

'What was so wrong about that?'

'Is that how you want to live the rest of your life? I mean, look what happened to you. Have you forgotten already? How can you carry on as if nothing happened?'

Roz fell silent and chewed her fingernails.

Diary: Monday 13 December

I spent the rest of last night on the sofa, watching Casablanca *dubbed into Czech. When you've seen a film so many times already then the language of transmission is no barrier. If anything, it frees your mind up to consider the characters, their motivations and reactions in a new light. You know when Ingrid Bergman looks at Humphrey Bogart in that dewy-eyed way, uncertain of where her true loyalties lie, between her lover and her husband? Could she really be in love with two men at once? I had never considered that a possibility. I'll never forget Douglas, and not only for what I had to do.*

It was a beautiful day yesterday, the kind of crisp sunshine and achingly blue sky that we would have yearned for on an English winter's day but I wasted it. Angela stole my afternoon and seeing Will again took the rest of the daylight hours. By the time I thought of going out for a walk to clear my head of everything, darkness had fallen and the flat pressed in on me. Roz suggested we go back to Černá Růže. I'm fed up of the place already. It was half-empty and I felt the hours drag by. Roz didn't even attempt to flirt with anyone. For once I looked forward to the bustle of a Monday morning.

This morning I rang the number of the hospital in the advert for a nurse.

Waste of time. I'd need too much re-training, the woman said. And my Czech wasn't good enough, apparently, which is stupid considering that most of the patients would be English-speaking. Back to square one. What the hell are we going to do for money? Roz said, 'marry money, worked for me'. She laughed. I didn't. I don't know which way to turn, what I should be doing. I had a routine, once, and I miss it, the comforting certainty of how to spend each day. I have a blank canvas now and am scared to paint the first line.

The days limped past. On Thursday morning Eva texted Will. *Yes, I'd love go to the mountains for the weekend.* Reluctantly, she accepted that Roz was right, that she had to learn to just enjoy the moment and stop worrying about what would or wouldn't happen.

She's heading for a fall, I just know it. One minute I think I've got the old Eva back – you know, feisty cow, takes no shit from anyone – then I think, no, she's still too soft. Falls in love too easily, that's part of her problem. Can't protect herself, not like me. Oh no, not like me at all. No crap like that.

Trouble is – well, I was wondering this morning what it would feel like, being in love. I can't say it's ever happened to me – well, you fancy a guy for a bit, get a bit wrapped up in them but it never lasts. How can it? They all let you down after a while, don't they, then you just have the memories of the shags, and some of them aren't that great either. When people say they're in love – well, they've just become used to someone, it gets too cosy. You give each other pet names, do the shopping together, buy a house, then the kids come along and suddenly you're wondering where's the person you used to be. You've just got these labels now of wife and mother or, in my case, society bloody hostess. Thank Christ Howard and I didn't have kids.

I'd forgotten what a bossy cow Eva could be, always trying to organize everyone. Why can't she leave me alone? Maybe she really should go off with this Will guy, but then, shit, I'm not sure what it would be like on my own. I want to go home, but I daren't. Fucking Howard, he's screwed up my life good and proper. Not my fault. Should I have put up with it, maybe? No. No longer.

What do I want, then? Someone normal who just wants some fun, no strings attached, fancies spoiling me a bit, then move on to the next one, and the next one after that…just like it used to be. What was so wrong with that? Eva says she doesn't want to go back to that life but I don't see what was so bad about it. Beats the shitty situation we're both in at the moment, doesn't it?

Eva can't go home either. We're both stuck in this hell-hole and I don't want to think about the future. What am I gonna do when she gets really sick? Need a drink. The coke's run out, have to get some more from Jiří tonight. Better hide it more carefully from Eva this time. I'm not hooked or anything but then, well, at this price why not? Whatever gets you through the night? And the next day.

Christmas soon. I fucking hate Christmas.

31

The outside doorbell buzzed just after three-thirty on Friday afternoon. Looking out of the living room window Eva could just about see the top of Will's head as he stood at the main door. Roz was behind her, straining to see. 'Bugger off, Roz,' Eva muttered.

'Why are you hiding him away from me?' Roz demanded. 'Is he that ugly?'

'I'll be down in a minute,' Eva called through the intercom.

'Aren't you going to invite him up?'

'It'll waste time,' Eva replied. 'He said it would take nearly two hours to get there.'

'Now listen, have a good time, shag his brains out and don't say anything stupid like "I love you".'

'Or that, by the way, I killed my father-in-law?' Eva's face darkened and the silence hung between them. 'Roz, how could I ever tell him?'

'You can't. You just can't. Go. Now. Just go, all right?'

They hugged each other briefly then Eva grabbed her case and hurried down the stairs. As she opened the front door Will turned to face her, his expression neutral.

'Hi,' she said, sounding cool, but not feeling it. They stood there, looking at each other, and she wondered whether he would lean forward to kiss her. Instead he picked up her bag and walked to his car, a dark blue Saab.

'How was your week?' he asked lightly.

She told him about the phone call to the hospital. 'Don't worry. Plenty of better opportunities out there. Stick to your dreams, right?'

'You need time to build your dreams,' she retorted.

They drove in silence for a while. The traffic leaving Prague was heavy as they headed southwest out of the city. 'This is normal,' he told her. 'Lots of folks here go to their weekend places to see family and friends.'

'I didn't realize they could afford weekend houses.'

'Don't get the wrong idea. Some places are pretty basic, but they've been in the family for generations and it's a tradition here. It's the tourists that fill the city at weekends.'

'How many people will be with us in the cottage?'

'The house belongs to Petr's family. It'll be him, his girlfriend Simona and us.'

'Oh.'

'There's a third bedroom you can have, if that's what you want.' He was looking straight ahead as he overtook a convoy of Lorries. She stared down at her hands in her lap, unsure of how to answer. Instead, she watched the scenery as it changed from the motorway to narrow and increasingly steep rough roads, passing through quiet villages of mostly wooden chalets with the occasional flash of wealth evidenced by a newly-built Western-style family house. The car drove well, despite the thick layer of snow on the road surface. Will had put on a Miles Davis CD and listening to the music felt like a good excuse not to talk.

It was dusk when they arrived. They passed through a small scattering of wooden houses, seemingly deserted. After another turn to the left Will stopped the car outside a long one-storey stone-built house, the snow in front of it swept aside to create a pathway for them. Through the windows she could see the soft yellow glow of lamplight.

'This is it,' said Will as he turned off the ignition. He turned to face her now. 'Like I said, no pressure. Petr and Simona are really nice people. Let's just try and enjoy the time, OK?'

She nodded but inside was wondering how to handle this changed situation between them. How could she have got this so wrong? *I'm not playing games, it's just that…I don't even know how to explain it to myself.* The front door of the house opened and a tall slim man in his thirties strode out, smiling broadly. Eva and Will got out of the car and the two men embraced.

'Will, so nice to see you! And this is Eva? *Ahoj!*' He nodded to me and then offered his hand to shake. 'Will told me you speak

Czech well, yes?'

'Very badly, actually.' She glanced at Will but he was now walking ahead to greet a petite dark-haired girl, almost lifting her off her feet in a close hug. Eva's stomach churned.

'Eva,' said Petr, 'this is Simona.'

'*Ahoj!*' Simona offered her tiny hand shyly to Eva who felt like a lumpy elephant beside her. 'I am sorry, but my English is not as good as Petr's.'

Petr and Simona were kind and inclusive but Eva felt like an interloper in their presence over dinner. Clearly they had all known each other for a while and she sat through the anecdotes and reminiscences, smiling politely. Simona had cooked a delicious veal stew and Petr placed bottles of beer and Moravian white wine on the table. Petr and Simona smoked constantly, whilst apologizing for their habit. Eva accepted a cigarette from her. Will raised his eyebrows but said nothing. She tried not to look at him during the meal even though they sat directly opposite each other. She was starting to wonder whether she should have come at all. As the men talked Simona asked her how she was finding Prague. They spoke in Czech and each glass of wine Eva drank improved her fluency. It turned out Simona was doing a PhD in Economics at Charles University. Eva thought how Roz would have hated Simona's combination of looks, brains and a sweet nature. Eva asked Simona if she had come across Angela at the University but she shook her head.

'So, Eva, what brings you to Prague?' asked Petr.

Eva avoided Will's gaze as she replied lightly, 'oh, well, I wanted to see where my family was from.'

'And do you still have any family here?'

'I've no idea. I hope to find out.'

'What was your family name?'

'Polák was my father's surname. He died here, during the '68 uprising. So did his brother, father, uncle and my maternal grandfather. In Pankrác prison, I understand. My mother died soon after I was born.' Petr and Simona murmured understandingly, their expressions solemn. *How many stories like this have they heard in their lives already, maybe from their own parents?* 'My grandmother was called Ludmila Šimková and she got us to England,' she went on, encouraged by their obvious interest. 'I don't know much else beyond that. She never wanted to talk much about what happened. She's dead now too.' She quickly took another sip of wine. The others all nodded gravely.

'Those were terrible times,' said Petr quietly.

'But now things are much better, aren't they?' Eva asked.

'For some, yes,' he shrugged.

Simona cut across the gloom. 'Eva, you must be tired after your journey.' She looked at her watch. 'Would you like me to show you to your room?' She led Eva down a dimly-lit corridor, past two other bedrooms and then opened a door into a room that held just a single bed and a slim wardrobe.

'I am sorry, it is very small,' Simona smiled shyly.

'It's lovely, thank you.' Eva followed her back down the corridor and reached for her case in the sitting room. Will and Petr were discussing the possibility of hiring skiing equipment the next day.

'I'll say goodnight, then,' Eva offered.

'Sleep well,' called Petr. She thought he stole a glance at Will but she couldn't be sure.

'Goodnight,' said Will, barely looking up, and then he went back to his conversation with Petr.

Eva lay in her bed. The room was pitch-black and the density of the darkness felt stifling after so many years of sleeping in urban half-light and so she left the curtains open for the moonlight to stream in. The memory of that one night with Will flooded back to her but she tried to banish the stirrings it raised in her body. The sedating effects of the wine kicked in and she felt herself drifting off when the door opened slightly.

'Eva?' came Will's soft voice.

She sat up quickly and pulled the duvet around her. He came over to the bed, towering over her. 'I wanted to say goodnight.'

'You already did.'

'No. Properly.'

He bent down, took her face in his hands and kissed her, lightly at first and then deeply. *Oh God.* 'Stay with me,' she breathed.

'There's more room in my bed,' he said, pulling the duvet slowly off her.

Eva had never learned to ski, never having had the inclination or time. She tried to slide a few yards the next day, and endured Will's roars of laughter at her clumsy efforts to stay upright. She should have been offended, but found she didn't mind. When she had awoken next to Will that morning there had been no sense of confusion this time about where she was or why. They had made love again, at her instigation, in their half-awake state, slowly, gently, wordlessly.

The time slipped through her fingers like melted chocolate and all too soon it seemed that Sunday afternoon was upon them and they were all sighing about the need to return to the city. She was envious that at least the others all had jobs or studies to return to and resolved to get Christmas out of the way and forge ahead after the New Year to create some new purpose for her own existence, suddenly feeling that there would be plenty of time after all.

It was on the return journey that evening that Will told her he would be flying to Toronto on Tuesday morning for the Christmas holidays.

'When will you be back?' *God, does that make me sound desperately needy?*

'After the New Year. I'm flying back on January 3rd.'

The date jarred. The Eurostar return tickets for her and Roz had been booked for that date. Her heart skipped a beat at the memory. *I should have torn the bloody tickets up.* 'So,' she said at last, 'you'll have a long break with your family.'

'Yeah. It'll be great to see them again. How about you?'

'What?'

'Don't you still have people to visit back home?'

'I'll be staying here. With Roz.'

'Oh, OK. So, you'll be having a wild time, two single girls together out on the town, right?'

She tried to laugh it off but her chest felt tight.

They reached Josefová at six in the evening. She wondered about whether to invite him in but didn't want the prospect of Roz interfering with their farewells. As it turned out, Will said he needed to catch up with work in the office.

'On a Sunday evening?'

'Have to. Need to finish everything before I go. Sorry.'

They kissed for a long time in the car but he eventually broke away. She wanted to say she'd miss him. He stroked her hair. 'I'll call you over Christmas,' he said.

She climbed the stairs to her flat slowly. Her head had started aching on the return journey and fear of her reality was creeping into her heart, eating away at the dreams of the last couple of days.

As she passed Angela's flat the door was just closing, but not before the short dumpy figure of Pani Havlová turned in the doorway and gave Eva a long appraising look.

'Are you sure, Ivana?'

'My contact at the British Embassy is very reliable, *Hraběnka*.'

Angela sighed, removing her dark glasses for a moment to rub her sore eyes. Ivana Havlová sat passively.

'What am I to do, Ivana?'

'You must tell her. Tell her the truth.'

'And what would that achieve? How much more pain must be inflicted? Hasn't everyone suffered enough?'

'Forgive me, *Hraběnka*, but are you thinking of yourself or of her?'

'But how much of the truth has to be revealed, though? We all keep something back from others, do we not? Where's the harm in that?'

'That depends on which part you hold back.'

'And what has total honesty achieved for me so far, Ivana? Look at what I lost because of it.' Angela replaced the dark glasses on her nose. She rustled the documents in her lap. They could not be ignored but she had to think about the implications before she decided how to act. From upstairs the sound of loud rock music could be faintly heard and Angela frowned. *That Roz woman has to be separated from Eva.*

32

Diary: Monday 20 December

I haven't written anything for a week. But I have to now because even if it's only talking to myself it's better than nothing. Roz wouldn't understand. She was home when I got back last night and full of her latest conquest. I just don't believe it. I told her she must have the memory of a goldfish, going out and picking up another guy like that, but she said this was different. She really seemed to believe it too. He's called Steve Burns, an Aussie working here as a commercial director for international property developers and already they've decided to spend Christmas in Vienna and she said, why don't you come and bring Will, it would be a nice foursome. She'll be planning little dinner parties next and to think she had the cheek to call <u>me</u> suburban! She went on and on about him, about how much money he must make. Not a question to me about how my weekend went. When I had the chance to say something all I could think of was, it was very nice, thanks, and that cracked her up. Like she thought I was going to tell her every little detail of what we did in bed.

    I miss Will already and I want to tell somebody but she'll go on at me again. I told her he was going home for Christmas and she said that maybe things would cool a bit. I don't want them to. But I don't want to be the first one to ring, either. How long will he leave it before he rings me? But what if he doesn't and I end up not ringing either and then he comes back and what happens then? Christ, it's like being eighteen again. I should have grown out of *this years ago.*

I was sick again this morning. I don't get it, I was fine over the weekend so I've rung the doctor's number and made an appointment for tomorrow. If it's a tummy bug maybe she'll give me some antibiotics. I want to be better for Christmas but I don't think I want to go to Vienna. Seeing Roz with someone would make me feel worse. But then, I've never spent Christmas alone before. What will Alex do, all alone now? But he was going to end up alone anyway, sometime, so why feel sorry for him? Last Christmas Douglas was still doing OK on chemotherapy, I was all right and Alex seemed normal, everything felt under control. Now everything's up in the air and I don't know which way it's going to turn out. What had we done wrong, as a family, to deserve all this?

I wonder if I should send Will a text tonight, just to wish him a good journey? Or would that sound desperate? If we're still OK when he gets back, what should I tell him? How much should I keep back?

The plaque outside the doctor's surgery proclaimed that MuDr. Hana Blaníková was a *praktický lékař* – a general practitioner – and that she shared her consulting rooms with a *dětský lékař* – pediatrician – called MuDr. Jan Husítský and a gynecologist by the name of Prof. MuDr. Karel Dohnál. *Children to the left, adults to the right. Something for all the family,* Eva thought, as she entered the reception area. The room was spotlessly clean, its whitewashed walls hung with colourful posters advertising vitamins and food supplements. Three people, two women and a man all appearing to be of retirement age, intoned the familiar greeting of *dobrý den* in flat voices to her that Eva was becoming accustomed to hearing from complete strangers whenever they met in whichever circumstances. *Is this a rule taught in their childhood education?* She hadn't felt so bad this morning but Roz had urged her to go, saying she still looked like death warmed up.

The uniformed nurse behind the reception desk confirmed Eva's appointment and asked her for her health insurance card.

'I'm sorry, I don't have one,' she confessed.

The nurse frowned. 'Then you must pay for the consultation before you go in.' She looked up a chart of rates and Eva paid eight hundred crowns and duly received a receipt. 'You should arrange something soon. If you need more treatment it will become expensive,' the nurse scolded.

There were no magazines or papers to read. The patients who went in before Eva certainly received far more of the doctor's time than the NHS back home would have allowed. The nurse was in and out of the consulting room frequently, carrying notes, syringes and various trays. After about forty minutes of staring at the grey lino floor looking for non-existent dirt Eva was beginning to regret not having brought a book with her when her name was finally called. It seemed strange to be called Pani McKinley, or something similar as the nurse struggled to pronounce her name.

MuDr. Blaníková was, Eva guessed, about her own age. Slender and dark-haired with a firm jaw set in a rigid line, the doctor beckoned her to take a seat. Eva explained that Angela had referred her and briefly described her symptoms. MuDr. Blaníková weighed Eva, measured her height and took her blood pressure.

'A little low but we can fix that. So, you speak a little Czech?'

'My family was from Prague.'

'Ah, I see. Now, how often have you been vomiting?'

'Um, well, I haven't actually been sick for nearly a week, apart from once again yesterday, and I still feel very tired.'

'Have you had a temperature?'

'No.'

The doctor measured it anyway and then leant over and gently inspected the inside of Eva's lower eyelid, frowning slightly. 'Hmm. A little anaemic, I would say. I can give you some iron tablets. Now, lie down on that couch and I will examine you.'

She pushed and prodded various parts of Eva's abdomen and looked to her for a reaction. *No pain*, Eva said.

'When was your last period?'

'I can't remember.'

'You don't know?'

'I've had problems with irregular periods for a few years now. Sometime at the beginning of November, maybe?'

'Have you had any children?

'No.' *And I'm not going to go into the whys and wherefores, OK?*

'I should like to do some tests. Come back tomorrow morning at seven-thirty to see the nurse. Bring a fresh sample of urine with you in a clean bottle. She will also take some blood tomorrow.'

'When will I have the results?'

'By Thursday lunchtime, I would say. We need to expedite

quickly, with Christmas in just a few days. I will see you Thursday afternoon. My nurse will make the appointment.'

'And then what?'

'And then we'll see.' She wound up their meeting by advising Eva to drink plenty of water and to avoid fried food.

As Eva glanced at her watch upon leaving the building she wondered whether Will's plane had taken off yet.

33

'Good thing I bought some red wine, then,' said Roz when Eva told her the doctor thought she was anaemic.

'I don't think it's going to do my guts much good, though.'

'Oh, just a sip, come on, to keep me company.'

'Thought you were going out tonight with Steve, anyway.'

Roz grimaced. 'Working late. He sent me a text. Looks like we've both got a couple of workaholics on our hands.'

'You make it sound so cosy when you say 'we'.'

'Yeah. Funny that, isn't it? Both ending up with a fella. Maybe we can start having a good time now. Have you thought about coming with us to Vienna, then?'

'Thanks, but I'd rather not.'

'You can't spend Christmas on your own, Eva. It's not, well, normal.'

Eva thought briefly back to last Christmas when Alex had been working throughout the holiday. 'I'm used to it, aren't I? The TV will be perfect company, thanks.'

'Tell me you're joking.'

'I wonder what Angela will be doing? Maybe I'll cook something for both of us.'

'Eva, I don't think that's a good idea – she'll bore the pants off you.'

'Actually, she promised to show me some old photos. And I want to ask her some more questions about how I should start my research.'

Roz stifled a yawn. 'Look, chick, you should come with us. It'll be a blast.'

'What will Steve think about that?'

'Listen, you're my mate and I'm not going to leave you here on your own and that's final. You'll be, well, suicidal on your own. By the way, do you know how to cook *guláš*?'

'Never tried. Baba did all that kind of cooking when I was a kid. Why?'

'Because Steve says he likes it and I'm going to cook it for him tomorrow when he comes over.'

Eva threw back her head, laughing. 'But you don't know how to cook! When was the last time - ?'

'I know, I know, but, well, I thought I'd give it a go.'

'Jesus Christ, you'll give us all food poisoning now!'

Roz laughed too and threw her shoe at Eva.

The next morning Eva rose at six and washed out an old bottle of bubble bath to use for her urine sample. She hadn't done anything like this for years and her hand shook as she tried to complete the procedure. She arrived at the doctor's surgery just before seven-thirty. The thick needle the nurse used to take Eva's blood sample left a livid bruise in the crook of her arm. *I'd have done a better job of it than that.* She paid twelve hundred crowns this time. The nurse said she would ring tomorrow lunchtime.

The call came through soon after twelve-thirty the next day. Eva was told to return to the surgery at four to see MuDr. Blanīkovā.

'Want me to come with you?' asked Roz.

'No, I'll be all right,' Eva replied.

The reception area is empty today. The nurse nods to me and gestures for me to go into the doctor's room.

'Please sit down, Pani McKinley,' *says MuDr. Blanīkovā.* 'I have the results now of your tests. They suggest that you are pregnant.' *She looks me full in the face.*

I feel I'm going to be sick again. 'What? But that's not possible!'

'When was the last time you had intercourse?'

I hate that word. It doesn't describe what Will and I have been doing. But that was Sunday morning and this sickness started nearly two weeks ago. My throat is tight and dry.

'I see that you were not expecting this,' *she says quietly.*

Alex? Alex??I can't bear to think about that night. 'Look, maybe the tests are wrong.'

'There is only one way to be sure, of course. My colleague,' *she gestures to the door,* 'will perform an ultrasound examination. I have asked him to stay and see you today. I'm afraid you will have to pay for that too.'

Why are they always talking about bloody money? She stretches out her hand, her face and voice softening now. 'Come with me now, please.' *She leads me back into the reception area. The nurse is nowhere to be seen. We pass through a door on the opposite side and I see a grey-haired slightly stooped man standing at a bookcase beside a desk. She speaks to him rapidly in a low voice, and then turns to me.*

'I will see you a little later.' *She manages a half-smile. How many times this week has she had to break news like this? The man introduces himself as Prof. MuDr. Dohnál and I remember his name from the plaque outside. He signals me to go behind a screened area, tells me to remove my trousers and knickers, and to climb on to the reclining chair. Although he does not smile his eyes look kind and tired. I wonder how many other women he has seen today who have also been given unexpected news. Were they thrilled, or repulsed? I can't feel a thing right now. My mind is a complete blank and my movements are slow and uncertain. It seems to take me an age to undress, my fingers clumsy with the zip of my jeans which jams half-way down. I struggle and finally free myself.*

I clamber on to the chair. MuDr. Dohnál places my feet in the stirrups so that my knees fall open. Above his head is a TV screen which he switches on. He slips on latex gloves, picks up a probe and starts spreading gel over it. He signals that he is going to insert this into my vagina. The sensation of its cold wet hardness as it is slowly pushed inside me instinctively makes me clench my muscles. He tells me to relax and to take deep breaths in and out. Eventually the probe slides all the way in but my body tightens again around it.

Whooshing sounds are now emanating from the TV screen. He wiggles the instrument around inside me and a swirling grey image appears on the screen, its form constantly changing. How often, in my nursing training, did I see a screen like this, with an anxious patient lying there, waiting for the pronouncement? Then he stops the manipulation and peers closely at the picture, pointing. And I know what I'm seeing.

'Yes, it is very small but it's definite,' *he says slowly, his eyes still on the screen. Another wiggle of the probe and he seems satisfied, nodding.*

My heart is beating wildly now. I stare at the image. My vaginal muscles feel like they are going into spasm. 'Please take it out!' *I cry.*

His face hardens fleetingly. He removes the instrument and my vagina feels sore, squidgy, violated. The image has disappeared. He switches off the monitor and tells me sharply to get dressed, leaving me to it whilst he goes back to his desk behind the screen. I hear him speaking on the telephone in a low voice. Within a minute or so, once I am dressed, MuDr. Blanikova's face appears behind the screen and she beckons me to follow her out. My legs are trembling as I pass MuDr. Dohnāl at his desk. He is typing at his PC and does not look up.

'Na Shledanou,' comes his slow voice behind me as I leave his office. I do not reply.

MuDr. Blanikova tells me to sit down. It hurts to sit and I squirm.

'So,' *she is saying,* 'it is certain, then. About four weeks, we think.'

My mind is in freefall now, counting back the weeks frantically. Alex, what you be thinking, if you knew? Didn't we use a condom, for once? I couldn't remember.

'Would you like a glass of water?' *she asks gently. My hands are shaking as I raise the plastic cup to my lips, spilling a little.*

'What happens now?' *I must be speaking because I can feel my lips moving.*

'That is up to you. Do you need some time to think about it -?'

'No. I can't.'

'Can't what?'

'I can't keep it.'

She looks at me, sympathy in her eyes. 'Perhaps you should talk this over with your husband or boyfriend first.'

'No, no, you don't understand.' *My heart is doing somersaults.* 'I can't keep it because – because, I may not live to look after it.' *I don't know why, but suddenly I feel free, cleansed, even if that sounds all wrong. Her face is frozen. She struggles to speak for a moment. So then I tell her my prognosis. No, I don't know exactly when it could happen. Yes, I could still be here in a couple of years. But my mind is clear: no child should be brought into the world with no family to care for it. I had lost my own mother soon after birth but, for this child, there would be no Baba around to save it.*

She sighs but nods. 'So, you are saying that you want to have the pregnancy terminated?'

'It's not my fault!'

'I didn't say it was, Pani McKinley. I am not here to judge you.

But, you must understand, that under Czech law -.'

'I – can't – I - .' *My tongue feels thick and heavy.*

'I am trying to say that under Czech law two doctors must sign to agree to this procedure.'

I nod dumbly, exhausted.

'I think you should go home and rest,' *she says kindly.* 'Is there someone who can be with you over this Christmas weekend?'

Roz will be in Vienna. Angela – well, this isn't her problem. 'Yes,' I lie.

'If you still want to proceed with the termination, then you should phone me on Monday morning. The clinic will be open again then.'

'How soon…?'

'I will ring the hospital now. Maybe it can be done next week, before the New Year weekend.'

I put my face in my hands. Suddenly my world has closed in again and I can barely breathe.

'Pani McKinley, you should go home now and rest. I understand this must be terribly difficult for you.'

Does she assume I would have wanted this child, if things were different? Well, would I? We sit there looking at each other. There is a hint of sadness in her eyes as she bids me goodbye. As I slowly close the main door behind me my mobile phone bleeps the arrival of a text message. 'Missing you already. Will.'

34

Roz picked Eva up in a taxi soon after Eva called her with her news. Roz looked pale, her eyes red-rimmed as if she had been crying too. They rode in silence but as the taxi pulled up in Josefová Roz mumbled, 'I've cancelled the dinner with Steve tonight, so we'll be on our own.' Eva nodded dumbly. She had forgotten. But then, she couldn't even remember what day it was.

Roz got the duvet from Eva's bed and brought it to the sofa covering both of them as they huddled together. 'I can't believe it,' she kept repeating. They didn't drink or smoke. They just sat there, curled up together. Eva put her head on Roz's shoulder and Roz turned to kiss Eva's hair.

'Just as well that Will's not here, isn't it?' Roz said at last.

'I wish he were.' *It was his arms I want around me now and the feel of his body next to mine. But how would he react?*

Roz sighed. 'Don't get any silly ideas about telling him, chick. He doesn't need to know everything. Let's face it, most guys would be out of here like a shot.'

'I'm tired of living with secrets.'

'Eva,' Roz pulled away from her now, 'you're not seriously thinking of keeping it, are you?'

'You know I can't, even if I wanted to.'

'Exactly. You really don't need this to complicate things. Anyway, it's not a child yet. Right? It's just a blob, a few cells. So, easy to decide, right?'

Eva saw Roz's eyes searching her face anxiously as if for confirmation. When she'd cried out, 'please take it out', she wasn't sure whether it was just the doctor's probe she had been referring to. *Easy to decide? Yes and no. Do I have the right to tell this being that it's better that it should not live at all, rather than as an orphan?* 'Why do I have to decide who lives or dies? It's not fair to ask me to decide when I don't get to choose what happens to me.' She buried her face in Roz's shoulder.

Roz hugged her. 'I know, chick, I know. Look, I'll go with you to the hospital when they do it.'

'So, when you come back from Vienna?'

'You think I'm going to leave you like this?'

'But you really wanted to go!'

'Some other time. I've got plenty of time to do that. Come on, we'll go find some great food somewhere, treat ourselves. The rest of the world can go to hell.'

'I feel sick.' Eva suddenly rose to go to the bathroom, her insides still tender from the examination. As she reached the corridor the door buzzer sounded.

'Oh, what the fuck does she want now?' muttered Roz.

Eva paused in the doorway of the bathroom, listening, clutching her stomach which felt as if it was going to explode.

'Oh, good evening, Roz. I was wondering, is Eva here?' Angela's voice drifted in. Eva stepped slowly forward into the hallway. 'Ah, there you are, my dear. Please forgive the intrusion but I thought I'd catch you before you went out for the evening perhaps and –.' She hesitated, looking between Eva and Roz. 'Is anything wrong?'

'We're fine,' snapped Roz. 'Is it important?'

Angela ignored her and moved towards Eva, who was now gripping the door handle to steady herself.

'My dear, what has happened - you look - .' Angela reached out her arm but Eva shrugged it off. 'Are you still unwell? You should have gone to the doctor - .'

'She did, and it's all under control now, so if you'll excuse us,' Roz stood in the doorway of the living room, hands on hips, glaring.

'Eva?' Angela reached out to touch Eva's face, which was now wet with tears she was trying frantically to wipe away. 'Oh my dear child, what has happened?'

'Eva - not a word! Don't let her interfere!' Angela reached out and drew Eva into her arms. Roz grabbed Angela's arm. 'Leave her alone – just go!'

'Please, let go, both of you!'

Eva sinks to the floor. The room is spinning around her. She feels the vomit rising in her throat and drags herself along the floor, desperate to reach the bathroom. Too late, she is violently sick in front of them. Between her legs she feels warm liquid trickling down her thighs.

'Oh Christ!' Roz stares at the trickle of blood now visible below the hem of Eva's dressing gown. She turns to Angela. 'Get an ambulance! Now!'

'Oh! Oh my dear! What's happened to you?'

Eva looks down. She knows what the blood means. She and Roz stare at each other. 'I'm losing it Roz, help me - .' And then the vomiting starts again, the floor seems to slip away and she starts to convulse.

Roz chews her fingernails, glancing occasionally at Angela who shares the padded bench in the hospital corridor. The harsh overhead lighting exaggerates the lines in the old woman's face. Roz is irritated by Angela's dark glasses. *What's she thinking? And why the fuck is she here, anyway?* On the way to the hospital Roz had told Angela about Eva's pregnancy and was taken aback by how upset she appeared to be.

The doctor who first saw Eva when she was admitted now appears through the security door. His blue scrubs are heavily creased, as if he has been wearing them non-stop for days. 'Are you her family?' he asks.

Angela looks up, breathing fast. 'How is she?' she asks in Czech.

'Excuse me, can we do English, please?' Roz cuts in.

'Of course.' His tone is brisk. 'Well, I'm afraid we could not save the child. I am very sorry.'

'She won't be,' mutters Roz.

Angela turns sharply to Roz but then back to the doctor. 'But she is all right, isn't she?'

The doctor folds his arms and rocks on his feet. 'We would like to run some tests. The paramedics tell me that in the ambulance Pani McKinley appeared to have some kind of fit.'

Roz closes her eyes briefly and her shoulders slump. 'You need to know something, then.' She tells the doctor about Eva's condition and prognosis. She hears Angela gasp beside her. The doctor nods and says it will take a few more hours for various tests to be conducted. He suggests they go home and he takes Roz's mobile number, promising to call the next morning.

'Right, let's go, nothing we can do right now.' Roz stares down at Angela who has sunk down on the bench again.

'Why didn't she tell me?' Angela's question is directed at the wall and then she turns her face up to Roz.

'Why should she? What is it to you? I'm looking after her now.' Roz picks up her handbag. 'Let's get out of here. This place gives me the creeps.' She will phone Steve later. Vienna can wait. Maybe they can go for the New Year weekend, if Eva feels better by then.

35

Angela takes to her bed as soon she and Roz return to Josefová, lying awake all night. The dark hours bring shapes and sounds back to her of thirty-six years ago. In this flat she had cowered, the sounds of gunfire in the square reverberating around the walls, the cries of Czech resistance fighters as they clashed over the barricades with Warsaw Pact troops, fearing the day when she might be dragged off to Pankrác prison as Štefan and so many of their friends had already been. Štefan. She had shared his ideals and his bed but even those links had not prevented her from the folly of her one mistake, her deep betrayal of his love and trust. And the vivid memory of the outcome of that fall now returns to haunt her as she recalls the long night when she had screamed in agony in the pangs of childbirth.

September 1968

Will this agony never end? I stagger around the room, reeling with each contraction, Ludmila's arm around me. That she should be with me now, after what I have done to her, tells me she is a far better person than I will ever be. 'It is the child who is important,' *she says,* 'not you, not me.'

'Promise me,' *I say over and over again,* 'that you will take it somewhere safe.' *Any day now, the knock on the door will surely come. Maybe I will be allowed to join Štefan in Pankrác prison. Even to know that he is in a cell somewhere close by, some hope may remain. But prison is no place for a baby. Either death or adoption by a state agency would be its fate. I lost Ilona before her time. This child may, at least, know me through my dear friend, Ludmila Šimková, whose loyal service I have repaid by shamefully breaking her trust and lusting after her husband.*

Finally, in the early hours - a daughter! Ludmila wraps her up tightly. The child appears healthy. I thank God for not having punished me with a stillborn again, as with Ilona. My few days with her are precious. Ludmila steals out at night time to bring food and water. I cuddle my daughter fiercely like a tigress. I cannot bear the thought of releasing her to the care of another, even to Ludmila. But what other choice do I have? The day of letting go comes too soon. I howl and hug her closely. I take her to the window and show her the sky. 'We will both see this sky, my little one, even if we are in different places for a while.' *'She is mine now,' says Ludmila, and I think she may enjoy inflicting this pain on me. But the child's safety must push aside my own selfish needs. Ludmila and I were meant to fight together as comrades, to die for each other in the Prague streets if we had to, so that our vision of true freedom would be restored to Czechoslovak citizens, not the Soviet version which was being foisted on them. But in the midst of this comradeship I took what I wanted, Ludmila's husband Tomaš for just one night, and this is now my punishment, to lose my second child.*

'We must go now', *says Ludmila.* I beg her, 'you will get a message to me, that you are safe? How? When? Where will you go?' *She says,* 'there is a group leaving tonight. We will cross the border by morning. After that, it is in God's hands where we finish our journey.'

I hold my baby daughter one last time and my tears flow without end. There is nothing I can give her to remind her of me. Please God, if I survive, then one day I will go to find her, for I cannot imagine, as things are right now, that this country will ever be the place to which she will want to return. I kiss Ludmila's hand and ask her forgiveness for my betrayal. I beg her to tell my daughter, one day, that I had no choice.

I will call her Eva.

36

Roz poured herself a generous measure of Scotch and sank into the leather sofa. The flat was too empty. There was no Eva to fuss at her to tidy up, scold her for the overflowing ashtray or to make lists for the week's shopping necessities. It was up to her now to look after Eva and she wasn't sure whether she was ready to face up to that responsibility. She had a sudden vision of being left alone here one day, to have to stare at these walls with just memories of angry exchanges to keep her company. She chided herself for her morbid thoughts – Eva would surely be allowed home in a few days. No point in thinking about what-ifs right now. She'd smuggle in some treats for her, something to make Christmas more bearable in that place. But one day, this flat really would be hers alone – she shook her head free of the thought. She texted Steve. *Have a good time in Vienna. Miss ya.* But she didn't want him to have too good a time. She wanted him to miss her too.

There was a beeping sound coming from Eva's handbag, still lying discarded on the floor from the mad rush when the ambulance had arrived. Two missed calls and a text alert from Will. A tide of jealousy rose within Roz – just a few weeks ago Eva needed her the most. *Well, what's he gonna do when it all comes out? Who's gonna pick up the pieces?*

Roz got up and crossed over to the window overlooking the square. Tomorrow would be Christmas Eve – Steve had told her that this was a bigger deal to Czechs than Christmas Day itself – and it looked like some people were starting to celebrate already. The restaurant opposite was brightly lit and packed with revellers. A blanket of snow made the world look innocent and she thought of fairy-tale book illustrations from her childhood, where Christmas pictures had indigo skies and powdery snowdrifts through which animals and small children cavorted. She remembered, that first meeting with Angela in Kavárna Slavia, how she had joked that she had come here to have a white Christmas for a change. Well, that wish at least had been granted.

Roz slept fitfully and was woken by her mobile soon after seven. In broken English, a nurse from the hospital announced that Eva was in a stable condition but that the doctor would like to meet with Roz before midday. Roz grunted and agreed. As she finished her shower, the door buzzer rang. Angela's anxious face peered in. 'I am sorry if this is too early for you, but has the hospital been in touch?'

Roz yawned and scratched her head. 'Yeah. I'm due to see the doctor before twelve.'

'May I accompany you?'

'Please yourself.'

They set off together, Roz feeling discomforted by Angela's presence beside her in the taxi. 'Did she know she was pregnant when she left England?' asked Angela quietly.

'No. It would have been too soon. And she never imagined, well, she and Alex...'

'Her husband?'

'Who else?' Roz laughed briefly at the possibility of Eva having an affair.

'But she knew she was ill?'

'Yes.'

Angela shook her head and fell silent. As they walked through the hospital entrance Roz muttered, 'you'd have thought they would try to cheer the place up with a few decorations.'

The doctor was the same as yesterday, and Roz wondered how long he had been on duty. His expression was sombre but the words were neutral. Eva was indeed stable. The miscarriage had not resulted in any complications, as far as he could see. However, the brain scan was causing them some concerns. There was a small amount of swelling. The next few days would be critical.

'How critical?' said Roz.

'If the swelling continues, we may need to intervene to reduce it. There are risks in such procedures.'

Angela said, 'she is young enough to recover from surgery?'

He sighed. 'Pani, we cannot tell. Overall - ,' he stroked the stubble on his chin, 'we know that things will deteriorate, but no one can say for sure how soon.'

'Come on! Weeks, months, years? You must have an idea!' Roz said, her voice rising.

He frowned. 'We are not in the gambling business! Pani McKinley understands the situation. She is accepting it.'

'Well, I'm bloody well not! I want a second opinion!' Roz said.

'As you wish. Now, she is awake but please do not exhaust her with your company.'

Angela fiddled with her glasses and took Roz by the arm. 'Come, my dear. We will be gentle with her, won't we?'

Eva was drifting in a soft morphine-induced haze, a half-world in-between sleep and wakefulness, light-flashes bursting through her eyelids like fireworks from time to time. Her hand rested on her stomach. An empty womb now. Thank God for not having had to initiate the loss herself. A thought flitted through her mind – how swollen would Camille's belly be now? Or had she already taken the path that she herself had been able to avoid? Within the space of a few weeks Alex had unintentionally created two children and lost at least one of them. Eva felt a stirring of pity for him. *This Christmas will be unimaginably hard for him*, and she was surprised at how sad that made her feel.

There was a loud thud as the door flew open and Roz strode in, all tossing red hair and stiletto boots clicking on the floor. Behind Roz's figure Eva could see Angela following, her normally erect figure looking slightly stooped.

'Hiya, at least you've got a room to yourself!' Roz's strident tones seemed to echo off the walls and made Eva wince.

Angela placed her arm on Roz's shoulder. 'Roz, please remember what the doctor said. Eva, my dear, it's so wonderful to see you at rest. How are you?'

'Bit sore. High as a kite on drugs.'

'The best way to be, chick!' Roz grinned.

'Eva, I am so sorry that you will be spending Christmas here.' Angela smoothed the bed blanket and fussed with the pillow.

'What can we bring you, my dear, to cheer you up?'

'Here,' said Roz, throwing Eva's mobile and charger on the bed. 'Lover boy will make you feel better! He's been trying to call you.'

'Oh!' Eva's face brightened. She reached out for the phone and saw the missed calls and text alert. She wanted Roz and Angela to go, to be alone with whatever Will had written and to think deeply about what to tell him.

Roz chuckled and turned to Angela. 'Told you it would help!'

Angela managed a half-smile. 'We so want you to come home soon. It would be wonderful if we could all celebrate the New Year together.'

'Oh!' Roz frowned and looked at Eva.

'It's all right, Roz. You should join Steve in Vienna. I'll be fine.'

'Yeah, well, we'll see. Get you home first, right?'

'The doctors aren't sure when - .'

'Yeah, well, you know what they're all like. Bunch of misery-guts. You're a fighter, you'll be up in no time.'

Eva turned her head away. 'Sure.'

Angela said, 'we'll come back this evening with something nice. The food is bound to be awful here, and Christmas Eve dinner won't be the same, will it?'

Eva recalled Christmas Eve with Baba from her childhood, the fried fillet of cod which replaced the traditional carp dish, the carols sung and presents opened after dinner, the stories of Baba tramping through knee-high snow in the mountains as a child under a clear blue sky. That weather was here now. But without Baba to comfort her.

'I want to sleep some more.'

Angela reached out to stroke Eva's hand. 'Sleep, my little angel,' she murmured, as Eva's eyes started to droop. 'We'll see you later.'

'You can't possibly take alcohol into the hospital!'

Roz scowled as Angela took the bottle of Scotch from her hand and carried it back to the kitchen. 'Well, it'll keep, I suppose.'

Angela had forced Roz to accompany her on a trip for food

and presents to take to Eva later that evening. She had then busied herself in her own kitchen, preparing the traditional carp and potato salad meal as she would always do for herself, setting aside a portion to take to the hospital. A few small cakes had been purchased at Maruška's and then some expensive toiletries as a gift. All in all, a small offering of Christmas. The main gift would wait until Eva was home.

'Jeez, this bag's heavy!' Roz picked up the small holdall beside Angela as they waited for the taxi.

'Just a little something. No one should be alone for Christmas.' Even if she usually was herself, but Roz didn't need to know that.

Eva was sitting up in bed and Angela was relieved to see a little colour had returned to her face. She seemed a little embarrassed by Angela's gifts but they chatted amiably, Eva laughing at the incident with the Scotch.

'We'll celebrate properly when you get home, chick,' Roz said.

'Thanks. It's a bit lonely here.'

Angela smiled. 'You won't be lonely once you're home. We'll celebrate all week, won't we Roz, and make it a Christmas to remember.'

'Steady on, Angela, or we'll all be back here with alcohol poisoning.'

Angela threw back her head and laughed. It seemed to her the world was suddenly brighter. As she and Roz walked part of the way home at her insistence – 'smell the air, Roz, look at that indigo sky, doesn't it make you feel glad to be alive?' – she observed all the lights in apartment blocks around them, and wondered at the family gatherings inside, remembering how she had always envied her friends with their children around them, however imperfect, on this one day of the year. But *I have my daughter back now and that's all I could ever wish for.*

37

'Happy Christmas, Eva.'

'You too, Will.' *I swallow hard.* 'Having a good time with your family?'

'Yeah. Catching up and stuff like that. You OK?'

'Yes.'

'Did you get my message?'

'Yes.'

'What are you up to?'

'Oh well, you know, just relaxing. Roz and I are cooking.'

'That sounds great. Listen, I've got to go, we've got more family coming in, it's getting a bit crazy here – will you be around when I get back?'

'Sure. When does your plane get in?'

'Late afternoon on the 3rd. Meet me then?'

My eyes close. 'Sure.' *Does that sound cool enough, or too much so?*

'Great. Look, I've really gotta go. Take care, Eva.'

'Will?'

'Yeah?'

I grip the phone. 'Miss you.'

There is silence for a moment, and then he says, 'I'm glad.' *The phone goes dead.*

What a good liar I have become. I lie about what I don't reveal – the hospital bed which is my Christmas dinner table too. The changes in my body that I can't control. How much of the truth will he ever be able to cope with?

Christmas Day morning found Eva depressed after the surprising gaiety of the evening before, surprising because of Angela's animation, like a young girl on a party night. Roz had joined in but had been pushed to the side-lines. Angela had prattled on about nothing in particular and Eva wondered whether she had taken a few drinks before leaving the house. Coming off the morphine drip last night hadn't helped. It given her the false sense of euphoria she had seen in her patients over the years and now her mood plunged. Knowing it would pass didn't make her feel any better about it. Will's call hadn't succeeded in cheering her up, reminding her only of the gulf that her secrets had created between them.

Hers was not the only mood to have taken a downward turn. Roz and Angela returned in the early afternoon. Angela was subdued and Roz looked like she had been up all night on a bender. *Can't she stay sober even for one night?* They all made some small talk but there were long silences too.

One of the nurses came in. 'Pani McKinley, you can go home tomorrow. The doctor will be here shortly.'

She should have been pleased to hear that. But going home meant facing reality. Her seizure in the ambulance had been a sharp reminder. *How am I going to get through each day now?*

'Well, that's great news, isn't it, chick?' Roz managed a smile.

'Yep.'

Angela leant forward and patted Eva's hand. 'We'll take good care of you. Don't worry.'

Angela asked Roz to come into her flat when they returned. The previous night she had grappled with a question. How Roz would react to it would give her an insight into what she should do.

Roz looked nonplussed to be invited in but made herself comfortable. Angela offered tea, then paused. 'You may wish for something a little stronger.'

Roz's eyes widened a little. 'Won't say no to that.' Angela poured them both a small measure of brandy, thought for a moment and then drank half of her glass in one go. 'Hey, steady on! You'll be competing with me soon!'

Angela forced a smile. 'I suggest you take some more yourself.' Her heart was beating furiously and she took a couple of deep breaths.

'Are you OK, Angela?'

Angela bowed her head. 'I have a story to tell you.'

Roz tilted her head. 'Go on.'

'A lot of things happened in the 1968 Prague uprising. You may well know the main events from what people have written over the years. But not everyone's story has been told. And maybe not all those stories should be told, in fact. People behave differently, in those kinds of situations. Life, truth, morals, they get distorted. People don't always think through the consequences of their actions.' Angela paused to take another sip. 'I take it you knew the lady who Eva calls Baba?'

'Yeah. I met her granny quite a few times. Scary lady. Can't say we got on.'

Angela smiled briefly. 'Scary? Yes, she could be. Incredibly brave woman.'

Roz nearly dropped her glass. 'Oh my God! So, you knew her! Jesus, and there's Eva wondering how she's going to – but why are you telling me, not her?'

'Because – because I don't know how much I should tell her.'

'Why? What's so bad about telling her about her granny? Not in the secret police, was she?' Roz dissolved into giggles.

'Please! This is difficult enough as it is!' Angela reached out to the brandy bottle for a refill. She placed her fingertips together as if in prayer before continuing. 'This lady, Baba, was a close friend of mine. We worked together, first in supporting Prime Minister Dubček in his Prague Spring movement, and then helping the Resistance when the Soviets invaded. Her name was Ludmila Šimková - .'

'Yes, I know that - .'

'She is not related to Eva.'

Roz's jaw dropped. *Is this how Eva will react, if I tell her too?*

Roz exploded at last. 'What the hell? Then who was she?'

'Ludmila was the only person I felt I could trust,' Angela gripped her hands together as she stared at Roz, 'to take my baby daughter out of the country to safety when I feared I might be arrested for helping the Resistance fighters.'

Roz frowned. 'So, what about your daughter? Why's that important?'

'Ludmila said she would care for her as if she were her own family. My daughter. Eva.'

'*Your daughter? Your daughter?* Is that what this is all about?'

Angela started breathing quickly. 'How can I tell her, Roz?'

'I don't believe it! Why are you talking such crap?'

Slowly, Angela removed her dark glasses, rubbed her eyes and turned to face Roz full on. Roz screwed up her face, then leant forward. 'Oh my God,' she said slowly, looking from one eye to another.

'Not a very common combination, is it, one green, one brown? Like Eva's? Does that help you believe me?'

Roz leant back on the sofa, eyes closed. 'What a mess!' Then her eyes flew open. 'You've had years to do something about this! Why did you never - ?'

'Because Ludmila would never permit me to contact Eva directly. All I had were a few photos she sent me when Eva was growing up. Then they must have moved because my letters were returned by the postal service and I could not find a way - .'

'What do you mean, she wouldn't let you contact her?'

Angela bowed her head. 'It was Ludmila's way of punishing me for what I had done. I had hurt her terribly. Eva's father was Ludmila's husband. It was a brief flash of love on my part – believe me, I have regretted it every day since - .'

'You cheated with your best friend's husband? Fucking hell, the high and mighty fake countess who has the cheek to look down her nose at me - .'

'Believe me, Roz, you couldn't say anything worse now than what I have told myself all these years. Yes, I was cruel, but not intentionally. I was selfish and everyone has had to pay for that. I am so very, very sorry.' She swallowed hard.

'You shouldn't be telling *me* that, you bitch, you should be apologizing to Eva!'

'Well, that's what I have been grappling with. You see, knowing now how things are with her, well, could she cope with the truth? Do I have the right to bring this misery into her life when she needs so much help to face her future? Roz, I need your help. You know her better than anyone else. How could she bear to hear the truth?'

Roz was silent for a few minutes. 'Baba was her life. She idolized her. For eighteen years they were the only family each other had. Everyone else had died in the uprising, she said.' She shook her head. 'I don't know. Right now, I couldn't tell you what to do.'

'But how can I look at her every day, knowing what I know, and not share this? I am so overwhelmed to have her back in my life and want so much to show her I love her - .'

'Because it's not just about you, is it Angela?'

38

Eva groaned slightly but managed to shuffle a few steps.

'You're doing great, chick.' Roz held Eva around the waist.

'So, why does it feel like I've gone thirteen rounds with Mike Tyson, then?'

'Stop moaning, woman, and get a move on!'

Nurses and doctors make the worst patients, Eva grinned to herself. It felt good to be leaving hospital and Roz had promised to wait on her hand and foot when they got home. Eva knew that wouldn't last more than an hour or so, but it didn't matter. Her mood had lifted. Will had sent a couple of loving texts. No, not those three words. They weren't necessary. The feelings were clear anyway. She had made up her mind to tell him about the miscarriage, about Douglas, her illness, everything. If there was any point to this relationship, they had to be honest with each other. If he cared, she felt they would find a way to work through it all. She was tired of lying, half-truths, and the whole mess that had triggered her escape. She was running towards something now and she would make sure to enjoy it for as long as she could.

Roz loaded up the kitchen with food and drink – not the run-of-the-mill daily groceries but special treats - smoked salmon, good champagne ('not that fizzy Czech Bohemia Sekt stuff,' Roz sniffed), wild boar pate and fresh salads, French bread and olives. 'No bloody overcooked turkey for us this year, chick.' As they stuffed themselves with food, she asked, 'will you be OK if I go to

Vienna, then, on Friday? I'll be back Sunday night, promise.'

'Sure. You'll have a great time.'

'You could come too, you know?'

'If I need anything I've got Angela.'

'Never mind her! You phone me if there's a problem – right?'

'I'll be fine. Honest.'

'Oh yeah, I forgot.' Roz scrunched up her face for a moment, but then brightened. 'I've made a New Year's resolution.'

'Oh? Long time since you bothered with those.'

'Yeah. I'm gonna get clean. No more of the white stuff, you know?'

'Oh Roz!' Eva's eyes filled with tears. 'If you really mean that, then that's one of the best Christmas presents I've ever had!'

They hugged each other. 'Keeping the booze a bit, mind, I'm not going that far!'

'We'll work on that!' Eva grinned.

The snow was still thick under their boots as they strolled through the streets each day, Eva holding on to Roz's arm for support, still a little dizzy at times. The city was filled with more tourists than locals and Eva wondered whether many Czechs had disappeared off to their country cottages for the whole week. Lying in bed on Wednesday night she resolved to start this very week her research into Baba and the rest of her family. She had looked again at the old photos in Baba's box. What had happened to her mother's body after she died in Austria? Would it have been returned to Prague? Eva decided to ask Angela where to start the process. There had to be a death certificate from a registry office and maybe that would lead to discovering a burial place. She had a sudden crazy idea of trying to get Baba's remains transferred from London to Prague, to re-unite her in death with her daughter Tereza. Then, Douglas' comment returned to her, when she had told him she would want to return to visit his grave. 'Sure, lassie, but I won't be there anyway.' It was a romantic notion, this idea of bodies buried next to each other. The dead had no need for it.

When Ivana phoned this morning I told her what I had done.

'Hraběnka, why did you tell that woman? She has no right to know.'

'But she knows Eva better than anyone else. I needed to know how she might react.'

'And now?'

'She thinks I should keep quiet, that it would hurt Eva too much to know the truth.'

Ivana went quiet. I could guess what she was thinking. We have all become used to the convenience of half-truths and deceptions, hardwired into us during the Communist era when truth could be dangerous.

'You must keep her distracted from the idea of family research, Hraběnka.'

'Well, she may become disheartened when she faces the bureaucracy of the process. She would not be the first person to start and then give up.'

I was so happy to see Eva return from hospital on Sunday. Roz seems to be more solicitous, no longer abandoning Eva for her own jaunts. I saw her staggering out of a taxi heavily-laden with grocery bags from the more expensive food shops. Eva deserves to have the finer things in life. If she outlives me she will have this house and what other assets I have. I phoned my lawyer this morning to start the process of making a new will. But if I outlive her…I can't bear to think about that right now. I promised Roz I would say nothing. Too much harm has been done in the name of good intentions.

Since that night I have not slept well. Old sins will not allow me peace now. Ludmila would understand that. We had both seen too much of what people could do to each other. But then there were the heroes and heroines too. I should like to be able to tell Eva how Ludmila nursed the wounded, ran messages despite the danger to herself and rendered me a service to prevent me from losing my child to enemies, despite the insult of her husband's adultery with me. And yet, I ended up losing my child after all. Ludmila had every right to be angry with me, to withhold Eva from me. But could she not have found it in her heart, eventually, to allow us to reconnect once Eva was old enough to understand? Maybe she would have, one day, if her early death had not cheated all of us. There is too much pain in my heart. I am not sure how much more of it I can take. To find Eva again, now, but with the knowledge that she will be taken from me once more, irrevocably this time, is the cruellest stroke of retribution.

I am so tired today. This morning I managed to get out at last to my doctor's appointment. He was delighted that my eye infection was clearing up. 'No more dark glasses, Hraběnka!' *I should have been glad about that. But these eyes of mine will ruin everything, if I allow them to. I told him I had got used to wearing them. He shook his head.* 'You are glamorous enough, Hraběnka, you do not need to add to your mystique!'

Perhaps I am going down with a virus. I am clumsy and nearly trip over my living room rug. I think of retiring to bed but the worst of my thoughts crowd in on me when I lie down. I am too tired to paint but I could try a little sketching, before the light fades. I sit myself down by the window. Below, in the square, I can see a taxi waiting and then Roz emerging from the house and getting into the car. Where is she going? I think of Eva, alone now, and I am tempted to go upstairs on the pretext of checking her well-being.

This sketch is a poor creation. I rub it out, and start again. The effort of concentration should be good for me, to lose myself in something of beauty which can restore my mental balance.

The door buzzer sounds. Eva is standing there and my heart lurches. She asks me if I am all right, concern in her eyes, and I have to resist pulling her into an embrace. I try to sound irritated at her interruption, telling her about my sketching efforts. She says, 'I'll come back another time, then,' *and my resistance melts as I invite her in. Every moment with her counts now.*

She tells me she wants my advice about where to start her family research. I ask, 'what's the hurry?' *She replies that it would make her feel better, that this is why she came here and that her seizure has brought the urgency of her situation back to her. A shiver runs through me. She is so accepting of her fate, so matter-of-fact — is that a product of her nursing experience? Can she have neutralized her feelings to such an extent?*

'Eva, it's so complicated here. You need to have a certain

amount of information already before you can even start. And the process could take months, years even.'

'Well, I'd better make a start now, then. Will the archive offices be open this week?'

'Probably not – look, you need to have her address at the time of her residence and dates and - .'

'Address? I'm not even sure whether it was in Prague itself or the surrounding area. How on earth do I find out?'

I want to throw out a false trail, something to keep her occupied but which will take her only to a dead-end. How unfair this is! How can I play this cat-and-mouse game with her?

Then, from a carrier bag beside her, she takes out a box I recognize. A carved oak box I gave to Ludmila many years before as a Christmas present. A blood vessel in my left temple starts throbbing as Eva opens the box and extracts three black-and-white photos. My dark glasses obscure some detail but as she holds the pictures out to me, I remember. I should remember. After all, I took two of them with my little box camera.

She starts to talk about the little she knows, how Ludmila/Baba told her who they were. Their faces stare back at me accusingly. Tomaš, her husband, my lover for one night. Tereza, her daughter with her own husband Václav. Others, friends who were with us in the struggles, all gone now for one reason or another. The third picture I did not take. Who took it? I cannot remember now. I freeze when I see it, then look at Eva to see what happens. She carries on talking. She has not recognized the woman in that third photo. I hardly recognize myself. What have the intervening years done to me?

I listen to her without hearing the words, only the longing in her voice. The urgency of her tone. I can't bear it. I rise, offering to make tea, but as I turn I feel the room spinning around me and I fall. My head hits the side of my armchair. My dark glasses fall on to the rug. She and I both scrabble at the same time to retrieve them and our eyes meet for a second. She appears startled and I snatch the glasses back up, cramming them on to my face. We are both sitting on the rug now. Her eyes register a question.

Neither of us have any more tears left to shed for now. I did it mostly for her, not just me. But now she must hate me, even though she has not spoken those words. It is her silence which hurts me more than anything she could say to me now. I betrayed the person closest to her - mother and grandmother combined – and who can say whether that can ever be forgiven? I rambled, it all spilled out of me like a burst pipe, and I saw confusion, rejection, and disbelief all register in her face as I sought to tell the story in some kind of order. Half the time it was as if I was talking to myself, justifying every action, trying to pre-empt every objection. I fizzled out, too exhausted to continue. I could not have repeated it. Her tears were of anger to start with and then the depth of grief was plunged. At the end I thought, she might have another seizure right now from the shock and it would all be my fault, just like the whole catalogue of errors. She had wanted to tear up the photos. 'No, if you must destroy something, take mine.' *I could have said, you could kill me now, I deserve it, but what would that achieve?*

Secrets and lies. They kill you slowly from within, like a cancer. The truth is quicker, cleaner, a quick sword-thrust rather than the slow sawing of a blunt knife.

She threatens to leave, go home, and then says she can't. I say I don't understand and she laughs, a hysterical edge to the sound. She is leaning against the window and I have a sudden fear that she will fling it open and jump out. I beg her to sit but I don't think she can hear me. Then she turns back to me.

'You will never be my mother. You are not fit to mention Baba's name, ever again. I don't care why you did what you did. Wanted to replace Ilona? You could have adopted one of those poor bloody orphans you and Baba picked up, you could have helped them get over the parents the Soviets murdered. That's what real love is.'

Those last words of hers hang in the air for the rest of the evening after she has stormed out. Did I do the wrong thing? Would she have found out anyway and then accused me of deception? Must I lose her again, even now?

39

I now feel like a stranger in both lands, neither Czech nor British. Throughout this whole mess, this series of messes, only Baba has not let me down. We didn't need to share a bloodline to be a family. If Angela didn't deserve to be a part of my life when I was growing up, why should she now?

I can hear them downstairs now, Roz screaming at Angela, 'why did you fucking have to tell her?' We'll have to find another flat. I can't bear to stay here now. Roz knew. She told me Angela had prepped her. So, if the old woman hadn't broken down then Roz would have been holding it back from me too. I'm the last one to know, just like with Alex and Camille. They can all go to hell.

Roz is mad at me because I'm mad at her. She doesn't get it. She says she was trying to protect me and that she couldn't help it if Angela had chosen to tell her first. I'm too wiped out to figure it out now. I go to bed without eating. Roz has turned the TV up loud so I can't even hear myself think.

In the morning I am surprised to find I slept at all. I hear Roz stomping around. Her flight to Vienna is due to leave late morning. A soft knock on my door.

'I'm going now, chick.'
I don't answer.
'Eva, you OK?'
'Just go, Roz.'
'Don't open the door to her, chick, if she comes calling. Phone if you need me?'
I think she must be gone, then I hear, 'I'm sorry, Eva. I wanted to protect you, that's all.' *I turn over and bury my face in the pillow. The muffled sound of the front door shutting. Alone for the New Year. I don't care.*

I stay in bed most of the day. I hear the door buzzer about six-thirty in the evening but remain under the duvet. If it's Angela then she has a cheek to try to see me. Does she think this can all blow over so quickly?

At just after seven a text message beeps. I don't want to talk to Roz. As I glance at the screen my spirits lift for a moment. Will's number. 'How are you? Can I call you?' But how can I talk to him without talking about all this? A few days ago I decided I would tell him everything, take the chance. Can I bear to add this story to the sorry pile? I have to think about what I don't want to think about. But I need to hear the voice of someone who hasn't betrayed me, who makes me laugh, who may know how to comfort me. 'I'm here now', I text back and he calls within a minute.

'I'm sorry I didn't call before – my family is driving me crazy! Are you OK?'

'Sure. Well – I haven't felt that great this week.'

'Oh, I'm sorry. What's wrong?'

Where do I start? 'Just – run down I suppose. Feeling a bit weird.'

'Wish I was there with you now.'

'Do you?'

He laughs. 'I don't do phone sex, I'm afraid.'

I giggle, despite myself. He is still laughing.

'What are you doing tonight? Going out with Roz?'

'She's in Vienna for the weekend with her latest man.'

'You're on your own? That's not right. Look, we'll have our own celebration when I get back on Monday. Promise.'

'I wish it was Monday now.'

'Me too.'

We talk for an hour and I can't believe how good it feels to be distracted from everything going on here. He tells me stories about his wacky aunt and the tricks he and his cousins have played on her. He's like a child, warm, trusting, spontaneous. I can't imagine him as a serious lawyer. So different from Alex. Why couldn't I have met him thirteen years ago instead? He promises to call again later when it's midnight here. 'That way I can see the New Year in twice,' *he says. It's early afternoon in Toronto, he tells me, and they're all going skiing tomorrow. The conditions are perfect this year, he says. I try to imagine him, swirling, whooshing through a cloud of powdery snow.* You can join us next year, *he says, and I fight back the tears.*

When the call is over I stand by the window and think how much I will miss the view of this square, because I know I cannot stay here now. The fact that Angela told me I was born in her flat one floor below makes it even harder. What about Roz? Who knows? Maybe she'll be moving in with Steve if they get serious. She'll dump me again like she did when she married Howard. A new life for her, and maybe she deserves a break too. If she can clean up her act there's a future for her. I'll find somewhere else. I won't throw myself at Will. If something develops naturally, well, I'd be lying if I said I wouldn't want it to. But, equally, I can learn to be on my own now. If I can find work that stimulates me and pays the bills I will feel happy enough. The rest is optional.

I curl up on the sofa with a glass of red wine and my duvet wrapped round me, watching a dubbed version of an American rom-com without following it. My mind is elsewhere, thinking back to Baba, wondering how she could have stayed silent all those years about what had happened here. How often did she feel tempted to tell me even part of the story? The woman in the photo, 'someone we knew, not important,' Baba had said. How could I not have spotted the younger Angela? Her eyes, obscured by those damn glasses, had held the key. How could she have lived with herself, all these years? Did Baba see her husband's infidelity every time she looked into my eyes too? It must have been unbearable for her. I feel myself dozing after a while, the gentle pull on my eyelids and the soft slip into a dream.

When the phone wakes me I think, why is Will calling the landline? Then it stops suddenly. I check my mobile for missed calls or texts. Nothing. It's nearly midnight. He should call any second now. Then the landline rings again. I hear thumping music and raucous laughter in the background.

'Hello?'

The caller's voice is muffled, stumbling over words. Not Will's voice.

'Hello? I can hardly hear you. Who is this?'

He said her body had turned blue.

At least, I thought that's what Steve said. The background noise, his garbled speech, I couldn't take it in at first. I had to keep asking him to repeat things and his tone, at first desperate, became irritable. 'It's not my fault', he kept saying and then, 'I didn't know who else to phone. This was the only number in her phone memory apart from mine. I don't know what to do,' he finished lamely.

Roz had promised me she would stop the drugs. What was it, one last shot before the New Year resolution kicked in? One bad tab dropped in some backstreet dive. It could have been anyone's bad luck. But Roz had never taken chances like that before. Had Steve egged her on? Had she been just too drunk *to think properly? I should have been with her. It wouldn't have happened if I had been there to look out for her. It's my fault.*

'What happens now?' Steve asked again, and I could hear the panic in his voice. I didn't know either. I had no choice but to seek help from the one person who could shortcut the process with her connections. Angela was bleary-eyed when I rang her door but she said she would phone Patrick Jennings at the Embassy who would, in turn, speak to his counterpart in the British Embassy in Vienna. She appeared shocked by the news but turned surprisingly calm in her practical handling of the situation. When I called Steve back she took the phone from me when it fell from my shaking hand and asked Steve quietly for his location and the name of the police officer in charge. She told me to go to bed whilst she called Patrick but I couldn't move from where I was sitting. Whilst she was on the phone to Patrick I managed to rise and moved to the door. I could hear her voice behind me, suddenly calling out, 'where are you going?', but I rushed down the stairs and out to the church in the square which was lit up by inset lights as a beacon in the surrounding darkness. In the falling snow I leaned my forehead against the wall, clenched my fist and started hammering it against the cement, repeatedly, feeling no pain until the blood began to trickle down my forearm.

When Patrick called back the next morning I was still awake. Angela had tried to stay up with me but eventually gave in about three a.m. I don't remember the hours passing or even what sounds from outside accompanied the arrival of dawn. I had been, in my mind, in another place, the school playground in Finchley, with Roz defending me against the bullies. And then the flat in Little Russell Street with her underwear strewn all over the bathroom floor and me screaming at her that it was her turn to clean the toilet. Roz hugging and laughing with Gianni in his restaurant. Her toast to our first week of freedom here. I couldn't even cry to release the pain inside me.

Patrick's voice was gentle. 'I'm sorry to ask you this, but would you agree to identify the body?' *That's all Roz is now, a cold body on a slab somewhere. He hadn't even used her name. You could fly to Vienna on Sunday evening, he said, I'll arrange a hotel and you can go to the city mortuary the following morning.*

'What happens then?'

'I'll make arrangements to fly her back to England and for you to return here.'

'There's no one back there to help. I want to go with her.'

I could hear a soft sigh at the other end. 'Of course. I understand. I'll make sure it's all sorted out.' *He paused.* 'I'm so sorry, Eva.'

Angela didn't fuss around me. I don't think I could have coped with that. I didn't want to be touched by her. 'You should eat something and try to snatch some sleep, at least,' *was as far as she pushed me.*

Walking back into Roz's bedroom was the hardest thing to do. I sat there and breathed in her musky scent and the essence of stale cigarette smoke on the bedclothes. I lay down on the bed and buried my face in her pillow. Later, I laid her suitcase on the bed and opened her wardrobe. As I folded up all the items carefully in her case and returned to close the wardrobe my eyes were drawn to the holdall. Howard's money. I picked up the bag and unzipped it slowly. It was still half-full. Should I count it? I couldn't bear to touch the notes. Blood money, I thought. If Howard had treated her better she wouldn't have had a reason to leave. He didn't deserve to have it back but I couldn't bear to keep it either. Burn it? The thought did cross my mind. It should go to charity, I finally decided. I wanted no more of it now.

I left the bed as it was. To strip it and wash the sheets and covers would have been to eradicate Roz's presence forever from this place and I wasn't ready to do it. When I closed her bedroom door behind me as I left her room the dull thud seemed to echo through the flat.

The flat was my prison until it was time to leave on Sunday afternoon. Roz was around me, in the clothes she had left strewn on her bed, the half-empty coffee cup and ashtray on her bedside table. I couldn't bear to clean it up just yet. I ripped up the diary I had started a few weeks ago. There was nothing about the last week I wanted to remember. In all the chaos I had forgotten about Will's planned call until the Saturday evening. Two missed calls and three texts. How could I not have heard them? He was concerned, that much was clear from his messages. He deserved to know why I wouldn't be here when he returned to Prague, but it was a hard call to make. He fell silent and I sat there, weeping silently. Finally, he said he would change his plans and fly directly to Vienna instead. That just made me cry even harder.

I had been embarrassed at seeking Angela's help and maybe she had sensed this as she made no attempt to disturb me through those long hours. She must have heard me on the stairs because as I waited for the taxi outside, she suddenly appeared at the front door. 'Is there anything I can do for you whilst you're away?' *I shook my head and picked up my case and Roz's as the taxi pulled up. The wind cut my face and I couldn't stop trembling.* 'God go with *you,'* said Angela and I stood stiffly as I allowed her to embrace me.

I sat in one of the departure lounges at Prague airport, watching a mother try to calm her fractious toddler. He was howling and pulling at her clothes, trying to nestle into her chest but he couldn't seem to get comfortable. She looked worn out and embarrassed by the looks other travellers were casting at them as she tried to shush him. It must be close to his bedtime, I was thinking, why on earth would she be taking him on a long journey now? Where was everyone going? Were they on their way home from family visits after the Christmas break? Life would be returning to a normal routine for many of them. I couldn't remember what a normal life felt like now.

When I saw on the departure board that my flight to Vienna was boarding at gate B6 I had a sudden urge not to go. I sat there, wrestling with the what-ifs circling around in my mind, until the flashing red lights appeared beside the flight number on the board and I grabbed my cabin bag and sped down the corridor, brushing past dawdling family groups.

The official at the mortuary is very kind. He says I can stay in the room for as long as I like. She will be laid out on a bed, he says, not in a coffin yet because the post-mortem will be held tomorrow morning. I wish he had not told me that. The thought of her being sliced open, the organs removed and examined....He leads me down the corridor. It's so cold and quiet, our footsteps echoing on the polished linoleum floor. I can't smell anything. I had expected it might smell like a hospital, all bleach and overcooked vegetables, but the air seems pure and sweet. There's a window in the wall of the room where he stops. My heart starts beating fast as I see a draped form on a trolley, nothing visible. An image of Douglas flashes into my mind.

The official goes before me, opens the door quietly and stands at the head of the bed. He looks up at me, enquiringly, and I nod my head quickly. With both hands he lifts back the sheet swiftly.

My hand flies to my mouth. He steps to my side and I feel his hand briefly on my arm as he steers me to a chair nearby, and then leaves as quietly as he had entered.

How could that bundle of energy have been transformed into this waxen effigy? Death has smoothed out the creases around her eyes and mouth and between her eyebrows – the perfect cosmetic surgeon. Her red hair is matted and tangled and I'm angry that no one has brushed it. Her skin has a bluish tinge.

Any moment now and her eyes might shoot open, blazing green and from that wide mouth would issue a shriek of laughter or a stream of expletives directed at me, perhaps. She had incinerated herself from within.

'You stupid bitch,' I say over and over again, as I rock back and forth on the chair, my arms wrapped tightly around my waist, tears dripping on to my coat. Then I lift my handbag and slip my hand inside the inner compartment. I find it at last and smooth out the creases on the pink-tinted paper that bears her name. I place the Eurostar return ticket beside her head and bend down to kiss her gently on the forehead.

'We're going home,' I whisper and I feel I can hear a soft sigh in the room.

40

After Eva left the mortuary she sat in a café and wondered whether she had the courage to see where Roz had died. The police would probably tell her, if she dared ask. What would be the point, though? She thought about the gestures some people make by the side of a road where a loved one has lost their life, a small bundle of drooping flowers with a battered sheet of paper, words scrawled in grief with the ink running and faded through exposure. Such a simple gesture, simple yet empty – or it would be for Eva because that could never represent what Roz had been about. A candle snuffed out before its time.

The day was overcast, clouds threatening rain or sleet with a keen wind cutting through her layers of clothes. Patrick had said it would be a few days before she could travel to England but that he would do his best to speed up the bureaucratic contortions. *There's no rush,* she had said, *Roz isn't going anywhere without me* and she wondered whether he was shocked at her levity. She didn't know how to feel anymore. Back in Prague was a mother she couldn't accept as her own. Baba, Douglas, Roz....why did they have to leave her?

Will's plane was due to land in an hour. She wanted his comfort but dreaded the conversation to come.

Will's sitting there, staring at the floor. Not at me. Sometimes he rubs his eyes but mostly his hands are still, clenched in his lap. Can't he bear to look at me? Would I, if I had just heard the whole damn story?

I wish he'd say something, anything. No. Not anything, not 'goodbye'. But maybe that's all I can expect. I have to clean up this mess myself, by myself. I feel drained, every ounce of energy has seeped away with every word and now there's just a dull thudding in my temples and an acidic taste in my mouth.

Then he lifts his face to me at last, his expression bewildered, and I start to shake uncontrollably. 'My God, Eva,' *is all he manages to say and I feel it's all over.*

'Yes, well, now you know everything. I'm sorry if – look, just go, all right? You shouldn't have come – this was a dumb idea - .'

He shakes his head and looks down at his hands again. 'How the hell have you lived with this all this time? Why didn't you tell me before?'

'Tell you? For God's sake, Will, I don't even know why I'm telling you this now, only…so, now you know who, or what, you've been sleeping with.'

'Stop it, Eva, it's not a joke.'

'Look, that's it, I understand if you just want to walk out that door now. In fact, why don't you, just go. Just go now!' *My voice catches in my throat. Poor bastard, guess he wasn't expecting the rest of this, was he? He had walked into my hotel room, hugged me close, saying sorry about Roz, and then it had hit him like a tidal wave. I couldn't keep it in, desperate to confess everything, to have it pour out of me like a cleansing shower. As I had rambled on, I felt the urge to lash out at Angela and even Baba for keeping Angela's secret.*

'Just about everyone has lied to me,' *I keep repeating,* 'and I don't feel I can do the same myself anymore.' *So, I haven't spared any details, however grim. If I knew the predicted date of my own death I would tell him that too.*

Funny, but I had felt better for a moment, as if a huge tumour had been removed from my guts but then I shift my gaze from the window to Will, see the frozen pain in his face. He looks smaller now, deflated, and incredulous.

'Please go,' *I repeat but he doesn't move.*

'When do you go to England?'

'Day after tomorrow.'

'I'll go with you.'

A shudder of hope mixed with fear shoots through me. 'No. It's not your problem. I have to do this on my own.'

'Do what?'

'After the funeral, I'm going to see Alex.'

'But why?'

'I want to know – I want to know whether he went to the police, whether I should try to defend myself.'

'And what would that achieve? You could go to jail.'

'Maybe. But then, look at what I did. Or, maybe they'll suspend a sentence with my circumstances…'

'Eva, why put yourself through that at all?'

'Because I'm tired of looking over my shoulder, that's why! Wondering if someone's going to knock on my door one day.'

'You need a good lawyer. I can find someone for you -.'

'Please let me sort this out for myself! I don't want anyone to control me anymore!'

'It's not control, sweetheart, I want to help you. I'm not going anywhere till we talk this out.'

'Bastard,' *I mutter and suddenly his face softens.*

'Yeah, so I've been told many times.'

41

The plane circled for an eternity above Manchester, fog delaying the landing. Eva gazed out of the window at occasional glimpses of the sprawl of suburbia and industrial estates below. For the first time since she and Roz had fled from home she found herself wondering about Howard, whether she should tell him about Roz's death and whether he would care – beyond, perhaps, whether he would get back the rest of his money. *Have the DVD and Roz's letter to the police hit their target? Hope so. The bastard deserves to squirm.*

Patrick Jennings had made all the arrangements for a funeral on the Thursday of that week. Eva had taken Will around Moss Side where Roz had grown up before moving to London in her teens with her mother. 'I can see why they left,' remarked Will. It occurred to Eva that maybe Roz would have met a similar end if she had stayed here. Things were changing for the better around here but it still wouldn't have been Roz's choice to return to her home city. *But Prague is not her home either, and at least she can be reunited with her own mother Audrey in the same grave.*

Thursday morning was bright and crisp. On a day like this last January Roz had worn the silver fox fur coat Howard had bought her for Christmas. As she had pirouetted in front of Eva she called the present a guilt offering. Eva had managed to cram it into her suitcase before leaving Prague. Today they were burying Roz in it.

Will stood beside Eva, his arm through hers. She imagined

Roz rolling her eyes in mock despair at her tears. Eva wanted to say to her shadow – *did you mean to take that tab? Did it get that bad or just crazy?* The wind ruffled Will's hair but now was not the time to want to stroke it. He stood close enough to Eva so she could hear his breathing and that feeling kept her warm and strong. It sustained her as Roz's coffin was lowered into the cold unforgiving grave.

They were the only mourners, just the two of them with their coat collars turned up in a futile defence against the icy wind. The service seemed to drag on forever and Eva listened to the priest's dirge of familiar phrases and wondered whether she could believe a single word of it. She had never had time for the notion of an afterlife, apart from that moment at Baba's funeral, eighteen years before, when she had found it impossible to imagine a world without Baba and had clung to the idea that her spirit might still linger with her in future years. If it did, she had not been aware of it. *Where was your spirit, Baba, in the last few months when I needed it the most?*

As the service came to an end, Eva fancied she could hear a sigh in her ear and Roz muttering, 'for fuck's sake, can't we go for a drink now?' An involuntary smile spread over Eva's face but she hid it behind a gloved hand. It was a little flip of something that lifted her spirits, if only for a second.

Will had to return to Prague the next morning. A big case to work on, no way he could postpone it, he apologized.

'I'll be fine,' she said.

'When will you come home?' Will asked.

Where is my home now? The first words from the Czech national anthem came into her mind, '*Kde domov můj?*' *Where is my homeland?*

That question stayed with her on the train to London that evening. Will had accompanied her and they would stay in central London together overnight before he took an early-morning flight from Heathrow to Prague. She had only been away from England for six weeks and yet it felt as if she was seeing everything around her after a lifetime's absence. Nerves made her jumpy as soon as the Tube train neared Ealing Broadway. Will had wanted to come with her, fearful of Alex's reaction. 'I have to do this on my own,' she had insisted.

Just a few minutes now. It was a quarter to nine in the evening. *What if Alex is working on a night shift? I can hardly just march into the hospital to track him down. How many people there might know me?* She walked quickly from the station and stood outside her house – their house – in the darkness, hesitating. A solitary light was burning in the porch. *That means nothing. Alex could have left that on if he's gone to work for the evening.* Her finger hovered over the doorbell for a minute before she jabbed it. And waited. The front door remained shut. *Now what do I do?*

She turned to leave but a sound behind her made her jump. The sound of a door-chain being unclasped. A slit of light as the front door was opened a fraction. Then the light flooded her face as she saw Alex open the door fully.

'Christ Almighty – Eva!'

She took just one step forward.

'For God's sake, where the hell have you been? Get in before someone sees you!'

'I haven't come to stay, Alex.'

'Just get in!'

Even with the light on the hall seemed dim, smaller even, than the last time she was here. In this space she had been confronted with the evidence of Alex's adultery and here was the spot where she and Alex had fought after Douglas' death. She looked down the corridor towards the room which had been Douglas' and struggled with the urge to go in, as if he was still there.

'Where have you been, Eva?'

'Away.'

'I thought you were dead, somewhere. I've been worried sick.'

'That would have been convenient, wouldn't it? My punishment?' She sighed. 'I'm only back because – well, I wanted to say sorry. But believe me, it's what he wanted -.'

'I don't want to hear about that! Have you any idea what I've been through?'

'What did you do with the note?'

'Used it, of course! Did you not think the post mortem would show up the high level of morphine? They would have thought it was me or Miriam. What were you thinking? He probably only had a couple of weeks to go, you saw how he was going downhill.'

'He wanted it so much – he wanted to be with Catherine - .'

'You must have said something to influence him! He never talked to me about any of that!'

'No. He wouldn't. And you were never here, were you?'

'That's not fair!'

'That's just how it was, Alex.'

The anger burned in his face. *Why did I bother coming back?* She turned to leave.

'Did you do it to spite me, because of what happened with Camille?'

'Camille? Please, give me some credit! So, is she here now, in our bed?'

He breathed hard. 'She went back to France just before Christmas. She had the termination a couple of weeks ago.'

Two babies, now none. 'Well, now you can make a fresh start yourself.'

'And you? Are you – all right?'

'I had another seizure, if that's what you mean.'

'Oh!'

'Not dead yet, though.'

'Don't say that.'

'What do you care? Look, I shouldn't have come only -,' she bit her lip. 'I wanted to visit Douglas' grave.'

'Too bad. He was cremated.'

'What? Why?'

'It's what everyone does now, isn't it? He wouldn't have wanted anyone to bother with tending a grave. It's what we did for Catherine, after all.'

She felt cheated. 'Where are the ashes?'

'God, Eva, why do you care? If you must know, I sprinkled them in the crematorium garden.' He suddenly laughed. 'Maybe I should have done it on his favourite golf course instead, I don't know. What does it matter?'

She looked long and hard at him. Alex would never change. *Is he destined now to live alone, married to his job until, one day, no one wants him there either?*

'Bye.' She stepped to the door.

'Wait! Where are you going?'

She turned again. 'Are the police looking for me?'

'I don't know. I told them about your problem. I think they checked it out. Maybe they won't take it up. You don't have to run away again.'

'You don't get it, do you? I was running away from you too.' *He looks shocked. Did he not realize?*

'Is there someone to look after you?' There was fear in his face now and she almost relented.

'I've always looked after myself, haven't I? And everyone else?' She looked down. 'Roz is dead. She came with me, to look after me….' She burst into tears. He stepped forward but she shrank from him.

'Sorry to hear that. What happened?'

'Bad drugs. Look, we've all made mistakes. Let's just admit that, OK?'

She rushed out and ran down the road without looking back.

Baba's grave in East Finchley Cemetery was covered in rotting leaves and Eva spent an hour cleaning the white marble, scouring away the mould and adding some silk flowers to the embedded vase. A conifer nearby swayed in the gentle breeze. Today felt like an early spring day, the fierce winds of the past few days had abated and weak sunshine tried to warm her back. As cemeteries went, it was a cheerful spot. When she was younger she used to come and have silent conversations with Baba, pass on her news. Today, she had a different kind of story to tell. *Why did you never tell me? Did you think it was better left unsaid? What should I do now?* She listened for some kind of answer in a sign, but nothing came.

When she had returned to the hotel the night before, exhausted from her argument with Alex, Will had held her all night. The twists and turns of the past month had depleted her energy reserves and she lay in his arms too tired to focus on anything but the sensation of being cared for, the dawning realization that nothing was guaranteed to last, either good or bad, and that peace would only come if she accepted that fact.

Will said, 'OK, so what Angela did was wrong, but she's paid for it in missing you from her life. I guess she's just as human as the rest of us. Give her some time.'

'But how could she make Baba pay such a terrible price too, to raise the child of an unfaithful husband and a friend she thought she could trust with her life? She didn't deserve that. No one would. How can I forgive Angela for that? Baba will always feel like my flesh and blood. How does Angela think she can replace her?'

'She's bound to feel desperate to make it up to you in any way she can. Perhaps she can still be your friend, in some way? She doesn't have to be your mother too, right now. Maybe that will change for you. Maybe not. Just see how you feel each day.'

'I came to look for Baba's family. What's the point now, if there's no blood tie?'

'If she still feels like your family, then why not? What about her story? And your father's, too?'

'He betrayed her. I don't want to know any more about him than that.'

Nothing made sense to her at the moment. They had fallen asleep together and she had dreamed of Baba again.

The taxi is waiting for Eva outside the cemetery. As they drive through the North London streets she knew in her childhood she wonders whether she will ever return again. The Friday afternoon traffic around Heathrow is nose-to-tail but she has allowed plenty of time. There will be no mad rush on this particular journey, plenty of time to reminisce and plan. In Prague she will be reunited with the woman she cannot yet bring herself to call mother, the woman who has begged not to lose her twice. And yet that woman, Angela, is her only link to her past and to Baba who will always be her family in her heart. Perhaps, she thinks, it is time for people to forgive themselves and each other. Another journey to start without certainty of when and where it will finish.

Eva checks again in her handbag for her passport and her plane ticket to Prague. Tucked inside the passport-holder is her old Eurostar return ticket.

A one-way ticket is all she needs this time.

The End

ABOUT THE AUTHOR

Rebecca Clements writes about women who are facing major change in their lives. The themes will be familiar to anyone who has faced difficult decisions and who may feel isolated in their environments.
'Open Ticket' is Ms. Clements' debut novel. She has also written a number of short stories. Her next novel 'Does He Eat Broccoli?', a satire about motherhood, will be published in 2015.

Rebecca Clements lives in the UK.

To follow the author's writing, visit:
https://www.facebook.com/pages/Rebecca-Clements/1533831350192594

Printed in Great Britain
by Amazon.co.uk, Ltd.,
Marston Gate.